I0733985

Necessary Chances

Anne Louise Bannon

HH

Healcroft House, Publishers

Altadena, California

ISBN: 978-1-948616-51-5

Library of Congress Control Number: 2025921189

To my family

Acknowledgements

I t is a fact that writing does not happen in a vaccuum. Although, I must say that writing Necessary Chances sure felt like it. I was writing during the Pandemic, and what contact I had with other people was pretty much limited to phone calls and/or emails with some Zoom meetings tossed in.

Still, my support system that only begins with my husband, Michael Holland, and daughter Corrie Klarner, has held me through some pretty rough times. The good folks at the Repair Cafe. Meredith Taylor and other lifelong friends I have made through the writing community. Tracey Phillips and the other Blackbird Writers. G.P. Gottlieb who came up with the Author Pod. Bennie Thomas and Phoenix Smith, my journaling buddies. Carol Louise Wilde and Jane Neff Rollins, colleagues and good friends.

Thank you all.

Contents

Prologue

To Breanna, 10/23/00

Today's Topic: Spending the Holidays Together

So, your mom is cool with the two of you joining me and the Whole Fam-Damily. I'm glad. I'd really hate to be without you. Christmas is a big deal for us, and I want to be with the people I love, especially you.

But I think it's only fair to make sure you and your mom know what you're letting yourselves in for. You know our monthly birthday parties? It's almost a whole month of that, plus the Then-Somes, namely the various friends we all have.

This year is going to be even crazier, since we're all going to D.C. to see Darby and Alicia do the big New Year's Eve concert at the Kennedy Center. Every day we will be there, you know Sy is going to be rousting us out to see everything there is to see in the Nation's Capital, and I do mean every-thing. I swear, I do not know how he does it. He's seventy-six and does not stop when he's in touring mode. Trust me, last summer in New Zealand was nothing.

Okay. We've got Thanksgiving settled. I don't know why we split up more for that holiday, given how much everyone in my family loves to eat, but Aunt Mae and Uncle Neil want to see his family in Nebraska, and that gives them the chance to do it. Which makes it easier for Grandma and Grandpa Wycherly to go see their families in South Florida. So, our Thanksgiving will be just about us, your mom, and my parents, Sy and Stella, and Ellen. (Did I forget anyone?)

Saturday and Sunday of Thanksgiving weekend, though, is when the chaos starts. We go over to the O'Malleys' early in the day on Saturday to help them get the lights up at their house and otherwise decorate. And then there's a party. Then everybody comes to my parents' place on Sunday after Mass to do the same there, and there's another party. There will be multiple shopping trips after this, sometimes en masse, sometimes in smaller groups, during which we will probably hit every mall in the greater Los Angeles area. Yes, there will be lots and lots of presents, but the majority of them will be jokes, a couple things that somebody really needs or wants, and/or homemade. Not everybody has my parents' and my cash flow, so that evens things out and nobody has to compete or get loaded down with stuff they don't need, and we all still get lots of presents to open. If it rains, there will probably be a ski trip. You did great in New Zealand. And if your mother wants to learn, you know Mom and Aunt Mae will be happy to teach her.

On the second Sunday of December, Aunt Mae and Uncle Neil have their open house. The Whole Fam-Damily will be there, plus lots of friends, a lot of whom you've met already. There will be more outings and trips to malls. The last weekend before Christmas, the party starts at my parents' place. Everyone descends on it Friday night, some stay overnight, others go back and forth. Sy and Stella usually go back to their place since it's so close to Mom and Dad's and Stella doesn't have to wear clothes there. The Then-Somes usually come over after Mass on Sunday. Christmas Eve,

Darby and Alicia will be with her parents, aunts, uncles, and grandparents, but they'll be at Midnight Mass at my parents' parish, along with the rest of the Whole Fam-Dam-ily. Dad's usually playing organ for Frank Lonnergan and the choir.

For some reason, on Boxing Day, we do an outing, but this year I think that's when we're leaving for D.C. Yes, Dad got your mom a ticket. I bought yours. We'll figure out who's rooming with your mom later, probably Janey and Ellen.

And so it goes on until New Year's Day and sometimes after.

The worst of it is, Mom, Aunt Mae, and Grandma all get a little nuts. They are the anti-Scrooges. They make Whos look like Grinches. The annual Christmas pajamas and nightgowns are the worst of it, and Aunt Mae is already bugging me for yours and your mother's sizes. Mom not only wears Christmas sweaters, she makes them. One year, she wanted to make a set of matching sweaters for the three of us and the dogs. Thank God, Dad and I talked her out of it. I may not have as easy a time talking her out of matching sweaters for the two of us. This from a woman who despises cute so much that when someone gave her a bunch of cutesy potholders, she took them to the shooting range and used them for target practice.

December 1, 1989

Lisa's Voice

I took in a deep breath of satisfaction. It was Friday afternoon, the first of December. Christmas was officially in season. I love Christmas. We'd already decorated the outside of the house the weekend before. As I half-sang "It Came Upon a Midnight Clear," I scratched Blueberry kitty between the ears, then went back to the white, green, and red sweater I was knitting. The gray short-haired cat was snuggled up on my lap. Our other two cats and the two dogs had decided to make themselves scarce, and with good reason.

My husband, Sid, our son Nick, and my nephew Darby were engaged in a most delicate maneuver, that of moving the walnut baby grand piano from our library to the big living room. The guys had already turned around the ebony baby grand to make it easier to slide the walnut in next to it.

Yeah, I know. Two baby grand pianos seem a bit much. We also have an upright upstairs in the music and workroom next to Sid's and my bedroom, not to mention several electronic keyboards here, there, and everywhere. We have multiple pianos because Sid is a pianist. Four and a half years ago, when we originally laid out the plan for the house, Sid wanted a piano in the living room to play for what was technically my family, but by that point had become just as much his family. I loved having a separate library with a piano in there so that I could read while Sid played. Or knit while Sid played. Since we have money, Sid decided we might as well have baby grands in both rooms.

Then Sid had found and reconciled with Stella, the aunt who had raised him. She was the one who had taught him to play in the first place, and is a very accomplished pianist and teacher. So, rather than force them to switch off playing, it was kind of fun to let them both play at the same time. This year, they wanted to do the Brahms waltzes for two pianos, Opus 39. Which necessitated turning the ebony piano one-hundred and eighty degrees, then moving the walnut in through the front hall into the living room, then tuning both because the movement, no matter how gentle, would tweak something that no one but Sid, Stella, or Darby, who is also a musician, would hear.

It had to be done well before Christmas so that Sid and Stella had time to rehearse and, if I'm honest, fight over it. Those two are always bickering, but oddly enough, there's a fondness to it that belies the crankiness.

"Alright," said Sid. He's not a large man, just around three inches taller than me, and I'm average. He has a solid, muscular build with dark, wavy hair, a cleft chin, and bright blue eyes. "I think we've got it."

Darby pushed his glasses up on his freckled nose.

"The ebony needs to go a little more that way," he said as if Sid didn't know what he was doing. "We don't want them too close together."

Darby has red hair and green eyes. At sixteen, he was already six feet tall, and we were wondering if he'd get any taller. While his shoulders are fairly well developed - no surprise, he's a violinist - the rest of his frame is pretty slight. He was also getting more than a little smart-mouthed of late.

Sid shot Darby a quick glare, then looked at the pianos and grimaced. "You might have a point. Let's do it."

Nick sighed. I could tell he was getting antsy. He'd been six-one for the past eight months, so we were thinking he might have finally stopped growing. He, too, was sixteen, so it wasn't a given that he'd reached his adult height. His frame is well muscled, like his father's, and Nick has the same cleft chin, wavy, dark hair, and blue eyes as Sid. Unlike his father, though, he prefers to wear glasses. Sid wears contact lenses. Both are very near-sighted. Nick's hair was only somewhat longer than Sid's, though, because the Catholic high school Nick goes to won't let him wear it past his collar.

"Mom, can you take notes, please?" Nick asked.

"Sure." I put down my sweater and found the notebook that Nick had dropped on the end table next to the sofa where I'd put my feet up. Blueberry squeaked her displeasure at being disturbed, but turned a couple times, kneaded my leg, and curled up again.

The living room is a large, long, open space that runs through the middle of the house. A hallway from the front door and the library runs across the front of it to Sid's and my office. The walls are a very light blue. While there is normally just the ebony baby grand on the one side of the room, on the other are three conversation groupings. The center section has a long couch upholstered in a muted blue and green stripe, with matching blue wing-back chairs flanking it. Each of the two conversation groups on either side of the long couch has a love seat along the same wall and two overstuffed chairs. The two love seats have the same blue and green stripe upholstery, but there's green upholstery on the overstuffed chairs. The floors are shiny dark wood, so it's relatively easy to re-group things when we need or want to.

At the far end of the living room is the dining room, with its lovely dark cherry wood table and the beautiful Louis Fifteen breakfront. Then there's another hallway and the huge TV or rumpus room beyond that.

Along with Nick's wire-bound notebook was a sheet of mimeographed paper with a list of questions.

"Okay," I said, pulling a pen from the round wires binding the lined sheets together. "Where were we?"

"Um, we've got date of birth for both you and Dad," Nick said. "And places of birth."

I looked at the notebook. "Yep, except your dad was born in New York, not San Francisco." I sighed. "Do you have a date of birth and place for your first mom yet?"

"Yeah." Nick brightened, even as he grunted with the effort to move the ebony piano the micrometers that Sid and Darby had decreed.

It wasn't that hard. Both of the pianos have wheels on their legs.

"That's good," said Darby. "What do you think, Uncle Sid?"

"That looks great. We'd better get on the tuning. Thanks, Nick."

Nick sighed, then flopped into the wing-back next to me and took the notebook and pen from me.

"New York, Dad?"

"Yeah," said Sid. "We didn't move to San Francisco until after I was two. Or was I three?"

Darby laughed a little. He and Nick were working on a family history. Both boys went to the same high school. They and their mutual best friend, Josh Sandoval, all had the same project. The assignment was for their religion class. According to the letter that had been sent home with each of the boys, the idea was to get the kids to not only think about faith as something that happened within a family experience, but also get them talking to their parents and grandparents in a non-judgmental way that would lead to better communication.

I suppose I could afford to be a little complacent about the communication thing. Not only did Sid and I have an excellent relationship with Nick, Darby enjoyed a darned good relationship with his parents, too. Well, most of the time, he did. The assignment had purposely been given right on top of the Christmas holidays because that's when extended family tended to be around.

"I want to know what your mom said about her sibling," Darby said to Nick. He grinned as Sid got out the tuning forks and started plinking the keys.

Darby's mother is my older sister, Mae. Her one and only sibling is me.

"She didn't yet." Nick grinned at me. "Well? Describe your sibling."

"Oh." I took a deep breath. "That's always been kind of a weird relationship. I mean, we love each other, but for some reason, she gets really competitive about me. I don't know why. She was always the one everyone looked up to.

She got the straight A's in school. Everyone always wanted me to be more like her because she was so well-behaved."

Darby laughed. "She said you always got what you wanted, and everyone paid more attention to you."

I shrugged. "Probably because I was causing more trouble."

Nick looked at Darby. "I can't wait to see what Grandma Wycherly says."

"You got it, dude!"

The two high-fived each other, then Sid asked Darby to play various keys on the walnut.

Nick and Darby weren't only cousins, they were best friends and had been ever since Nick had been brought to Sid's and my doorstep by Nick's first mother.

"Dad, your earliest memory."

Sid sighed and blinked. "Um. I think it was an Italian grocer who lived underneath us in Greenwich Village. I remember his eyes. They were really blue." He shook his head. "Not much more than that."

"And what were you doing around this date when you were sixteen?" Nick scribbled busily.

Sid laughed. "Probably working. I'd grown a mustache and gotten my job at the French restaurant. I was busing tables until Christmas Day itself, when I'd volunteered to work. They needed some extra waiters, so I got a shot at waiting that day and pulled it off well enough that they made me an apprentice waiter."

"Why'd you work Christmas?" Darby asked.

"Stella and I didn't celebrate," said Sid. "She didn't believe in it. I didn't think it was that big a deal. I knew others who didn't celebrate, either. So, when I had a shot at working and getting some extra bucks for the overtime, I went for it. Not to mention all the great tips I got."

Darby frowned. "You didn't celebrate Christmas?"

"Nope. Not until I did with you guys when you were nine."

Darby gaped. "Really? That was your first Christmas?"

Sid looked over at me with a fond smile. "Yeah, it was."

"I didn't know that." Darby shook his head in wonder, then plinked a key. "That E is still off."

"It most certainly is." Sid tossed Darby the tuning wrench, and Darby went to work.

"Dad, this is going to be a two-parter, 'cause it's about both my moms." Nick referred to both his birth mother and me as his moms.

"Okay."

"How did you meet my first mom, and how did you meet my second mom?"

I'm the second mom. It's not a rating. It's when I came into Nick's life.

Sid chuckled. "It's the same answer for both. I met them in a bar. It's where I met most women back then. Your first mom was looking for sex, which immediately made her attractive to me. Your second mom was in trouble, and I couldn't help myself."

Sid used to sleep around a lot. It wasn't the usual sleazy sort of thing. Stella had simply raised him to believe in free love. I'm religious and believe that sex is best within the commitment of marriage. Sid had been impressed by my willingness to stick to my standards and had hired me, and then we had to go and fall in love with each other.

As if it were ordained to come at the most awkward time, the pager I wore at my waist buzzed. Sid and I exchanged glances. He'd gotten the page, too. Nick saw us and knew what was up. Blueberry felt the vibration and fled. Darby, thank God, was oblivious.

You see, within the structures of the FBI and the CIA are several shadow agencies so secret that mostly only their members know they exist. Sid and I work for one called Operation Quickline. Nick knows we do top secret work for the government, but little more than that.

The page probably meant work coming in, and since it could sometimes be urgent, I decided I'd better answer it.

"Shoot," I said, getting up. "Darby, I just now remembered, your mom wants me to call. Are you staying here tonight?"

He shook his head. "Nah. I gotta go home. Mom's making us clean up the place for next weekend."

The O'Malley Open House was a big deal for the family. Mae and her husband, Neil, had almost canceled it this year because it was a lot of work, but the kids really wanted to have it. So, Mae decided that if the kids wanted it that badly, they could help get their place cleaned and fixed up. Which, of course, I already knew. I'd only asked to give Darby a plausible reason for my departure from the room. Not that Darby was likely to have noticed, but I didn't want to give him a chance to, just in case.

I checked my watch as I went into the office in the front corner of the house. It was quarter 'til four. Sid, Nick, and I were supposed to meet Sid's old high school buddy Tom Freeman and Angelique Carter (Tom's girlfriend and one of Sid's former lovers) at a restaurant in a nearby mall around six-thirty.

As I'd suspected, the page was from an agent fresh in from overseas. He had a floppy disk in his possession, and he also gave me the password to open the files on the disk once he'd passed it to me. I arranged to have him come to the mall by five. He told me he'd be reading a copy of some foreign newspaper and would leave it behind once I'd signaled him.

I also called Mae and told her that Darby was planning on being home that weekend instead of at our place.

"He'd darned well better be," Mae grumbled. "But thanks for confirming it."

The tuning was finished by the time I walked back into the living room.

"Dad said that he filed for his deferment right away," Darby was saying as he put his violin case on the walnut piano's bench. "He wanted to go to dental school, so he got it, and by the time he was done, the war was over."

Sid shrugged. "That's how it went sometimes." He glared at the keys to the ebony piano.

Sid and Neil are the same age and had turned nineteen in 1969, the age when a lot of guys got drafted to go into the armed forces.

"Why didn't you try for a deferment, Dad?" Nick asked. "Stella told me you had that scholarship to USF."

"They weren't going to give me one with an undecided major," Sid grumbled. He started arranging sheet music on the piano's stand. "Or a music major, or anything I was likely to be studying."

I was surprised that Sid was talking about when he'd gotten drafted. He seldom talks about anything connected to his time in the Vietnam War.

Sid winced. "Besides, I had no idea what I was going to do with my life. I decided to go in because it was something to do and found out what a colossal mistake I'd made about five minutes after I arrived at boot camp." He looked up at me. "What did Mae want?"

"Nothing much." I looked at Nick. "But she did remind me that Nick has some Christmas shopping to do before the party. Why don't I take him now and meet you guys at the restaurant?"

"I can drive you over there, Uncle Sid," Darby rosined his bow then picked up his violin. "That way, we can get some practice time in."

I walked over to the couch. "Am I dressed up enough for dinner?"

I had on a full, hip-length blouse with a pink back-ground and mauve paisley print over black leggings and a short black vest with fringe. I picked up my black flat boots and slid them on.

"Yeah. You look good." Sid smiled at me.

I went over and gave him a nice kiss. Nick scrambled up and followed me. He was wearing a t-shirt, a tan plaid dress shirt over that, and baggy jeans, practically formal wear for a kid his age. I could almost hear Sid sighing.

"See you later, Dad."

We got to the mall early for the drop. Nick agreed to play lookout. We found our contact right on time, and I gave the signal. The man folded up his newspaper, set it down on the bench he was sitting on, looked around for a minute or two, then checked his watch, and hurried off, leaving the newspaper. I ran over to the bench and grabbed the newspaper, as if I were trying to return it to him. Since he was gone, I shook my head and jammed the newspaper into my huge black purse. Nick and I continued our walk around the mall. Sometime shortly after five-thirty, Nick stiffened.

"Mom, we've got a tail," he said quietly. He is so good at spotting tails.

"How long?"

Nick frowned. "Just a second ago. I didn't see him or anyone else around when you made the pickup." Nick softly sighed. "Here he comes."

The man was just under average height. He had light brown hair that ringed a goodly-receded hairline. His face was long, and he wore wire-rimmed glasses. He had on a tan wool sport coat over dark jeans and cowboy boots. He walked up as if he were about to say hi.

It's one of those things you do in the spy business. Someone strange approaches, and you scan and assess for a potential threat. I don't even think about it. I just do it. Funny thing was, the man saw me and did the same thing. It took less than a second. Nick, on the other hand, got the man's full attention. The stranger smiled weakly.

"I apologize," he said. "I thought you were someone else." He gazed at Nick again and smiled oddly. "By God, you look like him, though."

I smiled. "No problem."

At least, Nick hadn't rolled his eyes. It doesn't happen that often, but he does look so much like his father that people (mostly women) sometimes think that's who he is. We continued shopping and got a couple of presents. I went to the Williams Sonoma store and got a bag from them to put the presents in to tease Sid. He loves Williams Sonoma, although he'd probably figure that there wasn't anything in that bag for him. I was much cagier than that. When it got close to six-thirty, Nick and I went to the restaurant where the dinner was supposed to be. Tom and Ange were already there.

Tom is a big guy with broad shoulders and wheat-colored hair just starting to show some gray. He wore wire-rimmed glasses and a black sport coat over a dress shirt and light blue jeans. Angelique had pulled back her full, brown hair and was still wearing the suit she'd worn to her job at the local FBI office that day. They got up to hug and greet us, then I sat down next to Ange, with Nick on my other side. I could still see the door to the restaurant from there. A minute later, Sid showed up, wearing a suit and tie. He patted Nick's shoulder, quickly kissed me, then hugged Ange and shook hands with Tom. He sat down on Tom's other side, where he could see the door to the restaurant.

"So, what's this all about?" Sid asked.

"That's just it," said Tom. "I don't entirely know. This private investigator said that he had a case that might involve us and some other guys, and wanted to have dinner with us. Ange was able to verify his license, so we thought, what the heck."

Ange coordinates programs and equipment for above-board agents and a few of us belonging to shadow agencies, such as Quickline. Tom didn't know about Sid's and my side business, but Ange did.

Sid suddenly gaped at a couple coming into the restaurant, and Tom did, too. The hostess pointed us out to the couple, and they approached, with the man gaping in the same way.

He was taller than Sid, but shorter than Tom, with a square face and dark hair cut short and parted on the side. He wore a suit that didn't quite fit his bulky frame and a loud tie. His wife, who was also portly with a round face, had on a silky polyester dress.

"Can it be?" the man yelped. "Sid? Tom?"

Tom jumped up and laughed. "Wallace! I'll be damned."

Sid was on his feet, grinning and shaking hands with Wallace. "You look good, buddy. How've you been?"

"Great! Oh, this is my wife, Lottie. Lottie, these are my old friends from high school. This is Sid Hackbirn, and Tom Freeman, and uh…" He stopped as he saw Angelique and me, but then laughed at Nick. "You, I'm guessing, are related to Sid."

"Yeah. My dad." Nick chuckled.

Wallace grinned. "You got caught?"

"I did, indeed." Sid laughed. "This is my son, Nick Flaherty, and my wife, Lisa Wycherly. Lisa, Nick, this is Wallace Merton."

"Married, too." Wallace cursed.

"And my girlfriend, Angelique Carter," Tom said.

We all shook hands, and Wallace and Lottie sat down, only to get up another moment later, when another man walked into the restaurant and gaped. He was about the same height as Wallace, but thinner with light hair and a decided paunch hanging over his dark dress slacks. He wore a dress shirt with a colorful sweater over it.

"Bob Kinney, as I live and breathe," said Tom, getting up, also.

There was another round of introductions, with Nick provoking yet another jab at Sid's former lifestyle.

"So, Sid, you're married?" Bob asked.

"Yeah. Three and a half years now. Four in March."

Wallace, Lottie, and Bob all glanced at Nick, then at me.

Sid's grin got just a touch tight. "Lisa is Nick's second mom."

"You were married before?" Wallace asked.

"No. In fact, I didn't even know I had Nick until he was eleven. How about you guys? Wallace, how long have you been married?"

"Too long," said Wallace. Lottie backhanded him lightly on the arm. "Well, maybe not too long."

"Sixteen years now," Lottie said, smiling. "And we have two kids. Our daughter is fourteen and our son is twelve."

"I'm a bachelor and likely to stay so," said Bob. "If I have any kids, I don't know about them and don't want to. What about you, Tom?"

"My first wife and I got divorced in nineteen-eighty. No kids. I met Ange at Sid and Lisa's wedding, and we've been together ever since. So, what all have you guys been doing?"

Wallace Merton was an electrical engineer and worked in Torrance for a firm specializing in printer interfaces. Bob was a medical doctor and general practitioner, with an office in Walnut Creek, a suburb of San Francisco and Oakland, although he lived in Berkeley. Tom teaches American Literature and creative writing at a high school in the city of Los Angeles.

"I used to teach at our old high school," Tom said. "Until I met Ange."

He would have continued, but Sid looked at the man coming into the restaurant at that moment and gasped. It was the same man who had talked to Nick and me earlier. The other men looked, and a hush fell. They recognized him, but couldn't believe what they were seeing at the same time.

"It's gotta be his brother," Sid finally said, swallowing.

"He didn't have a brother," muttered Bob.

"Cousin."

"Hi, guys. Wallace, Bob, Tom." The man paused as he looked at my husband. "Sid."

"Loser?" Bob asked. "Loser Renfrew?"

"In the flesh," the man said.

"You're dead." Sid looked at him in utter shock. "Your name is on the fucking wall. You're dead."

"There are a few mistakes on that wall," Loser said, referring to the Vietnam Veterans Memorial in Washington, D.C.

Tom frowned. "But your sister and your mom... There was a funeral. I was there."

"I, uh, know." Loser found a chair, pulled it up to the table, and sat down between Lottie and Bob. He looked at Sid. "You know how bad it was. I couldn't take it. I had to get out of there. A guy in my unit was about to go home. Had the orders in his pocket when he got his face blown off. I swapped dog tags with him and ran like hell. They thought he was me, and I disappeared."

Sid glared at him. "You swapped dog tags?"

Loser looked pleadingly at him. "Sid, you know what it was like. I had to."

"And I stayed. Two years, I stayed."

I had never seen Sid so shaken and so angry before. I looked over at Nick, who looked vaguely terrified.

"That's it." Sid scrambled to his feet. "I'm leaving. You guys have all the fun you want. I'm leaving."

He strode to the restaurant door. I shot a quick look at Angelique, who nodded, then Nick and I hurried after him. Sid trembled as we caught up with him outside the mall movie theater. I pulled him into my arms and just held him. Nick slid his arm across his shoulders. Sid finally swallowed, and we took him home.

December 2, 1989

When Angelique called the next morning, I made sure that Sid was in the large workroom next to our bedroom that houses both his music stuff and my sewing stuff before putting her on hold. I went downstairs to the office and shut the door, praying that Sid was not listening in on the extension. Our phones are set up so that you can't tell if someone is listening in on you.

I yawned as I picked up the phone. It was barely eight a.m., and I am not a morning person. The night before had been pretty rough, too. Sid sometimes has nightmares about his time in Vietnam, and he'd had three that night. Two were about the first time he'd killed somebody, which was the usual one. But then, there was a new one with people he'd known coming back from the dead to get him.

"How is he?" Ange asked.

I sighed deeply. "He's a complete mess. I've never seen him this bad. I got him to make love last night. I thought it would help, but not even close."

Angelique cursed. "That's bad."

"No kidding."

Ange is possibly the only person I can talk to about my sex life. While there are a lot of women out there who have a good idea of what my husband can do in bed, Ange is one of the very few who know and does not hate me because Sid is faithful to me. Her relationship with Tom is so much better than it ever was with Sid. And, yes, I am friends with several of Sid's former lovers. I was before he gave up sleeping around. There was no reason to ditch the friendships just because he'd stopped having sex with them. If they were okay with being former lovers, I was okay.

Ange groaned. "The worst of it is, Tom wants Sid to help Loser."

"What?"

"Loser is in trouble, and it sounds pretty serious."

"Can we start calling him Louis? I hate that nickname."

"I know. No wonder he's so messed up." Ange swallowed. "Wallace and Bob are pretty much useless. I mean, they'll do what they can, but they don't have the first clue. Is there any way we can get Sid to meet with Louis?"

"Sid won't even talk about it. He knows better than to do that, so I'm hoping it's just a matter of him getting used to the idea. The problem is, Ange, he is really, really angry. I kind of don't blame him. You know how he is about the war. He was just starting to sort of talk about it with Nick and Darby, and then this kicked him in the family jewels."

Angelique snorted. "I totally get it. Alright. We'll have to take this slowly. I'll talk to Tom."

"Thanks, Ange. I appreciate it. Please tell Tom that we'll do the best we can."

"I will. Thanks, Lisa."

I put the phone on the hook and wondered what to do next.

"You know," said Sid. He stood in the doorway. "Maybe the reason I can't talk about why I'm so angry is that I really don't know why I am."

"Oh, honey, that's okay."

Sid's chuckle was loaded with angst. "I know. That is one of the things I treasure about you. And it does make it easier to talk. I just..." He sighed deeply. "The thing is, if I'd had the same chance to swap dog tags, I would have. I wouldn't even have thought about it." He frowned. "If I had thought I could have gotten away with it, I would have. But that whole intelligence thing." Okay, he added a curse word. "I'm sure somebody would have found me and taken me out if I had."

Sid had been pulled into intelligence work when he was in boot camp, then pulled in again when he'd finally gotten home.

"You're smart enough. You would have found a way to escape them."

"Maybe. Loser was the smartest of the six of us. The guy was a genius."

You may have noted that there were only four friends and Louis at the table that night. The sixth member of that group was the unfortunately named Stan Ford. According to Tom, he still lived in the Bay Area and was doing a spectacular job of messing up his life at the time.

Sid shrugged. "So, did Ange say what's going on?"

"Not entirely. She just said that he's in trouble and that it seems pretty serious."

Sid snorted. "Loser was generally in some sort of trouble. Even worse than me."

"Really?" I frowned as I tried to remember what all Sid had said about him. "Didn't you say that you guys were the best and brightest at your school?"

"Yeah. That was kind of the problem they had with Loser. He was at the top of the class, grade-wise. How do you reconcile the fact that your best student is also one of your worst troublemakers?"

"So, now what do we do?"

Sid squeezed his eyes shut, then opened them. "Look, I've got to get my stuff together for today." Um. He did not say stuff. "We told Mae, and I'm willing to bet your parents are looking forward to it."

Sid and I had agreed to take Darby's youngest sister, Lissy, to a mall that day to get her picture with Santa, and my parents were coming along. Being three, Lissy was more hindrance than help when it came to the big cleaning operation at Mae's. Mama would probably have preferred to help with the cleaning. I guessed that Mae wanted her elsewhere. Mama can be a bit of a force of nature, and that can make life challenging. Mae needed to coordinate the other five children, ages nine through sixteen, and said force of nature has a bad habit of indulging those children.

I gave Sid a warm hug, then almost cursed.

"Shavings! I almost forgot. Where's my purse?"

"That's right. That pick up yesterday." Sid followed me into the front hallway and then through the living room.

I found the purse on the dryer. There's a large linen closet and a bay for the washer and dryer right next to the garage door, which is how we generally enter the house when we drive anywhere. Lots of stuff lands on the dryer because it's the easiest place to drop stuff when we come in. Usually, our housekeeper, Conchetta Ramirez, picks up the clutter and moves it off the dryer, only she wasn't in that day because it was Saturday, and she only works Monday to Friday.

I took the purse back to the office and retrieved the newspaper and disk drive. There was also a note in the drive's paper envelope.

Sid looked at it, reading the code as easily as regular writing. "It says the Dragon wants us to call at our convenience."

"Which do you want to do? Call or check the disk?"

"I'll call." Sid pulled his pocket watch from his jeans pocket. "Then we've got to get out of here. We told Mae we'd be there before ten."

Sid dialed the Dragon while I deciphered the code on the disk drive's envelope. The disk, it turned out, needed to go to New York. While Sid talked to the Dragon, I checked a couple of pins on our map of Quickline and picked a route, then coded the password for the files.

Sid hung up the phone, then yelped.

"Damn it, Bowser!"

Bowser was our eighteen-month-old mutt. We'd acquired him as a puppy when Stella had found a litter outside her music school. He's a good-sized dog, about sixty pounds big. He's just really short, with the stocky build and stubby legs of a basset hound or corgi, the head of a beagle, and longish, coarse hair that's black on the back and tan on the bottom. For some reason, he loves Sid and is constantly under Sid's feet, one of the reasons both he and our other dog, a liver-spotted springer spaniel named Motley, had been outside during the piano moving operation the afternoon before. Motley, who generally follows me when he's not chasing Nick on his skateboard, thumped his stub of a tail as if to point out that he didn't get under anybody's feet.

"So, what did Lillian say?" I asked.

Lillian's code name was the Dragon, and she was the head of Quickline.

"There were a couple requests for my service records," Sid said. "One from a Eugene Krakowski, a private detective, and another from Special Agent Harris Cobb. There's not a lot of information in the files, and anything intelligence-related wasn't included, anyway. But it's interesting that there were a couple requests."

I shrugged. "I guess we'd better get going, then."

I ran upstairs to put on my navy blue sweater with Rudolph on the front while Sid got the dogs outside in the backyard. I also thanked God that Sid had calmed down enough to take Lissy out.

We got Nick into Sid's BMW and got to the O'Malleys' house in Pasadena around a quarter 'til ten or so. Nick had agreed to help with the cleaning operation, so we only had to get Lissy's car seat into our car and Mama and Daddy, as well. Mama was easy. She's small and pert, like a bird. Daddy, on the other hand, is tall and filled out, though not fat. I volunteered to sit in the back with Mama so Daddy wasn't quite so cramped.

We headed down to South Coast Plaza, one of the larger and higher-end malls in Southern California, and one of Mama's favorite malls from back when Mae and Neil and the kids lived in Orange County. About an hour away from the O'Malley place in Pasadena, it might have been a long ride for Lissy, a redhead like her older brothers, but the kid fell asleep before we hit the freeway. And thanks to Sid's lead foot, it only took us forty-five minutes to get there.

Daddy and I chose to stand in line for Santa while Mama and Sid kept Lissy occupied elsewhere. Lissy wasn't as hyperactive as Nick, but being three, she could give him a run for his money. Not a good trait for standing in a fairly long line.

Once we got to her turn with Santa, however, Lissy took one look at him and screamed. None of us had any idea why. Lissy was usually very happy to meet strangers and loved new things in general. But Lissy did not want anything to do with sitting on the Guy in Red's lap.

"Lissy, it's only Santa Claus," Mama told her, as she gently tugged Lissy's hand. "He loves you. Why don't you sit on his lap like a good little girl?"

"Mama, she's scared," I said.

Mama shot me a glare, then turned back to her grand-daughter. "Now, Lissy, do you want a nice, big candy cane?"

Lissy only screamed louder.

"There's no point in traumatizing her," Sid said, sighing.

"Well, I suppose you're right." Mama looked back at Santa, and then we got out of line.

Sid picked Lissy up, and he and I both rolled our eyes at each other. Mama always knows better than me and makes sure I know it. But if Sid says anything, she agrees immediately. It's the same with Mae and Neil. Yeah, that's incredibly annoying, but you must allow for the fact that it's how Mama was raised, and she does try to be more open. Sid, that day, was not in the mood to be indulged.

Oddly enough, Mama picked up on Sid's mood. I'm still not sure how, but while Daddy and I took Lissy around the mall to the toy store, Mama talked to Sid. When we met up with them again, Daddy took Lissy to ride the mall's carousel. I looked at Mama and Sid as they gazed at Daddy holding a giggling Lissy on the brightly painted horse. Sid shrugged. It was plain Mama had gotten him to tell her what had happened the night before. Mama could do that. [Let's just say your ability to open me up comes honestly. - SEH]

"Well, I don't blame you for being mad," she said quietly. "Here, you've probably been grieving for him all these years and feeling guilty because you made it out okay, and he didn't. And it turns out he's still here. I'd be mad, too."

"Feeling guilty?" Sid looked at her.

"Of course, honey." Mama patted his arm. "It's called survivor guilt. I was reading some article about it not too long ago. It's been a real problem for the Holocaust survivors. But it can happen to people who've fought in wars, like you did. You'll get through it. You're a strong man."

Sid chuckled. "Thanks, Mama."

My mother's name is Althea, but she finally got Sid to call her Mama, like Neil does, a few years ago. Daddy's name is Bill, and it took him longer to get used to Sid calling him Daddy. But Mama had insisted on that, too. As I've already noted, my mother can be a force of nature.

When Sid and I finally got a moment alone together, I asked him about the guilt thing.

"Your mother may be right," he said.

"Then should we call Dr. Heilland?"

Dr. Heilland is a psychologist specializing in trauma who also happens to have the clearance to hear about the side business.

Sid frowned. "I suppose I should." He looked at me. "Just don't let me forget to do it."

Finally, it was way past time to leave the mall. Lissy had missed her nap and was getting cranky and whiny. She's usually a happy, pleasant child, except when she's tired. Fortunately, the kid passed out even before Sid could get out of the parking lot.

I called Mae from Sid's car phone. Things were in good shape there, but she had no idea what to do about dinner. I checked with Sid, and we offered to pick up pizza for everyone on the way home.

The house practically sparkled and reeked of furniture polish when we got there. Mae was exhausted, and Neil was unusually cranky. I found out why when Mae and I flopped onto the family room sofa with our pizza slices and a glass of red wine each.

"It's Darby," Mae sighed. "I think the only reason I haven't killed him sooner is that he's been at your place so much these past few months."

"Well, it is closer to school, and he does like practicing with Sid."

"You two can have him." Mae shuddered. "These past few weeks, he has been nothing but mouthy and all ego."

It wasn't that surprising. Darby's skills as a musician were starting to get noticed. He'd won a prestigious national competition earlier that fall and had been featured in the local newspapers. Mae and Neil had heard from a couple of agents at that time and flat-out told them not yet.

Then Darby was made first chair violin for the All-City Youth Orchestra of Los Angeles. After that, he'd been chosen as one of four young musicians to perform a solo with a professional chamber orchestra on December fourteen. As if that wasn't enough, the youth orchestra was playing in the big, free Christmas Eve concert at the Music Center in downtown Los Angeles. The county puts it on every year, and it's televised by the local public television station. It wouldn't be the first time the group, and Darby with them, had played for the event. This year, however, the orchestra was playing Winter from The Four Seasons, by Vivaldi, and Darby had been selected as the soloist. Worse yet, more reporters had interviewed him, and he'd been photographed several times and even had to get a formal headshot.

"He's been a little smart-alecky around us, too," I said. "You know, not quite going over the line, but getting close enough. I'm only glad he doesn't pull that ego nonsense around Stella or Sy."

Stella is Sid's aunt who raised him and Sy is Stella's lover. Sy is also Darby's mentor.

"I almost wish he would. They'd pound some sense into him." Mae sighed. "I'm happy that he's getting some attention for his talent. He does deserve that. And I suppose we can't be surprised that it's going to his head a little. But I swear, I am going to tan his fanny if I get any more of it."

I looked around. "There's another problem, too. Sid noticed that he was a little off last week, and he and Nick finally 'fessed up. Darby's been getting a lot of pressure to have sex."

Mae's face went pale. "Oh no. How? Who?"

"Some of the girls the guys have been hanging around with after school. It's been building since that first big feature after the competition. All of a sudden, Darby is the new cool kid, and you can't blame him for liking it. Nick's loving the attention, too. Even Josh is having fun with it. For the first time in any of their lives, they're considered popular. But some of the new groupies are looking for more than friendship, and they're getting a little insistent."

"Which may be why Darby's acting the way he is." Mae's eyes welled up.

She had good reason for her worry. When Darby was ten, he'd been molested by a neighbor. There was nothing good about it, but it could have been worse. The abuse was of relatively short duration, a few months rather than years. Also, the first thing Mae and Neil did when they'd found out about it was get Darby and them into therapy.

Darby had done very well, considering. He didn't show any signs of depression, a bad self-image, or even shame. Still, Darby did not like being alone in a room with an older man, and he had been freaking out at the least hint that a girl might want to have sex with him. Sadly, he was not freaking anymore.

"Well, Sid reinforced that no one, but no one, has the right to push when Darby says no. And he even gave Darby some nice ways to say no." I sighed. "Sid's just not sure Darby really wants to."

"Really?" Mae's eyes widened.

"That's what's worrying us and why I'm telling you. It could be just curiosity. I mean, he is sixteen, and believe me, he's got plenty of classmates who are sexually active. Hell, even Nick's getting curious. They'd have to be at this age, not to mention all the messages out there that there's something wrong with you if you aren't active. On the other hand, Sid said that Darby seems pretty uncomfortable, too."

"So, what do we do?"

I shook my head. "He's sixteen. I don't think there's much we can do short of hog-tying him and locking him in his room until he's thirty."

"You have no idea how attractive that sounds."

I looked over at Nick and Darby, who were talking to their grandmother.

"Yeah, I do, Mae."

Suddenly, Nick and Darby laughed loudly and looked at us. Mama tittered behind them. Mae and I both sighed.

"Family history project?" I asked.

"Oh, I think so. I wonder what she told them about us."

"Do we really want to know?"

Mae looked at me and we both laughed.

A spat suddenly erupted between Marty, one of the nine-year-old twins, and Ellen, who was eleven.

"Mom!" Ellen, a brunette with glasses, stomped through the dining room to the family room. "I'm trying to read, and Marty wants to play that stupid trumpet."

No matter how talented his eldest brother may have been, Marty, also a redhead like his elder and twin brothers and his youngest sister, was singularly untalented when it came to playing the trumpet. That may have had more to do with the fact that Marty only wanted to practice when he was most likely to annoy his siblings.

"Martin!" Mae called. "How many times do I have to tell you? No playing when the baby's asleep."

"I didn't know she was." Marty came running in with his horn in hand.

"You didn't check, either." Mae glared at him. "And if she wakes up, you're dealing with her."

Marty sighed and slowly went upstairs to put away the trumpet. Lissy was quite a charming, happy little girl most of the time. Except for the Santa incident, we'd had a lovely day with her. But that kid was hell when someone woke her up unexpectedly, or she got over-tired.

Nick and Darby had gone into the kitchen, where Neil and Sid were debating about the menu for the open house in one week. Darby suddenly let out a loud whoop of joy.

"We're going to have timbalo," he chanted and did the conga line dance out of the kitchen. "We're going to have timbalo." He stopped and turned. "I swear, Uncle Sid, you've gotta show me how to do it."

Darby, who loves food at least as much as I do, was also turning into quite the cook. Sid's timbalo, which is this incredible layered pasta dish, had become a family favorite. But it's labor-intensive in the extreme, so Sid seldom makes it more than once or twice a year.

Sid appeared in the kitchen doorway. "We'll see." He looked over at me. "Time to head home?"

"Sure." I got up.

"Come on, son." He turned back into the kitchen.

As we headed for the freeway, Sid shook his head.

"Darby seems a little hyper," he said, gunning the BMW sedan around a couple of cars.

"We're going on a double date tomorrow afternoon," Nick said from the back seat. "Dad, can I drive? Please?"

Sid looked at me.

"We've just got mass tomorrow, and we can take my car for that," I said.

"You know, it wouldn't be that big a deal if I had my own car," Nick added.

"Your six months aren't up until next week," Sid replied, sounding more annoyed than it warranted.

Nick was suffering the indignity of being without wheels. He'd gotten his driver's license on his birthday the previous February. However, Sid said that Nick couldn't have a car of his own until he'd driven for six months without a scratch on either of ours. Sadly, near the middle of June, Nick had totaled my little Datsun pickup when he'd pulled out for a left turn in front of another car, then stalled the pickup. Fortunately, he hadn't been hurt. However, the clock had been reset, and he would have to wait another six months for his own wheels. Darby had his father's old Toyota sedan, but he had a car.

"What's one week?" Nick said. "And you won't have to worry about juggling things."

I rolled my eyes. "But we will have to worry about you driving."

Nick heaved a sigh. "I'll be careful, Dad. I've got to practice, anyway."

"With Darby and two girls in the car." Sid shuddered, then paused. "Alright. You can take my car. But remember, you've only got one more week. The least ding or scratch, and you start your six months over again."

"It will look freshly detailed. I promise."

Sid glanced at me as if he had his doubts about that, but didn't say anything.

Nick flopped back in his seat and softly began chanting about timbalo in the conga rhythm.

As we pulled into the driveway of the house, Sid glanced back at the street, then pulled into the garage. He pushed the button on the car unit to shut the garage door before getting out, as well. Nick looked a little perplexed, but his brain was more occupied with the coming date and being able to get behind the wheel.

Nick kissed us both goodnight and hurried to his room to call Darby about the car. Sid went to the front of the house and left the lights out.

"What's going on?" I asked, following him into the library.

Sid looked out the front window. "I think somebody is watching the house. Huh. He seems to be leaving, though."

"Good. Let's go to bed."

Sid stopped and swallowed. I pulled him into my arms and held him.

"I know," I said softly. It wasn't as though I hadn't had to deal with the same thing. "But you've got to try to get some sleep, and I'll be there."

He kissed the side of my head. "Thank you, Lisapet."

December 3, 1989

At least, Sid only had one nightmare that night. It didn't help that I had one, too. It was one that had started when Nick began driving lessons. I dreamed that the boy and his car went flying off a cliff while I stood by helplessly to stop it.

We slept in until eight-thirty, a sure sign that Sid is exhausted because he seldom sleeps past six in the morning and is usually up by five. He was feeling frisky that morning, too, and I happily indulged him. We had to scramble to get to church in time.

Sid is an atheist, but he plays the organ at mass for the ten-thirty choir. It used to be the Guitar Choir, and our good friend Frank Lonnergan still directs it. Frank's officially a paid staff member at the parish as the music minister, not to mention working with a couple of other high school choirs and some other work for the archdiocese. Father John can only afford to pay him part-time, but Frank is in significant demand these days and can make it up. Even before he'd finished his master's degree in Liturgical Music last June, he was getting popular.

Well, let me rephrase that. The choir directing and diocesan work are Frank's visible living. The other reason he can make up for the low pay for all his gigs is that he and his wife, Esther Nguyen, have another job. The same one Sid and I do. So do our other friends, Kathy Deiner and Jesse White. They all got recruited because, apparently, the same qualities that draw us together are also the same qualities that make good operatives. Frank and Jesse are movers on our line, with Esther and Kathy being the hub team. Kathy keeps a small accounting practice going around raising hers and Jesse's little boy, Keshon. Esther owns and runs a small company making and selling electronic security devices. Jesse is a professional photographer. In fact, he did Darby's headshot when that was needed.

That Sunday, Sid passed Frank the disk we'd gotten on Friday - it wasn't that urgent, after all. Frank would take it to the next stop on the line, which was Phoenix and Desmond Moore. Desmond would take the package to the next stop and so on, until the disk got to New York, where it would be transferred to the CIA's keeping. Yes, it should have gone to Langley, Virginia, where the CIA is headquartered. But it's the CIA, and those guys are royal pains in the arse.

After mass, Frank and Esther followed Sid and me to Mid-City on Pico Boulevard to a little Thai food place not far from Koreatown. Kathy and Jesse were already there. Kathy is tall and elegant with rich, dark skin. Jesse is about the same height, but his skin is more the color of cocoa out of the box. Kathy generally keeps her hair cropped close to her head. Jesse let his grow a little more but cut it fairly round. Keshon was staying with Aunt Estelle, Kathy's sister, and Uncle Leon. Kathy and Jesse go to another parish that has more Black parishioners than ours.

"I need a break," Kathy said when I'd asked why they hadn't brought the kid.

Keshon was two, utterly adorable, and deeply invested in making his terrible twos as terrible as possible. He was exactly the sort of kid I would love when he got older. But as a toddler, he reminded me why I was ultimately happy that Sid and I couldn't have kids together. Having known all of Mae's kids at that age, I shudder to think what Nick was like as a toddler. I don't want to think about what Sid's and my combined genes would come up with.

"What did he do now?" Esther asked. She's a little shorter than me with a round face, black hair, and Vietnamese.

"Pitched a fit at church this morning when he couldn't get baptized like the other baby." Jesse sighed and rolled his eyes. "We tried to tell him he was already baptized, but he would not buy it."

Sid lowered his voice. "Listen, we need you guys to stay on alert. We may have a situation. Someone may have been watching our place last night."

"You need an extra camera?" Esther asked, her eyes lighting up. "I'm working on a longer-range lens for one that can be controlled from inside the house. One hundred and eighty degrees of surveillance."

I chuckled. "Sounds like fun, but we'll see."

"I could use some beta testers." Esther shrugged.

Frank looked at Sid. "You okay? You seem off."

Sid sighed. "I just got a shock and a half on Friday. I'm still trying to figure it out."

"What happened?" asked Esther.

Sid balked. As much as Sid does not like talking about the war, he and Esther avoid the topic like the plague. Esther left Vietnam with her father and brothers when she was fourteen in 1973. She's been trying to find her mother, who had gotten separated from the rest of her family as they escaped.

"Long story," Sid finally said.

Esther looked at him shrewdly. "Something about the war."

"Yeah." Sid looked at her. "Something that shouldn't have happened but did. Anyway, if any of you spot any surveillance, we need to know immediately."

"No problem there," said Jesse.

Kathy reached out and touched Sid's arm. "And if you want to talk, you know we're here."

"We're all here," said Frank as Jesse and Esther nodded.

Sid smiled softly. "Thanks, guys." He took a deep breath. "I appreciate it. We'll just have to see."

Lunch arrived, and we spent it eating and talking about other things. The time with our friends did Sid a world of good. Too bad that as we left, I got a call on my car phone. Sid picked it up since I was driving. He listened, then cursed.

"Just a second," he told the other person, and covered the mouthpiece. "It's Tom Freeman. He didn't get an answer on the house or office phone, then my car phone, so he called you. Our friend Stan died the other day."

"Oh, dear."

"The funeral's tomorrow. Do you mind if we go?"

"Not at all. What about Nick?"

"I'll call Stella. She'd want to know about Stan, anyway."

Sid got back on the phone long enough to tell Tom that he'd call him back, then called Stella, who didn't think she could leave her music school for the funeral.

"She probably doesn't want to go," Sid grumbled as he hung up, then dialed Tom.

I had to guess that Sid's conclusion about Stella had more to do with his grumpiness than Stella's actual preferences. Either way, Tom picked up the call, and he and Sid went back and forth on the arrangements. By the time they were done, we were home.

The first thing Sid did when we got inside was call his car. There was no answer, so he paged Nick. The boy didn't have one of our pagers. He had one that wasn't connected to the side business, although we'd gotten it for him because the side business meant that things changed on a dime, and he'd need to know. Several of his schoolmates had pagers, as well, but their parents were trying to keep tabs on them. Nick had scored multiple sympathy points for having been put on the pager leash.

It took a good twenty minutes for Nick to call back. In the meantime, I called a couple of my students from the community college where I taught Basic Composition to let them know that Off-Campus Office Hours were canceled for that day.

"We're at the beach and I had to find a phone," Nick said when he finally got through.

"What about the car phone?" I asked.

"Uh, it's further down the lot. This was here first."

"Okay." I explained about having to go up to the Bay Area because of Sid's friend, and that Stella would pick Nick up when he got his father's car home.

"We'll call you in the morning, honey," I told him. "I'm not sure when we'll be home, but I don't imagine we'll stay past tomorrow. Your dad and I both have to teach on Tuesday."

"Okay. Thanks." He sighed but said goodbye.

"Tom and Ange should be here any second now," Sid said, coming into the office with our overnight case.

I double-checked my purse. "I think I've got everything. Did you put flats in for the funeral?"

"No. I got your black suede and patent sling-backs."

Sid is amazing when it comes to shoes, and it was an excellent choice except for the spike heels on the shoes.

"Shavings. If it's a graveside service, I'll be sinking into the grass if I'm wearing those."

I ran upstairs and got a pair of black flats, and put them in my purse. By then, Tom had pulled into the driveway, Angelique at his side. Sid and I got into the back seat of their Honda sedan, and we headed to the airport.

The flight was to Oakland, and Sid had upgraded Ange and Tom's tickets so that they could sit across from us in business class.

"I've got the airline points and I'm not using them," Sid explained. "May as well."

Tom had also accepted an invite from Bob Kinney to stay at his place in Berkeley. Bob picked us up at the airport in Oakland.

"I scored us a reservation at Chez Panisse," Bob told us.

Sid's eyebrows rose. "That was nice of you."

Angelique and I glanced at each other. Something told us it wasn't about Bob being nice but trying to one-up Sid. We don't flaunt it, but even Sid's more casual clothes have that sheen that means he paid a fortune for them. So do some of mine, even though I generally made the outfit. Sewing is my therapy, and while I'll balk at spending thirty dollars for a blouse, I'll happily cough up forty bucks a yard for a print I really like, even if I need four yards of it. [You are the mistress of inconsistency. - SEH]

Still, dinner was insanely good. Bob asked Sid what had happened to his glasses as we began our salads.

"I got contact lenses," Sid said.

Bob looked at him. "You never did say what you've been doing for a living."

"A lot of things." Sid shrugged. "Some freelance writing. I teach piano."

Bob's look was skeptical, at best, which was understandable. Freelance writing does not pay that well, and the reason Sid had grown up dirt poor was that Stella taught piano for cash wages when he was young.

Sid cleared his throat. "I inherited some money at the end of seventy-two. From my grandfather, we've since found out."

"You mean you found out who your father was?" Bob's eyebrows rose.

Ange, Tom, Sid, and I all laughed softly. We all knew that story.

"We'll never know who he was," said Sid. [Okay, we did find out. But that wasn't until 2014, and who knew about DNA in '89? – SEH] "No, the money came from Stella's father. I have, however, spent a fair amount of time making sure it worked for me over the years. So, how did you get to med school?"

Bob rolled his eyes. "My dad finally coughed up. I did pre-med at UCLA, then med school at Stanford."

Sid laughed. "I did my undergrad there." He paused suddenly. "Stanford Med? When were you there?"

"Seventy-two to seventy-six. Why?"

"You didn't happen to know a Rachel Flaherty, did you?"

Bob's eyes opened wide, and he laughed crudely. "Everybody knew Rachel, and in the carnal sense." He laughed again. "Don't tell me, you knew her, too."

"Yeah." Sid's grin got just a touch evil. "I slept with her a few times in spring seventy-two, then that May spent a weekend with her and a bad box of condoms."

I couldn't help giggling.

Sid grew serious. "How well did you know her, Bob?"

He shrugged. "Not well at all. I mean, I slept with her a few times, but so did everyone else." He frowned. "She was an odd bird. When I knew her, she was just coming back from an academic leave, which is how she ended up in my year. Never said why."

Sid and I looked at each other and rolled our eyes.

"That was definitely her style," I grumbled.

Bob looked at me. "You knew her, too?"

"Later, yeah," I said.

Ange and Tom both sighed a little.

"I don't get it." Bob's brow wrinkled.

"Rachel was my son's first mother," Sid said. "That bad box of condoms was how I got caught." He shrugged and frowned. "I didn't see her again after that weekend in May, had no clue she'd gotten pregnant until she brought him to me the weekend before his eleventh birthday. It's just that Nick is working on a family history project right now, and I wish I could tell him more about his first mother."

"He can't ask her?" Bob asked.

"Not anymore." Sid looked over at Bob and sighed. "Rachel died about four and a half years ago."

Bob suddenly remembered the crude way he'd talked about her. "I'm, uh, so sorry to hear that, Sid. She was... She was a lot of fun."

Tom, Ange, and I couldn't help laughing as Sid rolled his eyes.

"It's okay, Bob," I said. "I wasn't one of Rachel's bigger fans, either. There were some things she did that really hurt Nick."

[Hello, Mama bear. - SEH]

Bob shook his head. "I didn't even know she had a kid."

"She tended to keep secrets," I said. "So I'm not surprised."

The junior waiter came and collected our empty salad plates, and a minute later, our entrees arrived. I'm not sure why, but Bob didn't notice that Tom was only drinking club soda and that Ange only had half a glass from the bottle of Pinot Noir that Sid had ordered to go with our entrees. Bob looked at the rest of us and frowned.

"I don't get it," he said, finally. "Tom, you said you and Angelique met at Sid and Lisa's wedding. So, Ange, were you Lisa's friend or Sid's?"

Ange laughed. "Both. And, yes, Sid and I had been sleeping together off and on long before Lisa showed up."

"That's actually how Ange and I got to be friends," I said. "Sid didn't give up sleeping around until I'd been with him for, what, two and a half years?"

"Lisa was initially my secretary," Sid explained.

"I gave up sleeping around," Ange said. "Then Sid gave up sleeping around, which was what kept Lisa from shacking up with him. Lisa and I were friends, and right before the wedding, we became poker buddies."

I giggled. I couldn't believe it, but the poker game that had started as my bachelorette party was still going every month.

"You girls like poker, huh?" Bob grinned.

"You don't want to play them," Tom said genially. He had lost more than a couple bucks to Ange and me. So had Sid. If they hadn't lost more, it was because we generally played penny ante.

"Trust me, you don't," said Sid.

Ange glared at both him and Tom. "Don't be such spoilsports."

Ange and I grinned at each other while Tom and Sid shuddered. They both knew what Ange and I were thinking. Fresh meat.

Bob was not to be deterred. "I think a game would be fun. We'll set one up when we get home."

"Sure, Bob," said Tom. "Why not?"

"Ten-dollar ante?" Bob said.

"We can manage that, can't we, Ange?" I said, slightly winking at her to let her know I could cover her.

Ange gave Bob the once-over. "We can manage that."

I caught her eyes. She was thinking it would be nice to win some real money for a change. Sid and Tom looked at each other and knew that Bob had just gotten himself in far deeper than he had thought. They both sighed. [Oh, come on. Bob was about to go on a fast trip to the cleaners and had no clue. So, we felt a little for the guy. - SEH]

We took our time finishing dinner, then went over to Bob's place. It was a split-level, built onto a hill overlooking Berkeley. In the distance, lights twinkled across the bay. The house had a definite mid-century style, but inside was modern, with lots of overstuffed furniture. Sid and I and Tom and Ange had rooms on the bottom floor. We dropped our bags there. I pulled a couple hundred dollars from my wallet. Sid pulled several from his, shaking his head.

"Honey," I groaned. "He is asking for it."

"I know." He smiled. "On one hand, he is an old friend. But on the other hand, it is a blast seeing you take on his kind of attitude."

We went upstairs to Bob's dining room, which was bland and next to his open kitchen. Bob had a set of poker chips on the table, along with a bottle of Wild Turkey White Label and a couple of bottles of white wine.

"Got any club soda?" Tom asked.

Bob again looked surprised. "Yeah. Why aren't you drinking?"

Tom grinned. "I got sober in nineteen-eighty and am happy to stay that way. But don't worry. I'm around people who drink all the time."

"Do you mind if I have a glass of wine or two?" Ange asked him.

He kissed her forehead. "You know I don't. You already give it up so often for me."

Those two were so cute together, I couldn't help but sigh happily.

"Oh, Tom, Sid, look what I found today." Bob handed them a couple of photographs.

One of the pictures I recognized.

"Sid, that's in our wedding album," I said, pointing to the print of the six teen boys in their altogether, sitting and laughing on a battered couch.

"Stella must have made extra prints," said Sid.

Tom smiled at the other one, then handed it to Sid. The six young men were all wearing caps and gowns and had their arms around each other in a line, with Stella in the middle.

"That's your high school graduation," I said.

"Oh, Tom, you were loaded," said Ange.

"I generally was at that time," Tom said.

"Bob, do you have a picture of you and your parents?" I asked.

Bob sighed. "No. Dad and I were not talking to each other then, and Mom didn't make it to graduation."

"Oh, no." I looked at him. "What happened?"

"She has a problem with agoraphobia."

"I remember that," said Sid.

"Yeah, well, let's play poker." Bob swallowed and held out his hand toward the table.

We paid in and got chips. I'd snuck my two hundred to Ange, and I'm sure Sid snuck some money to Tom. Sid bought my chips, but then I seldom have that much cash on me. He generally carried a lot more. Ange and Tom are not poor, but they are not high rollers on a government employee's and a teacher's salaries. With Bob determined to show off, that could have made things a little difficult for them. Ange, however, knew she'd be able to pay me back and probably cover Tom's bets, as well.

After three, almost four, years of playing poker together, Ange and I know each other's tells, and Ange has honed her skills playing me, and occasionally, my father, who is an even better poker player than I am. When it came to Bob, we were without mercy. Sid took a small splash of Wild Turkey. Ange and I each had a glass of genuinely nice sauvignon blanc. Bob filled his tumbler with the bourbon.

The deal went around the table at least twice before Bob made his bonehead move. Sid dealt a hand of five-card draw. I'd pulled absolutely nothing, and the odds of drawing anything were pretty much nil, so I folded in the first round of betting. I had a decent stack of chips in front of me. Tom was running low. Sid wasn't in much better shape. Ange had an okay stack, and Bob was behind both Ange and me.

Bob stood pat, i.e., didn't take any cards in the second deal. Ange and I glanced at each other. He was so obviously bluffing. We kept our faces straight, but dang, this was going to be fun. Tom took three cards. Ange took two. Then Sid took three. I spotted the momentary upward quirk on Ange's lips that meant she had something really good.

"Your bet, Bob," said Sid.

"Fifty dollars," Bob said, tossing in the red chip.

Tom folded. He had nothing. Ange frowned.

"Okay," she said. "And I raise it ten."

Sid folded with a brief flash of annoyance. He obviously had something decent. Ange usually folds fast and almost never raises unless she can back it up.

"Call and raise it another ten." Bob's grin was slightly evil.

The two of them went back and forth a few times, Bob's face growing slightly grayer as it did, until he had nothing left to bet.

"Okay, I call," he said.

"Ten high straight flush with clubs on it," said Ange, laying the cards on the table.

My jaw dropped and I laughed loudly.

Bob gulped. "Um. Beats me."

I glanced at Sid, then Ange. "I think it's time for me to cash out."

"I think I will, too." Ange winked at me and picked up the open bottle of sauv blanc.

She pushed her chips toward Tom as I shoved mine at Sid.

I grabbed our glasses and followed her. The two of us went downstairs, and Ange beckoned me into the bedroom she was sharing with Tom.

"I've got something for you," she said softly, glancing upstairs. "I went into the office yesterday after I called you. I told Tom I was Christmas shopping." She swallowed. "What Louis told us on Friday was that he wanted to come back as his real self and that he needed us to verify that he was who he said he was. The reason he wanted to come back was that he's a P.I."

"A P.I.?" I frowned.

"Yeah. He was using the name Gene Krakowski when he set the dinner up with Tom." Ange refilled our glasses.

I kept my face straight, but Ange caught me.

"Can't tell you," I said.

She rolled her eyes but understood. "Anyway, he was going after this drug dealer to get some back child support for the dealer's ex-wife and stumbled onto some crooked Feds. He even gave us the names." She handed me a file folder. "These Feds are pretty vicious, but Louis figures if he goes back to his real name and makes himself a cause celebre, it will be harder for the crooks to waste him. They have a motive, after all, and someone will be looking at them."

"Okay. But what can I do about that?"

"I know it's taking a chance on blowing your covers, but somebody has to check this out." She sighed and pointed to the file folder. "I have the profiles on the three agents Louis fingered. They're clean, at least on the surface. Here's the weird thing. You know how it is. People gossip, and the scuttlebutt on these three is that they're crooked as hell, and anytime they get caught, the evidence disappears, and their records are somehow scrubbed clean. Louis said they've been running deals since the war. He figures somebody has got to be protecting them, which would make sense based on the chatter I've heard."

I sighed. "I guess I can look into it. I just don't know what I'm going to tell Sid."

"What do you mean?"

"Ange, you saw him. Just because he's acting normal now doesn't mean he isn't still a mess. He's covering."

"Not that well."

"No kidding." I sighed. "He's sniping at the least little thing, poor guy."

Ange sighed, as well. "Well, we'll have to figure something out. Even if it weren't for Louis, we've probably got three crooked agents. We've gotta get on top of that."

"You're right. Let me think it over, okay? Maybe I can come up with something."

We finished the bottle of wine, then I jammed the file into my overnight case without thinking about it. I was tired and getting more and more worried about Sid.

December 3, 1989

Sid's Voice

The last thing I wanted to do was go to Stan's funeral. Still, I couldn't say no either, and I have no idea why. So, I suppose it's fair to say that I was not in the best of moods that evening. Worse yet, by the end of the poker game, Bob was really starting to get on my nerves. I should have gone downstairs with Lisa and Ange, but I needed to make the effort, I guess.

"We tried to tell you, Bob," said Tom as he sifted through the bills he'd gotten and handed four to me.

"Jesus," Bob grumbled. "It must be nuts to be married to those two broads."

I couldn't help rolling my eyes. "I like being married to a woman like Lisa."

"Whatever floats your boat," Bob grumbled.

"So, Bob, why aren't you married?" Tom asked. "Single doctor. You must have had plenty of opportunity."

Bob shook his head. "Nope. Not doing it. I don't even want to live with somebody."

"Were you in touch with Stan?" I asked.

"Hell, no." Bob sighed. "I was happy to leave high school behind. I know we guys had a good time, but honestly? Those were the worst years of my life." He shuddered.

"You mean, your folks' divorce?" Tom asked.

Bob winced but nodded. "Right before freshman year, Dad dumped my mom for the younger wife. That's why we lived in that crap apartment. Mom's still there. Won't leave. I have to do all her medical care, or she won't get any. My sister lives with her, and my brother checks in. Between hating my dad for what he did to my mom and having to depend on him for money, it was not a good time. Dad kept pushing me to go into business. Had this grand dream of his son following in his footsteps. Still hasn't gotten one to go for it. He's on his fourth wife. My half-sister keeps me up to date on him. But I don't talk to him. I only kept a relationship with him long enough to get through med school."

"Yeah," said Tom softly. "Wallace told me the other night it wasn't a good time for him, either. That's why he's not coming to the funeral." Tom looked at me. "I think the only time any of us felt okay was when we were hanging out at your place, Sid."

"Really." That surprised me. "Stella was hardly the maternal type."

Bob snorted. "I know you had problems with her, but she was more like a mom to me than my own mother was."

"Same here," said Tom.

"What was your mom's problem?" Bob asked.

"Buzzed all the time." Tom sighed.

"Stan's mom was a bitch," Bob continued. "I think she'd had to get married to his dad because she'd gotten pregnant with him and never forgave him for it."

I frowned. "I remember Wallace's parents seemed okay. Just really distant, even worse than Stella was. What I saw of them."

"That's because they were working all the time," Tom said.

"How is it you guys knew all this stuff and I didn't?" I asked.

Bob laughed. "You were too busy chasing tail."

"Not entirely," said Tom. "I didn't say anything about what was going on at my place. Wallace only told me about his folks the other night, after you and Louis had left, Bob. You didn't say anything about your mom's problems, either. We all knew you hated your father, but I didn't know why until tonight."

"Stan told me about his mom one night when we were drunk," said Bob, then he laughed. "Which was most nights for us, wasn't it?"

Tom shook his head. "Sadly."

Bob looked at me. "How is Stella?"

I smiled. "She's doing really well. She lives near me in L.A. Did you guys ever meet Sy Flournoy?"

"Not 'til your wedding," Tom said. "And then, I didn't get to talk to him much until he moved in with Stella. That was, what? A couple of years ago?"

"He's been there off and on since she moved to the condo in L.A. three and a half years ago," I said. "But he's been there full-time since last winter when he retired from Juilliard." I looked at Bob. "Sy was a part of our lives even when I was a kid. He just lived in New York and seldom came out here. Anyway, Stella had a music school in Florida when we reconciled a few years ago."

"Reconciled?" Bob asked.

"Eh, yeah," I said, squirming a little. "We got estranged when I got drafted and didn't speak to each other until about four years ago. After we reconciled, she moved her school out to Los Angeles, and when I got my master's in music, she talked me into teaching a couple days a week there. She's getting a big kick out of being Grandma, too."

"I'm not surprised," said Bob. "She really seemed to have a fun time with us. I could never figure out why you two fought all the time."

"It probably had to do with how she was raised." I shrugged. "I don't know. Those high school years were rough enough, but those two years in 'Nam put a whole different perspective on that."

"Two years?" Bob asked. "I thought the tour was only supposed to be one year."

My throat went dry. There was no way in hell that I wanted to talk about the war. I couldn't figure out why I'd brought it up. I shrugged.

"Got blackmailed into re-upping for a second year," I said.

"You never told me that," Tom said. "Were you dealing drugs or something?"

I had to laugh. "No. It was the usual. I got caught with my pants down."

Actually, the pants down was me humping the base commander's daughter stateside in boot camp. That's what got me blackmailed into doing intelligence work. The extra year was because I'd tumbled onto something hot, and they needed me to keep working it.

"Anyway, I don't talk about that time." I sighed. "I just want to keep it in the past where it belongs."

Bob filled his tumbler with bourbon for the third time. I got my second splash, then Bob pulled out a plastic baggie of roaches and tossed them onto the table.

Tom got up. "Go ahead and light up, guys. I'm going to go downstairs and avoid a contact high."

Bob pulled out two joints and got some matches and an ashtray. I looked at the joint and decided what the hell.

Believe it or not, it was Lisa who got me smoking pot again. In high school, I'd do a joint every now and then, with the occasional binge when the party got wild enough. I did a couple lines of cocaine once in 'Nam, then didn't do any more drugs at all because I wanted to stay alive, and being stoned in combat is not a good way to do that. Once home, it was back to the occasional joint at a party thing with no binges because pot, especially, is hard on the old libido.

However, a year and a half before, we'd been working a case and Lisa had gone to interview a suspect right after she'd wrenched her back. She was in a lot of pain, but the pain pills didn't help, and not doing anything didn't help, either. The suspect had a pot habit, and she talked to him at his place just long enough to get one serious contact high. She hadn't liked the sensation, but it did take the edge off her back pain long enough for her to get some sleep, which helped more than anything did.

So, on the rare occasion when Lisa puts her back out, we light up. We do have to make sure we've had sex first, and there's a hefty stash of crispy Cheetos and potato chips in the closet because she gets the munchies like no one else. But it is the only thing that helps her back enough that she can sleep, and she does not like getting stoned by herself. So, we share the joint.

Neither of us likes the sensation of being intoxicated, whether it's drunk or stoned. Bob's joint reminded me of why. Shit, that stuff was strong. I got about two puffs in and realized I did not want any more.

"You ever think about cheating on Lisa?" Bob asked me.

"No." I put the joint out in the ashtray.

"Not even a little bit?"

I looked at him. "Why would I? I have an incredibly intelligent, warm, loving, sexy, gorgeous wife. What else could I want or need?"

"What about when she gets old and fat?"

"Huh?" I blinked and coughed. "I'm going to get old and fat long before she does. She's eight years younger than me, and she doesn't gain weight. I'm the one who gains weight." I thought about it, trying to envision Lisa with rolls around her middle, and saw her mother and sister. Not that I'm attracted to either Mama or Mae - they are my mother-in-law and sister-in-law - but they are still lovely women. "And so what if she does? Lisa will still be incredibly intelligent, warm, loving, and really sexy."

Bob took an extra-long toke. "But that's my problem. It's all about how a woman looks. I have women who are friends, but I can't see myself sleeping with them. They're old. You don't sleep with old ladies. That's why I won't get married. Women get old, and I won't do what my dad did to my mom. They can't help getting old."

"Have you looked at yourself in the mirror, asshole?" I shook my head in a vain effort to clear it. "You've got a belly. You've got gray coming in. You're getting old, too. And, trust me, sleeping with an older woman is a blast."

"Because they're so grateful." Bob laughed morosely.

"No, fuckhead. They're fun. I'm sure there are plenty of them who have hang-ups, but most of the women I knew who were happy to climb into bed with some young stud were pretty confident, and better yet, comfortable in their own skin. It was the younger ones who were so insecure and constantly needing reassurance."

Man, I hated that lightheaded feeling. Worse yet, the last thing I needed or even wanted to be doing was listening to some fucking idiot getting maudlin on the night before a funeral I really did not want to be at.

I got up. "I've gotta get to bed."

I staggered downstairs. Lisa was awake and reading in bed.

"You okay?" She asked, putting the bookmark in her book and setting it on the nightstand.

"No. I'm a little high." I went into the bathroom to get my contacts out and get undressed.

She got a good whiff of me as I went past. "So, I guess we're not getting any tonight."

"Oh, you are. I need to get my self-esteem back." I sighed, popping out my lenses and cleaning them. "If you can still put up with me."

"I can. I'm just worried about you, is all."

I looked at myself in the mirror, then squirted some toothpaste on my brush. "I'm worried about me, too."

It wasn't just that I couldn't get it up. That generally happened when I smoked pot, so while I didn't like it, I could live with it. I finished brushing my teeth and getting undressed, then went back into the bedroom.

"You realize that us guys are all going to turn forty this coming year." I pulled the covers back and sat down on the bed. "Bob never got married because women get old, and he can't see himself sleeping with an older woman. What is it with these pricks that they keep asking me for relationship advice?"

She laughed in spite of herself. "Because you have a good relationship?"

I slid under the covers. "Lisapet, I have no idea how I got a good relationship. You just happened to me." I snuggled in close, then let my hand drift onto her breasts.

She purred. "But you did keep working on it. Now, make me happy and get your self-esteem back."

That woman is magic. Somehow, someway, I got my erection after all, and she got made happy a second time. Which, oddly, did not make me feel more like a man, whatever that's supposed to feel like. It did make me feel happy, though. Definitely happy.

December 4, 1989

Lisa's Voice

Sid, fortunately, had not drunk that much the night before, so while he was feeling pretty much like a wrung-out dishcloth that next morning, at least his head wasn't pounding. I wasn't thrilled that he'd been smoking pot with Bob that night, but decided not to worry about it unless he kept it up. He hadn't had a nightmare, either, and I thanked God for that.

I was glad that I'd grabbed my flats before leaving the day before. It was a graveside service, and chilly, with a steady breeze coming in off the bay. Stan's younger brother and sister were there, with their spouses and children, all the kids being younger than twelve. I never did find out whose child was whose. The kids seemed bored silly by the whole thing, and their parents weren't much more interested. Stan's mother was sort of there. Stan was about to be buried next to her.

"Oh, by the way," Bob muttered to Tom, Sid, Ange, and me. "I went to the viewing yesterday before picking you guys up. It really was Stan in the box."

It was, perhaps, a rather crass observation. However, given what they'd all dealt with the previous Friday, I could understand it.

There were a couple other friends present, none of whom seemed particularly sad. I couldn't help wondering if anyone had gotten close enough to Stanley Ford to genuinely grieve at his passing. There were two other men wearing dark suits that were probably polyester and fit like they'd come off the rack at Sears. One of them spoke briefly to Stan's brother, who pointed our little party out to him.

The funeral director gave the eulogy, which was sparse enough. Stan had worked as a car salesman at a local dealership and had been a good employee. His personal life was glossed over. No one else chose to speak.

As the funeral party began to disperse, the two guys in the Sears suits approached the five of us. Both flashed badges at us.

"Lafayette P.D.," said the first one. He was somewhat taller than average with thinning red hair. "I understand that you five are friends of the deceased."

Lafayette was one of the many suburbs in the Bay Area.

"Were friends," said Bob.

"I was probably most in contact with him," said Tom. "How can we help you?"

"Let's get your names first," said the partner, who was short with strongly Hispanic features. He pointed at Bob. "You?"

"Dr. Robert Kinney, MD. I've got a general practice in Walnut Creek."

"And how did you know the deceased?"

Bob swallowed. "He was a former friend. We hung out together in high school." Bob gestured at Tom and Sid. "All three of us hung out with him."

"And when did you lose touch with Mr. Ford?"

"Almost immediately after graduation," Bob said.

"I kept in loose touch with Stan," Tom said. "Um, I'm Thomas Freeman. I live in Los Angeles now."

The second detective looked at Sid. "And you?"

"Sid Hackbirn." He didn't even bother spelling it.

"And when were you last in touch with Mr. Ford?"

Sid thought for a second. "Sometime during my first semester of college."

Sid had started college at the University of San Francisco before he'd gotten drafted.

"And when was that?"

"Fall, nineteen sixty-eight."

The two cops' eyes narrowed at Sid. No surprise. He was the only person who wasn't offering more information than was asked for.

"Detectives," said Ange. "May I ask why you're questioning us?"

"And you are?" asked the redhead.

"Angelique Carter, Programs Coordinator for the FBI, Los Angeles office."

The two detectives glanced at each other with slightly worried frowns.

The redhead swallowed. "Uh, Mr. Ford was, unfortunately, murdered. His car had been tampered with." He looked at Sid, Tom, and Bob. "What can you guys tell us about Louis Renfrew?"

Bob's jaw dropped. Tom almost kept his poker face on. Sid, Ange, and I definitely did.

Ange cut in before Bob could say anything stupid. "What does this Mr. Renfrew have to do with anything?"

The two detectives looked at Bob, and I had a bad feeling they'd be leaning on Dr. Kinney in no time.

"He's a person of interest," said the Hispanic detective.

Ange stared both him and his partner down. "I see. And how did you learn about this person of interest?"

The redhead swallowed and glanced at the rest of us. "I'm afraid that's confidential, Ms., um, Carter."

She looked at us, then back at the detectives. "Thank you, detectives. Is there anything else?"

"Uh, no, ma'am." The redhead gulped, and the two detectives backed off.

We got into Bob's car.

"Holy shit, Angelique," he crowed as he pulled out. "That was amazing!"

Tom was in the front seat of Bob's Mercedes sedan, while Sid, I, and Ange were in the back seat. Ange was shaking a little as I squeezed her hand.

"Look, Bob," Ange said. "You can't say anything beyond that Louis was your friend in high school. You have no idea that he had any contact with Stan, which, by the way, you really don't, so you won't be lying. Just don't say anything more than that. Okay?"

"Why?"

Ange rolled her eyes. "Because we don't know what Louis was up to the other night. You could be endangering us unnecessarily. Or him. If you hear from Louis, though, I want to know about it. I do work for the FBI, and if there are bad agents involved, like he said, then I need to know. It's for your safety. And those bad agents, if they're there, they won't mind taking you out if it means they can get to Louis. Do you understand?"

I was so proud of Ange at that moment, as was Sid. I think Tom was, too, even if he didn't entirely understand what Ange was up to.

We ate an early lunch at a small diner in northern Oakland, then Bob took us to the airport. We grabbed the first flight to L.A. that we could find, even though we had to run a bit to catch it.

Sid usually sleeps when flying, but it's a short flight from the Bay Area to Los Angeles, so Sid kept his contacts in and stayed awake. Once in the air, Sid glanced over at Tom and Ange, across the aisle from us.

"Bad agents?" Sid asked.

"Yeah." I told him what Angelique had said the night before. "I don't think she entirely buys Louis' story, especially after today. But it's just hinky enough that she thinks we should check it out."

Sid shook his head. "We're too close."

"Who else is she going to ask?"

"I suppose, but not only are we too close, we've got the Whole Fam-Damily breathing down our necks. It's hard enough getting anything through this time of year."

"I know." I looked back over at Tom and Ange. "If you want to stay out of it, I can just take it on myself."

"I'm not going to do that to you. But I will call Lillian to see if she can offer any help."

"That's probably a good idea. And you asked me to remind you to call Dr. Heilland."

He stared straight ahead. "I need to do that. What else have we got on the docket for this week?"

I dug my organizer out of my purse. "No freelance deadlines. In fact, I don't think we have any for the entire month."

"We'll see what's in the mail."

I flipped through pages. "As far as the family is concerned, we've got dinner at our place Saturday night, and you've got a timbalo to make."

Sid shuddered. "I've got two of them."

"What? Are you crazy?"

"I don't think so." He winced. "Neil asked me to do two because it's the first thing that goes, and some folks were unhappy that they didn't get any last year. It shouldn't be that much harder to make two at the same time."

"I suppose. You're playing at Mass on Friday for Immaculate Conception. Workwise, besides this new thing, you've just got your usual lessons on Tuesday and Thursday. I've got to finish grading term papers today, then see if I can order Quackenbush's book. I'm only a quarter of the way through it, and already I've got notes to photocopy half of that. So, if I can order the book, then I've got Ashton and Scoresby to start, plus finals on Tuesday and Thursday, then getting those graded and grades filed on Friday. Mae wants me to help make cookies for the party one day this week. I'm thinking Wednesday, assuming I can get Tuesday's finals graded fast enough."

"I suppose I shouldn't be surprised." Sid blinked and glared out the plane window. "You did warn me that this PhD thing was more than full-time. I was hoping that once you finished your coursework that it would lighten up a little."

I snorted. "Working on my dissertation is even worse. All that research and I'm expected to teach at the same time."

"So, are you going to head up the English department somewhere?"

"Nah. I don't even know if I want to go for a full professorship. But I do want to do some teaching."

He nodded. "That's important."

The plane landed at two-fifteen, and since none of us had brought more than an overnight bag, we didn't have to wait for luggage and got back to Tom's car before three o'clock. Tom dropped Angelique off at the FBI offices in the federal building in Westwood, then drove us home.

"Monday is her hell day," Tom said as he steered his car down Wilshire Boulevard. "She has to clear up everything that came in over the weekend. Me? Getting a sub today was a Godsend. I can finally catch up on some grading, maybe get my lesson plans together on the Harlem Renaissance unit."

Tom teaches American Lit and Creative Writing at a local high school.

"So, when are you done with Frost?" I asked.

"Just finished. I've got Dickinson next, through Friday, and I think next week, we'll be doing some of the moderns. I forgot what I put down. It's not going to make much difference, anyway. These last few weeks before Christmas holidays, they are all on the ceiling, and it's only going to get worse between now and vacation time."

"I'm so glad my semester is almost done," I said. "Community college kids aren't much better."

"Say, isn't Nick in one of your classes?"

"Yep."

Nick is what they call a bridge student at the small community college where I teach two sections of Basic Composition. Nick's in an extra-curricular program that allows gifted high school students to take college-level classes and get credit for them. He had taken a bridge class every semester he'd been in high school, starting with chemistry, then moving on to biology classes. I'd started teaching at the college the year before, when it was made clear I needed to be teaching while I was working on my PhD. That semester, Nick had chosen to work on general education requirements and, for a joke, signed up for Basic Composition. The joke was on him. I'm a tough teacher and didn't let up on him for his sake.

Tom pulled into our driveway. We thanked him and got our overnight case out of the trunk, then went through the front door as Tom pulled out. As Sid waved goodbye, he sighed.

"Did you see it?" he asked, unlocking the front door.

"The van out front that's supposed to look like a gardener's and is probably a recon vehicle?"

"I guess you saw it." He shut the door. "Now what?"

"I'm going to change clothes, call Ange, then work on term papers." I paused, picking up the overnight case and grinning. "Do you have something else in mind?"

Sid smiled sadly, the exhaustion wafting off him. "Oh, that sounds nice. Sadly, if we do, I will not get up from wherever we land, and we have work to do. I'll page Nick to let him know we're home, then get on the mail. Oh, and did Ange pass on any paperwork on those Feds she's worried about? She kind of hinted to me that she had."

"Yeah. I'll bring the folder down after I change and unpack."

Which is exactly what I did. Sid had the mail spread out on his desk, although most of it was related to our various investments. There were two Christmas cards that we would open later, after dinner. I gave Sid the folder, then pulled the stack of term papers in folders off the file cabinet and brought them over to my desk.

"I called Ange, too," Sid said.

"What did she say?"

"That she wanted to get the police reports on Stan's death." Sid smiled. "She said she had a case number, which should help, and she gave it to me. She was surprised about the recon van, but said she'd check it out right away."

"Good. What about Lillian and Dr. Heilland?"

"Couldn't call Lillian." He opened the folder. "I didn't have the names of our targets yet. I'm assuming these are the guys in question."

"They are."

Sid cursed. "You know, one of them is a Special Agent Harlan Cobb."

My eyes widened. "That doesn't sound good."

Sid checked his watch. "It's getting a little late in DC, but I'll call Lillian now and leave a message. And I've got an appointment tomorrow with Dr. Heilland at eleven. Do you want to come?"

"I could. Do you want me to?"

"I don't know." Sid stared blankly at the desktop. "No. If this is about me feeling guilty, then I don't want to add to it by taking you away from your schoolwork. If things get serious, then I'll ask."

I smiled at him. "Okay. I'm trusting you to do that."

Sid made the call to Lillian and left a message while I started in on the top paper. If the prose seemed more than a little familiar, it was because I knew who had helped our son. The wording was all Nick's, and I'm sure Sid did little more than point out errors and offer a suggestion or two. But there was at least one transition that was all Sid's style.

Sid noticed what I was working on and lifted an eyebrow. "So... How is our boy doing?"

"Rather nicely indeed. I've only found three grammatical errors, one spelling error, and four typos. His bibliography is gorgeous. Oops. Make that five typos. Dang. He almost had a B."

"You're giving him a C for that?"

"No. B minus. He needs a little work on his clarity."

Sid sighed and shook his head. Well, I am a really tough teacher.

"Mom! Dad!" Nick bellowed from the front door. "I'm home!"

Sid pressed the intercom button. "You're clear, son. We're in the office."

Another of Nick's trials is that if he shows up when we're not expecting him, well, he's accidentally walked in on us a few times. Not often, but he does make sure that he announces his presence quite loudly, and we make sure he knows where he doesn't want to go if we're, um, otherwise occupied.

I slid Nick's term paper to the bottom of my stack as he came into the office.

"You guys okay?" he asked, giving me a solid squeeze and kiss on the cheek.

"We're fine, darling," I said. "It wasn't business."

He squeezed Sid and kissed his father on top of his head. Sid sighed. Nick sometimes delights in reminding his father that he's the taller of the two. I would have thought, given the car situation, that Nick would have been more diplomatic. He was sixteen, however, which meant he wasn't the most astute human being alive.

"So, how did you get home?" Sid asked.

"Drove Stella's car." Nick grinned. "She let me take it to school today. Darby will bring her over when he's done with his lesson."

Sid sighed and got up. "I'd better let Conchetta know there will be a crowd at dinner tonight."

I looked up from grading. "Who all is coming?"

"Just the rest of the team. But with them and Stella and Darby..."

I nodded.

Nick sat on the edge of my desk. "So. Did you get to my paper yet?"

"You'll get it on Thursday." I looked up at him. "We agreed. You are no different than any of my other students."

"You just grade me harder, is all."

I shrugged. "If that's what you want to think."

I probably did grade him harder. I'd done the same to Sid when he'd been in my class while we were on an undercover case in Wisconsin. My cousin Maggie had also gotten graded harder when she turned up in my class the winter before. In Nick's case, especially, I knew he was up to the challenge, and I did not want to play favorites, even if my darling son was the smartest and nicest kid there.

"Did you guys see the van out front?" Nick asked.

"We did. That's probably why your dad is asking Frank, Esther, Jesse, and Kathy to dinner tonight."

Nick grimaced. "Does that mean I'm going to have to babysit Keshon?"

I looked at him, surprised. "You've never minded before."

"He wasn't into temper tantrums before."

"I'll have to give you points on that. We'll see. Maybe Kathy can get him to sleep."

Nick rolled his eyes.

"Don't you have homework to do?" I asked.

"I got most of it done at school."

"Any reading you're behind on?" I looked at him severely. He generally was behind on reading, not that I could blame him.

"The Scarlet Letter." He shuddered.

I winced. "I couldn't finish that one."

"I'm a quarter of the way in, and I already know it's Dimmesdale. It's boring and stupid."

"I know, darling, but it is required reading. It could be worse. It could be Moby Dick."

The summer before, Nick and I had challenged each other to see who could finish Moby Dick first. I guess, technically, the challenge is still open since neither of us got far with it before we both lost the will to win.

Nick groaned and stalked off to work on The Scarlet Letter. I felt for him. I am not generally a fan of the nineteenth-century novel, American or British. I get that it sounds a little weird that I'm working on my PhD in English, and I have never read either The Scarlet Letter or Moby Dick. I've been dodging those two and the novels of Thomas Hardy most of my academic career, hiding behind my emphasis on English education with a minor in Shakespeare.

Kathy and Jesse showed first, with Keshon in full run. Sid and I hadn't entirely baby-proofed the house. But we had put covers on all the wall outlets before Lissy had started walking and had made a few other adjustments. Most of our cabinets tended to be locked, anyway, because several of them held things like a variety of rifles, handguns, night-vision goggles, listening devices, and other tools of the spy trade. By the time Lissy was old enough to avoid most trouble, Keshon had arrived, and he was one curious little guy. It generally took someone with Nick's hyperactive energy to keep up with him.

Kathy and I got Keshon into the rumpus room with a pile of toys, then put up a child-safety gate in the doorway. We weren't sure how long it would be before Keshon realized he'd been penned in, but we figured we had a couple of minutes. Kathy and I sat in the dining room just in case. Sid and Jesse were upstairs.

I gave Kathy a quick run-down on the three crooked FBI agents and handed her the notes I'd made on the file that Angelique had given me.

"So, we've got Harlan Cobb, Bruce Whitemore, and Peter Venkt." Kathy made a note in her organizer. "I should be able to get their information pretty quickly. Do we have a case number?"

"Yeah. It's there at the top."

"That will make life easier. It's Jesse's day with Keshon tomorrow, so I'll go to County Records in the morning. Then I'll use the case number for the DMV search. I'm thinking we'll want to see what we can find with the admissible searches first."

Admissible, as in admissible in court. We often did searches that provided the kind of evidence that wasn't admissible in court. After all, our job was to find out things, not necessarily get a conviction. It was something we had to be careful about. After all, constitutional protections are there for good reason.

Something went thump in the rumpus room. Kathy and I were on our feet in seconds. Keshon climbed up the bookcase on the back wall. Somehow, neither Kathy nor I screamed. We didn't want him getting startled and falling. Kathy got over the safety gate and pulled her son down.

He screamed, utterly furious that he'd been denied his adventure.

"In the corner with you," Kathy said tiredly.

She put him in the nearest corner and stood over him while he screamed for another minute or so. The good thing about Keshon's tantrums was that they didn't last long, partly because he was easy to distract and partly because he got tired of raising a ruckus when nobody was going to cave into it.

"What now?" Jesse asked as he and Sid stood outside the rumpus room.

"Climbing the bookcase," Kathy said.

Sid bit back a swear word. He was trying to keep his language clean around Lissy and Keshon because they were at that age.

"The pillows," Sid grumbled.

We have several oversized pillows that the kids lie on while watching movies on Uncle Sid's large screen TV, along with the three recliners in the room. The pillows were usually kept stacked by the blinds on the sliding glass door to the back yard and Nick's sun porch laboratory to make it easier for Conchetta to vacuum in there. Someone, however, had stacked the pillows by the bookcase this time, and sure enough, the pillows had fallen over just right to serve as a step stool onto the bookcase.

"Nick!" Sid called.

"Yeah, Dad." Nick wandered up the hall from his bedroom.

"Did you stack the pillows next to the bookcase?"

Nick looked in the room and groaned. "I'm sorry. Lissy hasn't climbed anything in a long time."

"Because we keep the pillows away from the bookcases."

"Yes, sir."

I patted my son's arm. "Honey, just assume there's always going to be a small child around here for the time being."

They hadn't succeeded yet, but Frank and Esther were trying to get pregnant. Keshon hadn't put Kathy and Jesse off having a second child, although they had decided to space the next one out a little further. Not to mention other friends of ours who had babies and toddlers or were about to produce some.

"Aunt Lisa!" Darby bellowed from the front. "Uncle Sid! I'm here!"

Darby had not walked in on Sid and me in flagrante delicto but had picked up the protocol.

"We're clear and in the dining room," I called back.

Darby wandered through the living room, Stella on his heels.

"I'm starving," Darby announced. "What's for dinner?"

"Chicken," said Nick, grinning.

Sid sighed. "Nick, that never was funny and still isn't funny."

"Well?" Nick spread out his hands. "It's not wrong. We always have chicken."

"Not always," Sid grumbled.

He rarely eats red meat, so we do eat a lot of chicken. And Conchetta had made a lovely chicken stew with fresh-baked whole wheat rolls. Stella, however, declined to eat with us. She and Sy wanted to go out to dinner that night. She left in her car. Frank and Esther showed up then, and she, Sid, and Jesse went back upstairs.

They didn't come back downstairs until time for dinner. Keshon had gotten his bits of chicken and vegetables before we sat down and was playing quietly in the rumpus room. I set up the Advent wreath on the dining room table. It's basically a green wreath with four candles, one for each of the four Sundays of Advent, which is the big preparation season before Christmas in the Catholic Church. Three of the candles are purple, the color of penance, since we're supposed to be preparing our souls for the arrival of Christ. One is pink, for joy that the Savior is on His way. I lit the first purple candle, then set the two Christmas cards we'd gotten next to the wreath.

"That new lens is looking really good," Esther told us after we'd said grace and started eating.

Now, Darby doesn't know about the side business. However, because Esther's visible living comes from her security device business, she can get away with talking about things that we, otherwise, would not.

"I think it's time for me to shave," Darby said suddenly.

"Not unless you want to shave those zits off," sniggered Nick.

Darby's beard was still barely there, and while his acne wasn't bad at all, he usually had a whitehead or two on his face. Nick, on the other hand, took after his father. Sid shaves twice a day; his beard is so dark and full. Nick was only shaving in the mornings, but was starting to get a decent five o'clock shadow. He was also, finally, zit-free.

Darby glared at Nick.

Sid glared at Darby. "Esther was telling us something just now."

"Oh. Sorry." Darby shrugged, clearly not sorry.

Esther chuckled. "Anyway, I can't wait to see the shots you guys got. If the light amplifying technology works at distance, then all we have to do is shrink down the size of the lens."

"It looked pretty good from the viewfinder," Jesse said. "We got some great shots of the gardeners across the street."

After dinner, the team members left. I sent Darby to finish his homework, which was not done, as usual. Darby is remarkably disciplined about practicing his violin, but anything else in his life, forget it.

"We need your dirty clothes, too!" I shouted after him.

Nick, Sid, and I opened the Christmas cards, then got into the usual debate about whether to display them or not. Nick didn't care. I wanted them displayed. Sid saw no reason to. I won that one and clipped them to the string I'd already run across the living room wall behind the pianos and around all the art on the wall.

Sid met me in the office a minute later. "We got shots of the shift change. From what I saw through the viewfinder on the camera, one of those three we're supposed to be chasing was there."

I sighed. "Now, what do we do?"

"We're going to have to go after them somehow. We can't have this kind of surveillance on the place."

"But why would they be checking us out?"

"I have no idea." Sid looked pained. "Just what I don't want to be doing."

December 5, 1989

I t being a school day, we all got up at five a.m. to go running for an hour at five-thirty. Darby had accepted running in the morning as the price he had to pay for staying with us most of the week. That didn't mean he didn't complain about it. Of course, I did, too.

I started breakfast while the guys showered and got dressed. We eat fruit salad and whole wheat toast almost every morning. With Darby there, we went through even more fruit and bread. Teen boys eat a lot. I also happen to eat a lot, myself, but I'm one of those rare types who can eat like a horse and never gain weight.

Some months after Nick had turned fourteen, Sid had given up on trying to restrain us and had bought two four-slice toasters in the name of efficiency. I popped bread slices into the toasters and ground the beans for the coffee maker. As the coffee dripped into the pot, the toast popped up. I took those out, put eight more slices in, plunged the switches down, then buttered the toast that had popped up. I got Sid's prune juice into a glass, and poured orange juice for the rest of us, then got out the skim milk and poured glasses of that.

By that time, Nick was out of the shower and dressed in his school uniform, and helped me get the table set.

"Where's Darby?" I asked.

Nick shrugged. I sighed. Even odds, Darby had fallen asleep again.

"Would you go chivvy him out?" I asked. "You don't want your dad to do it."

Nick winced. "Is he still in a bad mood?"

"I'm afraid so, and he is not going to take well to Darby dragging."

Nick trotted to the opposite side of the house, where Darby had taken up residence in one of the three guest rooms there.

Sid came downstairs, dressed in a two-piece suit and tie. He often wears suits during the day, even if we're only going to be at home. That day, he had his appointment with Dr. Heilland and would be teaching at Stella's school later, so he had even more reason to dress up. Well, from his perspective, he did.

"Where are the boys?" he asked, moodily picking up the morning paper.

"We're right here," said Nick.

Darby just yawned and plopped into his chair at the breakfast room table. It's a light, airy room, done in light green with buttery yellow accents, four white wood chairs, and a white wrought iron table with a glass top. Sid got his fruit salad and toast while scanning the headlines on the front page. The boys wait for Sid, then me, to take what we want first. Nick gets his next because his appetite was slowing, then Darby wolfs down the rest.

Breakfast is usually a quiet meal, and it got quieter when Nick nudged Darby and told him it was time to get to school. The boys took off. One of the nice things about having Darby at the house was that he was driving Nick to and from school. Sid and I continued reading the newspaper. I yawned and got up.

"I'll clear the table," Sid said.

"Okay. Thanks." I gave him a quick kiss, then went upstairs to get dressed for the day.

I got my shower and put on a pair of khaki slacks and a brightly printed turtleneck sweater, made of a cotton knit with a nice, almost glossy sheen.

"My day for the phones?" I asked, coming into the office.

"Yeah. Thanks." Sid looked up from his desk, where he was reading the Wall Street Journal.

Long John Silver, a large gray short-haired cat with a mangled ear and one eye, was already curled up in Sid's lap. We have three cats. Long John was named before we knew she was female and pregnant, some five years before. The pregnancy had resulted in four kittens, two of whom landed with Jesse and Kathy. We have Fritz, a gray tabby with a strong preference for staying outside until dinner time, and Blueberry, who likes sleeping inside all day but is more likely to sleep on a shelf or a mantle.

Bowser was asleep on the floor next to Sid. Motley sat by my chair, thumping the stub of his tail. I gave him a solid pet, then opened Quackenbush and went back to reading. I hadn't been able to order the tome, which meant I was going to be doing a lot of photocopying sometime in the near future.

The first phone call was for Sid. It was an editor responding in the affirmative to a query Sid had sent three weeks before. Ever since Sid had finished his master's degree, he'd been getting back into freelance writing. I had to concede; I was a little envious. I hadn't been able to do any freelance work since I got my dissertation topic approved.

At ten, Conchetta arrived for the day and brought in the mail to us. I thanked her and took a break from rhetoric and grammar. There were a couple bills, which I paid, three more Christmas cards, and a rejection for Sid. He looked at it, shrugged, and filed it. He pulled his pocket watch from his pants and checked the time.

"I'd better get going." He sighed deeply.

"I can go with you." I got up.

He held me closely, then shook his head. "As nice as that would be, I'd better face this one head-on. I'll tell you all about it later, though."

"Okay. I'll hold lunch until you get back."

"Thanks."

He kissed me with a touch of extra warmth and left.

Sid was just barely gone when Lillian paged me. She doesn't like calling the house directly because, well, she caught Sid and me fully engaged a couple of times. Sid answers the phone no matter what he's doing and no matter what stage we're at while doing it. Lillian just can't handle that.

I called her back immediately.

"Why are you checking out Harlan Cobb and friends?" Lillian asked. She was curious, not challenging.

"Well, he did check out Sid's service record for a case," I said. "Is there a reason we shouldn't?"

"No. It's a good thing you are. After I got Sid's message yesterday, I did a little checking around and came up against a brick wall almost immediately."

"I don't understand."

"There is never any evidence against these guys. It always disappears. They get transferred. Their records are cleared. Still, everyone knows they're as crooked as they come, but no one can nail them for it."

"Well, we know somebody's protecting them."

Lillian sighed. "Probably several people. That's one of the things that makes these guys so dangerous. The scuttlebutt is that they've got dirt on just about everybody in Washington."

"You're sure that's not an exaggeration?"

"Not according to Dale O'Connor."

How to explain Dale O'Connor? He's a friend and yet not a friend. He is a member of the House of Representatives, representing South Lake Tahoe, where I'm from (which is not a coincidence), and serves on the House Intelligence Committee. He has been involved in intelligence work since the Korean War, has his fingers in the CIA, FBI counterintelligence, and a host of other shadow agencies, including Quickline. He's also a sexist asshole and the person responsible for blackmailing Sid into intelligence work when Sid was in boot camp.

We're visibly "friends" because Sid and I, along with Lillian and several other key personnel are members of a travel club that serves as a way for us couriers to stay on top of what's going on in Europe and South America so that we can route information to the right agencies and/or operatives here in the States.

The problem was that if Dale was saying these bad FBI agents had dirt on just about everybody, they probably did. Dale tended to know these things.

"Any chance they have something on Dale?" I asked. I could hope.

"I'm sure they do, and I'm also sure Dale doesn't care." Lillian sighed. "You know him. Utterly convinced he's invulnerable. In any case, the other problem is your friend, Mr. Renfrew."

I gasped. "You know him?"

"Well, not personally. Dale told me about him. Apparently, Mr. Renfrew is part of an operation to take out Cobb and company."

"Oh." I swallowed. "So, why is Dale involved?"

"He's also trying to bring down Agent Cobb and his partners. He's been trying to since the war. Back then, Cobb and his friends were involved in drug sales, equipment theft, pimping, child labor. About the only thing they weren't involved in while they were in Vietnam was espionage."

"So, Cobb and company were in the Army together." I bit my lip.

"Yes. They commanded Mr. Renfrew's unit. Even with as much corruption as there was among the officers, Cobb and his buddies were exceptional. Harlan Cobb's father, Marshal Cobb, was something of a political kingmaker. The story was that Marshal insisted that Harlan join the Army to straighten Harlan out. Instead, Harlan used his father's political connections and the dirt on those connections to keep him and his pals in the clear while they oversaw all manner of illegal activity. Since then, Harlan has been adding to his connections and dirt collection. Only recently, however, he tried to use some dirt that he shouldn't have, and according to Dale, the consensus is that he's gone too far, and something must be done about him."

"Terrific."

"However, the sticky wicket here is that Mr. Renfrew has worked off and on for Agent Cobb and his cronies after they returned stateside, and apparently under his real name."

"So, why is he turning on them now?" I asked.

"That I do not know, nor does Dale. At least, he says he doesn't." Lillian let out a soft groan. "He was acting a little cagey about Mr. Renfrew. I'm afraid it's all one miserable mess."

"Especially since it looks like Agent Cobb has set up surveillance on us. Worse yet, it's the holidays. My whole family, plus Stella and Sy, are in and out of here constantly. My nephew is pretty much staying with us during the week. The only good part of it is that our team members have an easy excuse to be here. Is there anything you can do on your end to get them to drop the surveillance?"

"I probably should." Lillian sighed. "I'll do what I can. However, given the number of people who would love to see Agent Cobb's operation die a quick, painful death, I'm afraid you and Sid must investigate and see if there's a way to get their dirt, then put them out of business. Dale insists that you do not let Mr. Renfrew know about your connection to Dale or covert activity. Mr. Renfrew is, according to Dale, highly intelligent, and Dale does not want Sid's cover blown. Oh, and we are not looking to build a court case, I'm afraid."

"Oh, dear." I swallowed. "You know we're not going to do the assassin thing."

"I am all too aware of that," Lillian grumbled. "As is Dale. He said he has made provision for some sort of capture."

"Great."

We hung up shortly after that. I like Lillian a lot, but she does tend to see people as assets that can be expendable. I am profoundly glad that she sees Sid and me as extremely valuable assets.

Angelique called some minutes later.

"How are you doing?" I asked.

"Okay." She sighed. "I was able to check the paperwork on the recon vehicles. Harlan Cobb is behind all of them."

"What do you mean, all of them?"

"He's ordered recon on you, the Mertons, Bob Kinney, and Tom and me. Well, Tom. I don't think Cobb's figured out about me."

"Why, in Heaven's name, would he do that?"

"My best guess, he's looking for Louis to contact us." Which would make sense if Louis were turning on them. Ange sighed. "I'm trying to get it all called off. We can't have recon going on your place, let alone mine and Tom's."

"I know. I appreciate it."

"And I can't get a hold of Louis. I tried the phone number at his P.I. office, but all I got was an answering machine. The home number on his license is disconnected, too."

I bit my lip again. "Okay. I'll see what I can do on my end."

I hung up feeling rather annoyed. At least, Sid was somewhat more relaxed when he got home from Dr. Heilland's. We met in the breakfast room for lunch.

"Well?" I asked.

Sid shrugged. "It's probably some survivor guilt on top of re-opening the old trauma wound. I'll just be going in weekly for the time being. How was your morning?"

I grabbed the plate of sandwiches that Conchetta had made and nodded toward the office. Sid raised an eyebrow but followed me. He doesn't generally like talking about work during meals, which is why we make a point of eating them in the breakfast or dining room. Unless the meal is an excuse to conference with somebody. So, when I headed for the office, Sid knew something was going on. I didn't want to risk Conchetta hearing what I had to say. She's got a clearance and knows something is going on, but we generally pretend there isn't.

"So, what's up?" Sid asked, shutting the office door. He laid the plates and napkins on our desks.

I plopped the plate of sandwiches between us. Our desks are butted up, facing each other. Taking a sandwich, I told him about the calls from Lillian and Angelique.

"I did take the liberty of sending Frank and Esther to case Louis' office on the off chance we'll want to search it," I said. "I hope you don't mind."

Sid took a deep breath. "No. I'm glad you did." He closed his eyes. "Investigating this is certainly going to complicate things. But I guess we must."

"Maybe it will help you come to terms with the war."

Sid smiled weakly. "Dr. Heilland said the same thing."

"Do you want to plan on searching tonight?"

"Not really." Sid looked out at the street, then took a sandwich. "It will be hard to pull off with our friends out there."

"Maybe if we go out early or something."

"That might work. But not tonight. Stella called the car to remind me about practicing tonight, and I promised I would."

There wasn't much to say or do after that. Esther called to let us know that they'd cased the building where Private Investigator Gene Krakowski's (aka Louis') office was, but wouldn't be able to get to us until after four. Both Sid and I had classes to teach, so we put Frank and Esther off until the next day.

Sid and I left around two. Sid went to Stella's music school to teach his two Tuesday students, and I went to give the final for my early Basic Composition class. I got home around six and got half an hour in on grading before Sid showed up with Stella on his heels. Darby and Nick were in the library, supposedly doing homework.

After dinner, Darby wanted to practice with Sid, and Stella told him to go ahead. I went to my office and blazed through grading finals. Well, I'd only asked one essay question, and the rest were short answer. I'd stayed in the classroom until five-thirty, too, and the class had mostly finished by four-thirty, so I'd gotten a jump on the grading.

As soon as I was done, I packed the papers away and started upstairs, only to stop when I heard Sid growling at Darby.

"I know what I'm doing, Uncle Sid," Darby complained.

"I'm not saying you don't." Sid was getting angry. "But I don't feel like practicing with people who are being rude. We're finished for the evening."

"But—"

"We're finished for the evening."

I hurried up the stairs and went into our sewing and music room. I had three projects, all needing zippers. I tend to sew in batches. I get more done that way.

I got my first zipper pinned into the pants I was making as Darby thumped into the room.

"Why are you here?" he groaned.

"This is my sewing room."

"But I need to practice. I've got that concert next Thursday." Darby's face was strained with worry.

I sighed and looked at him. "What's going on, Darby? I know the concert's important, but you're not usually this upset about things like that."

"I'm fine." He started arranging sheet music on a nearby stand. "I just need to practice."

"Are you sure?" I went over to him and touched his back. "You know it's not good to hold things back like this."

He closed his eyes and began breathing heavily. He knew darned well I was talking about the time he'd been molested. He had refused to talk about what was happening then and, I thought, knew better than to do it again.

"Is anybody hurting you?" I asked.

"No." He shook his head. "It's nothing like that, Aunt Lisa." He looked over at my sewing machines without really seeing them. "There's this agent. Mr. Crispin. He wants me to sign with him." Darby dug into his pants pocket and pulled out a folded bill. "He even gave me fifty dollars. I mean, he's not the nicest guy, but he does make sense. I should be touring. I should be trying to get more gigs. The problem is, Mom and Dad don't want me to yet."

"Neither do Sy and Stella."

Darby's face fell. "But what if Crispin's right? What if I lose my chance? Now, I'm the young whiz kid. That'll get me places, you know?"

"I agree. But it won't help if you're not ready and you blow it." I pulled him into my arms. "Do you really want to be nothing more than a flash in a pan? We want you to have a nice, long career, which is going to take longer to build, and that sucks. But it will be worth it in the end."

"Probably." Darby winced. "I probably need to be around more people who really understand what I'm dealing with."

"And you're saying Sy doesn't?"

"He's old. Things change."

"Not that much." I gave him another squeeze. "You're going to be fine, sweetie. It's tough now, but you'll be okay. You've got a lot of people around you who really love you, and that's the most important thing."

He couldn't argue with that. So, I went back to my sewing, smiling as he played. He really was incredibly good at it.

At nine o'clock, I sent Darby to bed. I had all three of my zippers installed, so I contemplated my next set of sewing tasks and decided I could work on them later. I went downstairs only to find that Peace on Earth was still pretty far off. Sid and Stella glared at each other over the music stands on their respective pianos. Sid sat at the ebony, and Stella at the walnut.

Stella is short, with dark gray wavy hair. Her bright blue eyes and cleft chin are also particularly familiar. She is rather stern by nature, which may be partly why she and Sid spend so much time butting heads with each other.

"You keep telling me to go for the interpretive instead of as strictly written," Sid snarled at her.

"But there is no ritard there." Stella's eyes blazed.

"That doesn't mean there can't be! Why are you being so obtuse?"

As if he weren't being the same. Stella, however, sighed.

"It's been a bad week," she finally grumbled. She looked at Sid. "You haven't told me how it went at Stan's funeral."

Sid sighed and glared at the sheet music in front of him. "It was dismal. His brother and sister showed with their families, and a couple friends besides us. But that was it. Even the funeral director couldn't come up with much to say."

"What about his mother?"

"They buried him next to her."

Stella shook her head. "Now, there's a sick joke." She looked at Sid. "You know how he felt about her."

"Yeah." Sid's reply was short, but very pained.

"That poor kid. He was always so angry. And it was no surprise given his mother."

Sid looked at her. "How did you know Stan's mother?"

"They were our neighbors, remember? They lived upstairs, all four of them in that little one-bedroom place."

Stella and Sid had lived in a similar one-bedroom place. Sid had told me he hadn't had a bedroom to himself until after he'd gotten his money.

Sid frowned. "Why didn't I remember that?"

"Probably because we didn't know them until you and Stan became friends in high school, and then he spent most of his time at our place. But I got to talk to his mother. Oh, my goodness, what a bitch she was. Hated her kids, especially Stan. She was constantly criticizing him."

"As if I don't know how that feels," Sid grumbled.

"I never came after you the way she came after Stan." Stella stopped and swallowed. "I may not have been the warmest, nicest mother to you, but I tried."

"I know you did, Stella." Sid looked at her. "I was out of line."

She looked back at him, her face softening. "This whole thing with Loser, it has thrown you off, hasn't it?"

"I'm afraid so."

She shook her head. "Well, I don't blame you for being mad. He shouldn't have done what he did, shocking you boys that way. But I can't say it surprises me. You know, his father was in prison the entire time you boys were in high school."

"That's right." Sid frowned, then looked at his aunt. "Did Loser ever tell you for what?"

Stella nodded. "He did. Fraud and extortion. His father was a con man."

"So was Loser." Sid shook his head quickly.

Stella looked at the music in front of her. "Let's try that last waltz. This time with a ritard."

Sid grinned. "Yeah. Let's."

The two went back to playing as I plopped down on the sofa next to the wingback chair in which Sy dozed. He's a tall man with a generous gut and light gray hair.

He snorted and sighed, then opened his eyes. "Gods be praised, they're back to playing."

"Yeah," I said.

Sy blinked, then looked at me. "How did it go with Darby upstairs?"

"Not well." I sighed. "He said there's an agent who's coming after him. Even gave him some cash."

"Alex Crispin." Sy's voice dripped with disdain. "I thought I saw him outside the school yesterday afternoon.

"So, why aren't you chasing him off?"

"It's not going to do any good." Sy sighed and blinked. "I'm afraid, my dear Lisa, that Darby is entering upon one of the more difficult phases of any young talented artist's career. He is beginning to be noticed. The sharks have smelled the new blood in the water, and he, alas, does not know yet how to tell a shark from a friend. The notice, of course and understandably, is going to his head. Many young artists never recover, in that they remain big-headed and convinced that being special entitles them to every consideration. I have every confidence, however, that Darby will snap out of it. He is very level-headed. He takes after his father that way, in addition to his more passionate nature. He has also been well-raised by parents and an extended family who deeply love him to the point that they will not tolerate his crap. This is a phase he must pass through, and better that he does it now, while he is still bound by the embrace of a loving family, rather than on his own with no one to guide him. Nonetheless, it is going to be a bitch to watch."

December 6, 1989

"Sweetheart?" I all but whined as Sid tried to nuzzle me awake the next morning.

"What, my sweet Lisa?"

"Are you going to mind if I'm not exactly at my coherent best today?"

"At this hour of the morning, it's normal."

I blinked. "Yeah, but I'm afraid I'm going to be a zombie for the better part of the day."

Sid winced and groaned a little. "My fault, I fear."

"It's not your fault. I mean, you didn't ask to have night-mares. I'm happy to be here for them. You know that."

"I do, and I appreciate it. It still doesn't make it any easier to function the next morning." Sid kissed me warmly, then rolled away. "Nonetheless, we do have the boys to get up and going, plus our normal workout." He paused. "With luck, that will wake us up."

I decided not to express my skepticism. Darby was, surprisingly, the most chipper among us. We ran. Sid got breakfast going while I got my shower, then put on jeans and a long-sleeved t-shirt. Sid didn't exactly glower, but I knew he was not thrilled that I had dressed that far down.

"I'm baking cookies with Mae this morning," I muttered at him as I brought the coffee pot to the breakfast room table.

He blinked behind his glasses, which he only wears when we're running. "Oh. That's right."

The boys got off to school in a timely manner. Sid and I still blinked at each other for several minutes, then he hauled himself upstairs to shower and dress. Sid and I can, and often do, shower together. Just not on weekday mornings. You would think that it would save time. Alas, not for us. I brought the breakfast dishes into the kitchen, then went into the office to be sure I had all my finals filed appropriately.

Sid came downstairs dressed in nice slacks and a dress shirt, but no tie or suit coat, and his contact lenses were in. It was going to be a more casual day. I looked at my watch.

"I'd better head out," I grumbled.

"You going to be okay?" he asked.

I shrugged. "Should be."

I headed to the garage, debating which freeway parking lot I wanted to brave to get to Mae's place in Pasadena. Interstate 10 into Downtown L.A. was guaranteed to be grim. The 405 was always dismal. I thumbed through my Thomas Guide and, on a whim, took surface streets and was pleasantly surprised that by the time I got to Interstate 5 south of Glendale, I was driving against the prevailing traffic and made decent time.

Mae was not in one of her better moods when I got there, however. Lissy was at pre-school, and Neil would pick her up, as well as Ellen and the twins, when he was done for the day. Neil teaches at the USC dental school, and his classes were still winding down for the semester. Thirteen-year-old Janey went to a Montessori school within walking distance of the house and would come home on her own.

"How is Darby?" Mae asked darkly after we'd hugged and said hello.

I rolled my eyes. "He's been difficult."

She sighed and sank onto a barstool in the corner of the kitchen. I told her what Sy had said. She nodded, then squeezed her eyes shut.

"That sounds about right." She gulped. "I really hate this phase."

"Darby's a good kid. I think Sy's right. He'll snap out of it."

"Hopefully before I kill him."

"Hopefully before we all do."

Mae sighed, then went back to laying out recipe cards on the kitchen counter.

"Where are Mama and Daddy?" I asked. My parents had been staying with Mae since the week before.

"Looking at another retirement village." Mae rolled her eyes. "Mama does not want to stay in Tahoe year-round, and you can hardly blame her. She is seriously fed up with the snow. But Daddy is still not sure what he wants to do about his business."

I winced. It was true that my parents were old enough to be retiring, and many of their peers already had. My parents owned a resort in South Lake Tahoe, which Daddy had set up so that the business would run itself, and it seemed to be. The problem they were having was where to settle and whether to sell out, since neither of their children was likely to take over the business. I did still feel a little guilty about that, never mind that my father had been on to me all along. One of my life plans had been to take over the business until I discovered I loved academia. Then Sid had come into my life and thrown all of that out the window when he recruited me to be part of Quickline. I loved being a spy, plus I was pursuing my dream of getting my PhD.

"I get the impression that Daddy doesn't want to let go just yet." I looked over the recipe cards. "Which one of these do you want to start with?"

"Anything that needs chilling." Mae picked up a card. "Here. Of course, he doesn't want to let go. But now that Grandma Caulfield is gone, it will be easier for them to live in two places."

Our maternal grandmother had passed away the summer before. Our father's mom had passed away not quite two years before.

I got out the flour and sugar. "Does Mama want to do that?"

"Who knows?" Mae shrugged. "She mostly wants to be around the kids more often before they all go off to college. She never really got to, having to stay in Tahoe while we were down here."

"I can understand that."

Mae and I both shuddered a little. That also meant potentially more interference from Mama when it came to raising those kids. I was once again glad that I only had Nick for her to interfere with.

"But what are they going to do about Spot and Richmond?" I began measuring flour and baking soda into a sieve.

Spot and Richmond were my parents' two dogs. Richmond was over ten and a half years old and a big old hound. Spot was a Dalmation-mix, three years old, and as hyper as a toy poodle. It wasn't a problem up in Tahoe, where Spot could run to his heart's content. Assuming my parents could find a retirement village that would allow pets, getting Spot out for enough walks was going to be a challenge.

Mae shrugged. "I have no idea. At least, Richmond shouldn't be much of a problem. He's so old, he mostly sleeps."

I went back to measuring ingredients. I made most of the dough since I could be trusted to follow a recipe. Mae did most of the cutting and baking, which she enjoyed. Then she had to leave to go work at the local library, where she's a librarian.

I got home around three-thirty. The surveillance van was gone, and there were no cars parked on the street around us. When I got inside, I found Sid in the office with Frank and Esther. Frank is tall with dark hair. Esther is closer to average size with a round face. I went over and kissed Sid, then looked at our friends.

"What's up?" I asked.

"They were just going to share what they found at Krakowski's office," Sid said.

"There wasn't much," said Frank. "According to the leasing agent, the rent is paid up through next June. Nor is Krakowski there that much. I got a look at the paperwork, and there's only a P.O. box listed as a home address, and the emergency phone number was disconnected when I tried calling it. The receptionist at the building said that Krakowski was a nice guy, but not there very often."

"The building security is pretty good." Esther jumped in. "Video surveillance on the lobby and on all outside doors. Code entry only, no keys. No entry except through the front, too. You can get out through the back doors, but you can't get in."

"And if we have to break in?" Sid asked.

"The significant vulnerability is the video system." Esther grinned. "It's unmanned. So, even if it catches you, it won't trigger anything. Breaking the door will set off an alarm. So will punching in too many codes at one time."

Frank grinned. "We did manage to get you a couple of the codes, though."

"We also found trip wires on the office," Esther said. "But it looks like they've been breached already, so you should be okay there. Didn't pick up any transmissions either, so it's not bugged. You sure you don't want me to come with you?"

Sid looked at me. "No thanks. Lisa and I can handle it now that the recon is gone. And we'll have a better idea of what we're looking for, too."

"Okay." Esther shrugged.

Frank checked his watch. "I've got choir rehearsal to get ready for."

"And I need to get back to my office," Esther said.

They took off. Angelique knocked on the door just before five.

"What's up?" I asked as I invited her inside.

"Are the boys home?" she asked.

"Not yet. Darby has violin until five, and Nick waits at the music school and does homework."

Ange chuckled. "Still stuck with the bus otherwise?"

"Just 'til Friday."

Sid came into the hall from the office. "Hey, Ange. What's up?"

"We need to have a secure conversation."

Sid's and my eyebrows rose, but we went into the office and shut the door. The office isn't as well soundproofed as the bedroom upstairs, but if we keep our voices down, it's almost impossible to overhear a conversation once the door is closed.

"What's going on?" I asked as Ange slid down onto the office couch.

"The reason the recon is gone. It's gone on all of us, at least, as far as Tom has been able to check. An emergency memo came down from the A.G.'s office in D.C. this morning. All reconnaissance needs to be approved by two department heads until further notice. Any current operations need to have their approvals verified by five today. And if you're a department head, you can't be one of the two approvals on any of your operations. The thing is, this won't affect the legitimate operations. Most are approved by two independent department heads, anyway. It looks better when the attorneys get hold of the case."

"But it will affect our targets," Sid grumbled. "Terrific. We've gotten some hints that their protection is getting fed up with them. Nice of the attorney general to spook them for us."

I shrugged. "It could be a coincidence, but the timing sure sucks pondwater."

"Even if it is a coincidence, it's not going to help if our targets panic." Sid sighed.

"On the other hand, it got them off your backs with a good excuse," Ange said. "And they don't have any specific person to go after. Look, Cobb is not an idiot. He's not going to cause trouble just because he can. He's got too much to lose. What we have to do is get the goods on him in such a way that he can't use his protection to cover him."

Sid and I glanced at each other. Getting Cobb and his pals arrested would be a good thing, but it wasn't necessary for the purposes of our operation. Still, it was the way we preferred.

"Um," I said. "We've gotten some intel that Louis is trying to help somebody bring Cobb and company down. In addition, Louis has also worked for Cobb periodically."

"Which means Cobb knows he's alive." Ange frowned. "We need to talk to Louis and find out what he knows."

"But we can't let him know that we're operatives," I said. I reached over and touched Sid's hand. "Maybe Ange and I can take over this part. You can stay away."

Sid glared at us. "It's not going to do any good for you two to walk on eggshells around me. We've got a job to do. We're going to do it."

"But, honey, if you're not—"

"I'm up to it." Sid's eyes blazed. "And if I'm not, I'd better get up to it and fast. Dancing around seeing Loser is not going to help." He looked at Ange. "Do you know how to get a hold of him? You said you were having trouble yesterday."

"He called Tom last night and gave him a phone number to call. I can set something up for tomorrow."

"I'm teaching until six," said Sid.

"I get out at five-thirty," I said. "But I'll have exams to grade. It shouldn't take too long. I've only got twenty-three of them, and I purposely made them easy to do. The department head expects a final exam, but in my class, the real final is the term paper. It's just that I have to have grades in by Friday."

"Okay. If I set it up for seven-thirty at my place, will that work?" Ange looked a touch anxious. "I'll pull Wallace in on the meeting, too. That should cover you two. We'll confront Louis about the harassment. That should be a believable in."

Sid nodded. "Sounds good."

"We're home!" Nick bellowed from the front of the house.

Sid hit the intercom button. "Okay. Go change clothes. Dinner in ten minutes."

"Stella and Sy are here, too."

"Okay, Nick. Go tell Conchetta and apologize for the last-second additions."

"No problem," Nick said. "I'll eat less."

Sid rolled his eyes. The good news was that Conchetta was generally prepared for last-second guests, especially at that time of year. Either she made a lot of soups and stews that could be stretched when needed, or she made extra food, in general, then remade any leftovers into lunches.

I looked at Ange. "Do you want to stay?"

She shook her head. "No. I need to get back to Tom. I'll see you two tomorrow."

We left the office. Angelique waved hi at Stella and Sy, who were relaxing in the living room. I saw her out as Sid went to chat with Stella and Sy.

Dinner on Wednesday nights was usually a little early. Sid had to be at church for choir rehearsal with Frank by seven. Conchetta had poached some salmon, which would normally mean we were going to have salmon salad for lunch in the next few days. Alas, not with Sy and Stella there. Not to mention Darby, who had the decency to wait until the rest of us had gotten enough before sucking up the rest.

Nick had gone back to working on the family history project. Although his next question made Sid grimace. My guess was that it was intended to induce warm, fuzzy feelings.

"Your thoughts and feelings the first time you saw me," Nick asked, his eyes dancing.

"Uh…" Sid glanced frantically at me.

"You, too, Mom," Nick grinned.

I shrugged. "All I could think was that I should have bet on the paternity issue. I would have cleaned up and then some."

"I remember that." Darby laughed. He'd been there the day Rachel, Nick's first mom, brought Nick to us. In fact, he and I had met Nick before his father did.

"A bet?" Stella asked.

"Sid and I had a bet going over whether or not Rachel had a kid with her, trying to pin it on him." I smiled at Sid. "I told Sid that I wouldn't bet on the paternity of said kid because it was so unlikely. Then I saw you, Nick, and thought I should have made that bet."

There was general laughter around the table, even from Sid. Even back then, at just shy of eleven, Nick looked like his father.

"Dad?" Nick looked at his father expectantly. Sid winced again. "Oh, come on, Dad. It's not like I don't know you were not happy to see me."

Darby snorted. "Uncle Sid, you were so not happy to see him. The look on your face, dude."

Sid finally shrugged. "I have to concede it was pretty startling." Then he chuckled as he saw me roll my eyes.

"Alright. My blood ran cold. I was in total shock." He smiled at his son, then added a few curses. "All I could think was that I got caught. I thought I'd ditched it, but I really got caught."

Stella chuckled. "Are you sure Nick doesn't have any siblings?"

Sid's face went white. "You don't know of any, do you?"

"No. But I suppose it's possible."

"I don't want to know." Sid sighed. "It's worked out a lot better than I would have anticipated. But that is not something I want to face again."

"How about you, Stella?" Nick asked. "What was your first thought when you saw Dad for the first time?"

Stella's face softened, and she smiled at Sid with her eyes filling. "What an extraordinarily beautiful creature. How wonderful and innocent. And he was mine."

Sid's eyes began blinking, too. We were all blinking back tears. Stella raised Sid because Sid's mother didn't want him, and Stella did. Sid's mother had also died when Sid was two.

"Um..." Nick swallowed and looked at his notebook. "Okay. We've got your first memory, Dad."

"Oh?" Stella asked, sending a quick smile Sy's way. "What was that?"

"The Italian grocer who had his store below us in the Village," Sid said, turning his attention to his salmon.

Stella looked perplexed. "We didn't live over a grocery store. It was just a standard brownstone."

"Oh." Sid shrugged. "Could it have been in San Francisco?"

"No."

Sid looked at her. "I mean, it's fuzzy, but I do remember some old man with really bright blue eyes. I didn't like him."

"Oh, my." Stella laughed oddly. "That had to have been your grandfather."

"Are you sure?" Sy asked.

"Sy, you know what happened. Who else could it have been?" Stella looked at Sid. "It happened when you were three, Sid. My father had found out that your mother had died and tracked us down through Juilliard. That's how he knew your name to put in his will. I let him see you, but would not let him pick you up or touch you. You screamed when he tried, and I was grateful. Father finally broke down and offered me ten thousand dollars to let him take you back to his home. He tried to give me a check, but I insisted on cash. So, he left to go get it, and I saw my chance. Sy came over and brought you to his place, along with the suitcases I'd packed for the two of us. Father came back with the cash. I met him in the hall to the rooms. As soon as I had the money and counted it, I told him that you were in the back bedroom and ran. When I got to Sy's, he took us straight to Grand Central Station and put us on a train to San Francisco. Father tried one other time to see you, but by that point, you had left for Vietnam. Those ten thousand dollars, though, kept the wolf from our door for a lot of years. Until that last school folded and I had to go try and teach lessons privately, and you went to San Fran High."

Sid looked at her. "Why didn't you tell me all this, Stella?"

"I probably should have." Stella sighed deeply. "I have to admit that is one thing I do regret, not telling you about my family. I just wanted so badly to erase them from my life. From your life, as well. I did not want you hurt by them."

Sid smiled. "I guess I can appreciate that much."

"Cool," said Darby. "Uncle Sid, you've got, like, the most interesting life. My parents are totally boring."

I mock-glared at him. "Which means your aunt is, too."

Sid glanced at his watch and swore. "I'm going to be late."

He kissed me warmly, gave Stella a quick hug, and ran off to the garage. Nick and I looked at each other and silently agreed to open that day's Christmas cards the next day.

Stella, bless her, decided to accompany Darby for some extra practice time. She and Sy left at nine, when the boys were supposed to go to bed (which they, presumably, did). Sid returned to the house around nine-thirty. We went upstairs and changed into our black break-in pants and light-colored shirts. I sewed, and Sid played through a couple of Broadway shows for me. It wasn't quite one a.m. when we looked at each other and nodded.

We took my car over to Louis', I mean Krakowski's office. I parked around the corner. Sid and I pretty much kept to the shadows as we walked over there, just in case, but didn't zip up our black sweatshirts or put on our all-over ski masks until we were ready to enter the building. We also had on black leather gloves, and the multiple pockets of our break-in pants were loaded with the whole panoply of the burglary trade. Not that we were there to steal anything.

The first code we tried worked perfectly. We shut the door after us, then went up to the second floor where the office was. I checked my bug finder, then nodded at Sid. Nothing was transmitting.

He picked the lock on the door quickly enough, and we slid inside. We were thorough, but the search didn't take that long. The file cabinets had been emptied, as had the desk. The credenza behind the desk didn't hold anything except a few office supplies and some weird bits of pottery. Sid and I even went through the reams of paper just in case, but came up empty. We were just about to leave when we heard scraping at the lock on the door. We looked at each other and got into position, me on the side where I'd be behind the door when it opened, Sid on the other, our Model Thirteen revolvers in our hands.

In the dim light from the window, we recognized Peter Venkt when he came in the door. Sid rolled into him, but Venkt recovered quickly and sent a punch flying Sid's way. Sid dodged. I nudged the door shut and tried to draw a bead on the two. I'm a darned good shot, but there are things I won't risk, and shooting Sid in a fist fight is one of them. Venkt drew back, and I fired into the floor next to him. It startled him enough that Sid was able to rabbit punch him in the temple and get him dazed enough that we could run.

Which we did. We got to the car without being followed and whipped off the sweatshirts, masks, and shoulder holsters. I hauled out. But as we got onto the freeway, I sighed.

"What?" asked Sid.

"We didn't get to neck," I grumbled.

There were times when Sid and I would start necking and simulating sexual activity [or engaging in sexual activity - SEH] to throw off people pursuing us.

Sid leaned back in his seat and laughed loudly and long. "We'll fix that at home."

"I know. But there's something about it when we're chased."

"True." Sid tried to get his laughter under control and almost succeeded. "My sweet, sweet Lisa, you are definitely not the woman I first met."

"Thank God." I grinned as I glanced at him. "Neither of us is."

He grinned back at me. "Nonetheless, my beloved, for all tonight's excitement, there is only one thing on my mind."

"Oh?"

His smile took on that really hot bent it did when he was thinking about having sex with me.

"All I want to do right now is make love to you slowly. And deliciously."

My breath caught. "Okay. That hasn't changed. And I am trying to drive."

December 7, 1989

Truth be told, after running, breakfast, and seeing the boys off to school, Sid and I went back to bed for a couple more hours the next morning. Nick figured we'd been up to something the night before, but we were there and in one piece, so he didn't bother to ask. It wasn't as though we could give him an answer, anyway, and he knew it.

We were still a little groggy when we got up in time for lunch. Sid looked at the mail, then handed me the incoming Christmas cards to be opened (hopefully) that evening.

"We still have to get ours out," I complained as we ate a nice salad, albeit without poached salmon.

Sid blinked. "After the open house. We might try to start before then, but you know how it goes."

Unfortunately, I did. I still held out hope, nonetheless.

The good thing for me about exam days is that I didn't have to be particularly on top of things. I felt for Sid. He didn't have exam days or term paper days. He had to be present every day he was teaching.

I really tried, but it was Nick's day to take his final, and I couldn't help the way my gaze kept falling on my sweet, adorable son. I will say this. He was one of the first to finish. First to finish does not always mean the student is on top of things. More often than not, the very first exams that come in fall short of the mark. But Nick had hit the sweet spot, early enough to have his stuff together, not so early that he was trying to BS his way through. Nick turned in his paper and then left the classroom. I had already started grading the three that had come in ahead of his.

Nick aced the short answer section, which did not surprise me in the least. But his essay was particularly good. I was impressed and gave him an A, then moved on to the next exam that had fallen on my desk at the head of the room.

Nick was not thrilled with the grade I'd given his term paper.

"B-minus?" he groaned as I drove us home at five-thirty.

"You had one too many typos," I said. "And did you read the notes about your clarity issues?"

He sighed deeply.

Darby was at the house when Nick and I got home. Sid arrived a few minutes later, carrying two fully loaded plastic grocery sacks.

"What on earth?" I asked, following him into the kitchen.

"A gift from the Mendoza family." Sid handed the sacks to Conchetta. "Alicia's mother brought them today. We've got four dozen tamales. Two dozen chicken with green chile, a dozen of pork with red chile, and a dozen sweet."

"These look lovely," said Conchetta. She gazed at the fridge. "Let's see. How am I going to do this?"

Sid would have put the tamales in the freezer himself, but then Conchetta would have been annoyed. She has a specific way of keeping the kitchen organized, and Sid has learned not to cross her. Conchetta has also learned to let Sid do the cooking when he wants.

"So, how did lessons go?" I asked as we left the kitchen to set the dining room table.

Sid grinned. "I gave Alicia a new piece to work on and she played it by sight first time through without missing a beat."

Alicia Mendoza is Sid's main student, and he works with her twice a week, which is why he only has two other students. Just fourteen, she had taught herself how to play piano when she was younger by listening to the radio and other classical records. Sid had been working with her for over a year and a half at that point, and it had been a struggle teaching her to read sheet music. Getting her to play a new piece without having heard it first was a significant breakthrough.

"That's terrific."

We had to eat dinner rather quickly, though. Sid and I had to be at Tom and Ange's place in Culver City by seven-thirty. We opened the new Christmas cards while we ate. I was delighted to see that Fran Mercer and Max Beard had sent one. Sid and I had met them on a case that had taken us to Wisconsin, and then met them again with Nick on a similar case in Kansas. They were two professors and had resettled about two and a half years before at Northwestern University, just north of Chicago.

"Nick," I said, holding up the card. "Have you and Josh thought about Northwestern? You know, Dr. Beard is there."

"Who's Dr. Beard?" Darby asked. He was headed for Juilliard and, given that Sy had recently retired from the strings department there, wasn't likely to land anywhere else.

Nick grinned. "He's a chemistry professor that Mom and Dad know. He's a really nice guy. His wife's cool, too."

"I've also heard that N.U. is a good acting school," Sid said.

It was one of those things that no one said anything about, mostly because Josh hadn't said anything, but we all sort of knew. Josh was probably gay, and I knew his mother, Lety, was worried sick about him going away to school. It had been Nick's idea that the two go to the same college and either room together in the dorms or find a place of their own. They'd even mapped out several plans for both getting accepted at the same school when they both had such different aspirations. Nick was waffling between majoring in biology or chemistry. Josh wanted to major in acting.

"That'd be awesome for the both of you," said Darby sincerely. He was just as much friends with Josh as Nick was. "Hope you both get in."

I looked at my watch. "We've got to get out of here. The usual rules, boys."

Both rolled their eyes.

Sid got up and glared at them. "You do not want to know what will happen when I find out that homework hasn't been done or the other rules broken. And I will find out. Are we clear?"

"Yes, sir," they both mumbled.

"Both of you, please clear the table, too." Sid smiled briefly at me as I ran to get my purse.

I was glad Sid's afternoon had gone so well. It didn't look like that evening would. I offered to drive. Sid shook his head, and we took his car. We were a touch late. Louis was already there. In fact, he, Tom, and Angelique were just finishing their dinner. Tom and I helped clear the table as Ange opened a bottle of chardonnay and poured some for Louis, Sid, and me. Although Ange will occasionally have a glass of wine, she usually prefers not to drink around Tom. It's her way of being supportive.

"Wallace called this afternoon," Tom told us. "He's going to be late. Has some school event for one of his kids that he needs to be at."

Louis shook his head. "How did we come to such a bad end?"

I bit my lip, and Sid sent me a mild glare. He was prone to asking the same question when it came to Nick, and my response was inevitably that the condom had broken. Which it had.

Tom settled into a chair next to Ange, then looked at Louis.

"The thing we're worried about is what you've dragged us into," Tom said. "Being watched by the FBI? If these are crooked agents, that's pretty scary."

"I totally get it," Louis said, smiling. "I didn't mean to expose you guys to that. I really didn't."

Sid's eyes flicked toward me. He didn't entirely believe Louis. I know I didn't. Louis looked my way for a second.

"The problem is, Louis," said Ange. "When I thought about it, given that your friend Cobb and his pals are looking for you by your real name, it doesn't make sense that you'd want to change back to it. And, believe me, there are other ways for you to verify your identity without depending on your mother being coherent."

Louis laughed. "Hey, it would be better to have you guys than not."

"Except that I have to agree with Ange," said Tom. "I don't think you're that worried about going back to your real name. So, what gives? Why drag us into this mess?"

"I didn't want to drag all of you," he said with a sigh. He glanced my way, then looked at Angelique. "But, well, I needed a way to get my information to a federal agent. Ange, you're close enough. I apologize, but these guys are scary. There's got to be some way to bring them to the attention of their superiors."

Tom and Ange sighed and looked at each other.

"We're doing the best we can," Ange said. "But it would help a lot if we could give them the correct information. So, how do you know these guys?"

Louis shrugged. "I've been following them for a lot of years." He sighed. "I am a P.I. I'm licensed in several states, by the way. Most of my work involves tracking down dads who don't pay their child support."

"And yet you used an alias for the name you gave us," Ange said. "The license checked out, but I only turned up the one for California under that name."

"Yeah, well," Louis shifted. "I may have licenses under a variety of names in different states. As long as they run my prints as part of a criminal record search, I'm okay."

We all gaped.

"That's got to be illegal," I said. "Aren't you worried about losing your license?"

Louis chuckled. "It's better than losing my life. I wasn't kidding the other night. These guys are coming for me. I've got to stay one step ahead of them."

Ange glared at him. "Still, one of my colleagues told me that you've been working for them off and on since the war."

"Of course, I did." Louis laughed loudly. "How the hell do you think I got the dirt on them?"

"Where is the dirt?" Sid asked.

"I'm not saying." Louis grinned. "I mean, seriously, do you really want to know, given that these guys are already looking at you?"

"I suppose not." Sid sighed.

"So, what are we going to do to stop the harassment?" Tom asked.

"The best thing to do would be to get these guys taken down," Louis said.

"And how are we supposed to do that?" I asked, a little indignant. "Isn't this the sort of thing we're supposed to leave to the police or something?"

The doorbell rang. Tom got up and let Wallace in.

"Sorry to be late," Wallace said as he sat down at the table. "Junior high choir concert. The wife made me go."

He sounded a little disgusted, and I saw Sid glaring at him. [I was disgusted. The odds were even, at best, that he had wanted to go but didn't want to cop to caring about his family so much. I don't know why that sort of thing gripes my liver the way it does, but it does. - SEH]

"Alright," Tom said, as Ange poured the last bit of wine from the bottle into a glass and gave it to Wallace. "We've got a problem here in that Loser dragged us into some nasty business."

"I say we leave it to law enforcement," I said.

Louis rolled his eyes. "Problem is, it's law enforcement that's after us."

"There's got to be somebody we can talk to," I said.

"What if there isn't?" Wallace swallowed and looked a little pale. "If these guys have as many connections as Loser said, then we're screwed."

"I don't know," said Sid. "Lisa's right. We're not professionals here, except for Loser. If these guys are that crooked, then there's got to be somebody in the FBI trying to capture them."

"Or maybe we should just try to be nice to them," Wallace said. "Then maybe they'll leave us alone."

Louis laughed loudly. "Cobb, Whitemore, and Venkt do not know from nice. They couldn't care less. Going along with them only means you're going to end up doing some of their dirty work. I oughta know." Louis looked at Tom, then the rest of us. "I do have some official help, though. We just have to get Cobb and his guys into a compromising position, preferably with witnesses, which makes you guys perfect. You don't have any skin in this game. I know how we can do this. There's a warehouse in North Hollywood, at the end of Laurel Canyon Road." He gave us the address. "I'll set up a meeting and wear a wire. Ange, you can be in charge of the recording. Anybody got a piece of paper?"

"I do." Tom got up and brought Louis a piece of typing paper.

Louis pulled a mechanical pencil from his shirt pocket and drew a rectangle on the paper. His plan made a lot of sense. I wasn't supposed to be a part of it, but Sid glanced my way a couple of times, as if he were preparing to add me to the scenario. The next big problem we had was finding a time to do it. Louis was adamant that we do it at night, probably because the warehouse was empty then. I pulled out my organizer, as did Ange. Tom got his pocket calendar from his briefcase, and Wallace pulled his from his inside suit coat pocket. Louis looked a little worried.

Friday night was out. Tom and Ange had the big faculty Christmas party at his school, and Wallace had promised to take his wife out to dinner.

"She'll kill me if I don't," Wallace said, and I saw Sid trying not to roll his eyes.

Saturday night.

"No good," I said. "My sister and her family are coming for dinner."

"And Tom and I have tickets for Phantom of the Opera," Ange said. "It's a miracle we got them. I am not giving them up."

"Sunday, Lottie and I are at her folks' place." Wallace sighed.

"And that's the Open House," Sid said. He looked at Tom and Ange. "You'll be there, right?"

They nodded.

Louis sighed. "What about Monday night?"

Wallace looked at Sid and Tom. "I'm clear."

Sid looked at me.

"We just have a Liturgy Meeting from seven to nine," I said. "Although you don't need to be there, unless Frank thinks you need to be for some reason."

Sid shook his head. "Nah. The Christmas music is set, and after that isn't usually any big deal, and there will be time to update me before Lent starts."

Wallace and Louis looked at Sid in shock.

"Liturgy?" Louis asked. "Is that church stuff?"

"Yeah," said Sid with a small shrug. "I play the organ and piano for the choir at Lisa's church."

"But you're an atheist," Wallace said. "Or you were."

"Still am. So?" Sid didn't quite glare at him.

Louis swore. "Stella must have had a conniption."

"She's gotten used to it." Sid smiled softly. "She's even played a couple times. She likes what the choir director does, and Lisa's church has an amazing organ."

"Alright, then I guess we'll set this up for Monday night," Louis said and waited as everyone nodded. "We'll meet here at eight-thirty, that will give us time to go over things and then get over there by nine-thirty. I'll set things up with Cobb and company for ten-thirty, eleven. That work?"

There was general agreement. Louis looked at Sid, though, and frowned.

"I thought I heard that Stella kicked you out when you got drafted."

Sid swallowed. "Yeah. She did. We were estranged for over sixteen years."

"She kept in touch with me, though," Tom said.

Sid reached over and took my hand. "And then Lisa found her and got us talking again."

"Nick helped," I said.

"Yeah. She's really enjoying being a grandma." Sid chuckled. He glanced at me. "Is there anything else we need to discuss?"

"Well, it's not late." Louis shrugged. "Maybe we can shoot the breeze a little. Catch up on our lives."

Sid glared at him. "Loser, I am here because you put my family in the crosshairs of three corrupt FBI agents. That's the only reason I'm here. And that family, by the way, includes Stella, someone you have professed to have some feelings for. Why would I give a damn about you?

Why would Wallace? He's got a wife and kids, too, that he presumably loves."

"Well, yeah." Wallace sat up. "Look, Sid, I... I don't think Loser meant to get us in trouble." He looked over at Louis nervously, then back at Sid. "He came to us because we're his friends. Th... that's who you turn to when you're in trouble."

I squeezed Sid's hand. "Is it going to help to keep hating him?"

I said it very softly, but he heard it, then looked at Louis.

"You damned bastard." Sid flashed a weak grin at him. "You are yet another person who has every reason to be grateful that my darling wife is here now."

"Look, Sid," Louis said. "I get why you're pissed at me."

"I don't care." Okay, that wasn't quite what Sid said. "The good news is that I do want to hear more about Wallace's life."

Wallace shrugged. "I've got two kids and a wife. Lottie's working as an office manager in an insurance agent's office." His face took on an odd stare. "We're normal. We're utterly normal people. We even have a dog and a cat. And two parakeets." He looked at Sid and Tom. "How did we end up this way? We were the new generation. We were going to change the world."

Tom shrugged. "And yet, we have, in some ways."

"I certainly didn't get to where I am in the normal way," said Sid. He smiled at me again. "But I have to admit, I'm liking where I'm at. I've got a great kid. My wife is beyond wonderful. We've got a crazy, fun extended family. We've got friends. We've got two dogs and three cats. And we live comfortably. What else is there?"

"Yeah, I was noticing that." Louis looked at Sid shrewdly. "You've got money."

Sid chuckled. "I do, indeed. Turns out that Stella came from a wealthy family. When her father died, he left money to her, and since my mother was dead, some to me. I just made it work for me over the years."

"What happened to your glasses?" Wallace asked. "That's been bugging me."

Sid is very nearsighted.

He smiled. "I got contact lenses shortly after I got my money. But you're doing well, Wallace, aren't you?"

Wallace shrugged. "Well enough. Lottie's income helps. But kids are expensive, man. Plus, with Lottie working, we need a cleaning lady and a gardener because I have a black thumb. I kill everything. I have a wood-working shop."

Tom smiled. "That's right. You really liked being in wood shop."

"I've even made some of our furniture," Wallace said. "Tom, you always wanted to be a teacher, but how did you get into the American Lit thing?"

Tom grinned. "I read Moby Dick."

Sid fell over laughing as my eyes widened.

"Please tell me you wanted to spare innocent children that monstrosity," I yelped.

"What?" Tom looked at me, bemused. "It's a great book."

Sid laughed some more. "Nick said he'd lost the will to live after reading the first chapter."

"Yes, it's challenging," Tom said.

Wallace blinked as Tom and I went back and forth, our conversation veering into the concept of the Nineteenth-Century Novel, in general. I did get dangerously close to ripping Phantom of the Opera. Sid, Nick, and I had seen the show with the rest of the Whole Fam-Damily in New York during the previous Christmas holiday, and while Nick, Neil, and I had thought it was okay, if a bit showy, Sid and the other musicians ripped the music up one side and down the other. Angelique had been dying to see it and had the CD playing on her office stereo with some regularity, so I did not want to rain on her parade.

Louis just watched. It was kind of obvious how he listened, but didn't say much, kind of like how Sid gets when he doesn't want to talk, as well.

As it got later, Sid whispered something into my ear, and I nodded my agreement.

"Listen, Lisa and I do have to take off," Sid said, getting up. "You know what, Wallace? Loser? I think Stella would love to see you. Lisa and I have a party for our friends."

"We usually do it on the Sunday before Christmas, but that's Christmas Eve this year," I said. "So, we're having the friends' party on the twenty-third."

"Anyway, the Whole Fam-Damily will be there, which means Stella and Sy." Sid smiled at the guys. "Why don't you come? Wallace, bring your wife and kids." He looked at me. "The Sandovals will be there, right?"

"That's what Lety says."

Sid turned back to Wallace. "Kids of all ages, so yours should fit right in."

"I'd like to see Stella again." Wallace nodded. "We'll do it."

"Well, we'll see you guys on Monday, then." Sid smiled, and we left.

I waited until Sid had pulled onto the freeway.

"How are you feeling?" I asked.

He frowned. "So-so. I do not trust Loser one bit."

"Can we stop calling him Loser?"

"His mother called him that."

I groaned. "You know, that says a lot about how he ended up."

"Maybe." Sid sighed, then glanced at me before gunning the engine to get around a couple of cars in the right lane. "But I meant what I said to him tonight. He has no idea just how lucky he is that you exist in my life."

"As long as you do," I said.

"Oh, I hope I do." He smiled at me with delightful lechery.

I smiled back. "I hope I know how lucky I am."

Sid chuckled. "I'll do my best to show you when we get home."

And he did, too.

December 8 – 10, 1989

N ick was on the ceiling that morning. It was my turn to get breakfast ready while Sid showered, and Nick bounced into the kitchen well before anybody. The excitement was infectious, since Darby was dressed and helping out even before Sid got downstairs.

"My six months are up, Dad," Nick announced as Sid walked into the breakfast room, dressed in a lavender Oxford shirt and off-white chino slacks.

"I am well aware of that, son." Sid smiled but didn't sound all that thrilled. [I have to concede, there was part of me that really wanted to keep Nick grounded, that wasn't quite ready to let go of him. - SEH]

Nick gulped. "You're not going to hold me to the minute, are you?"

"However, tempting, no." Sid settled into his seat and dished out fruit salad onto his plate. He looked at his son. "You are getting a car."

Both Nick and Darby whooped in joy.

"Don't get too excited. You're not getting the one you want."

"If it's got four wheels, an engine, and it runs, that's the one I want," said Nick.

Which was nonsense, and all of us knew it. Nick had been lusting after the little Mazda Miatas ever since he'd seen a commercial for one. I had sort of been lusting after the cute little roadsters, too, but I needed a back seat, and had only gotten my little BMW convertible late in June. We'd ordered the car the previous spring and picked it up in Munich over Easter vacation. Sid and I had a blast running the little car over the German Autobahns. Nick couldn't drive because in Europe, you must be eighteen. But we had to wait until the car was shipped here, and it took a couple of months. I'd just gotten it when Nick got into the accident with my truck.

Sid sighed. "The one you're getting will be in the garage by the time you boys come home from school."

There was another whoop of joy, and I couldn't help laughing. Minutes later, the boys were rushing off to get to school on time, and Sid and I looked at each other, our ears ringing.

"When are you going over to the college?" Sid asked me.

"I'm not sure." I had my grades to enter into the college system, and couldn't do it from home. "Why?"

"I've got to pick up Nick's car and could use a ride to the garage. Do you mind?"

"Not at all. Let's see. The boys are going to be home around three."

We eventually decided to leave sooner rather than later. Then our pagers went off. It was Sid's turn to take the pickup, so he arranged to do it after he picked up the car. He'd call me from the car's cell phone. [I was not going to let Nick drive without one. - SEH] We'd meet for lunch, depending on how close I was to finishing entering grades. Then Esther called, wanting a conference with us. Since we figured we'd have work for her or Frank, anyway, we offered to meet for lunch. Then Kathy called because she had the information from the searches she'd done, so she got invited to lunch, as well.

"Looks like it's going to be a morning," I grumbled as I backed my car out of the garage.

Sid shrugged. "It's how our life is. You don't like it when it gets slow."

"True."

Grades did not take that long to enter. I try to stay on top of that sort of thing. Sid had gotten the pickup and Nick's car home by the time I was done, and I still had time to pick him up and get to lunch to meet Esther and Kathy in Hollywood.

Esther was not in a good mood. She'd opted for a diner on Sunset and was waiting for us when we got there. Kathy was not much happier, though for a different reason.

"Where's Keshon?" I asked her as we got settled at a table.

Kathy yawned. "At home with Jesse. He ran a little fever last night, which means he didn't sleep, which means we didn't sleep." Kathy blinked. "He's fine this morning. Just cranky."

We all winced at the thought of a cranky Keshon. We ordered lunch, then Sid asked Kathy and Esther which of them wanted the drop.

"I'll take it," Kathy said. "It'll give Jesse a chance to get out of the house for a while."

"Fine with me," grumbled Esther.

"What's going on?" I asked.

"I'll tell you in a minute."

Once the waitress had brought our food, Esther told us and then some.

"I got harassed this morning," she said, interspersing curses freely. "Right in front of a client. Special Agent Bruce Whitemore wanted to know what Frank and I were doing casing that building where the P.I.'s office is. He actually said casing the building. I told him what we'd told the building manager, that we'd been referred to Krakowski and were making a cold call. Whitemore wanted to know what we found, so I told him about the basics of the building security and the trip wires, but not that they'd been breached. Whitemore said the office had gotten broken into that night, so I pulled up the security tapes on my place, and it's clear we are there all night. Which was good for my client, and I just said maybe the break-in was why Krakowski wanted to beef up security. But what an asshole!"

Sid cursed, as well. "The question is, was this due to your connection to us or because you were checking out Krakowski?"

"He didn't say anything about you guys or anyone else." Esther frowned. "I just wanted him out of there. I almost lost that client, you know. You can't get a bad rep like that in my business."

I looked at Sid. "So, now what?"

"I don't know." He shrugged. "It's not going to help if you guys got made."

Kathy shook her head. "Sid, the only way they could have made us is if they already know about you two, and if that's the case, then we're all pretty much screwed."

"Well, let's keep you guys out of it as much as possible," I said. "At least, in any visible way."

"Fine by me," said Esther.

"I don't have much for you, but I do have some information," Kathy said, handing us a file folder. "Our guys are definitely living above their means, at least, visibly. The interesting thing is that it's not so bad as to call attention to it."

"So, what are they doing with the money?" Sid asked.

"Stashing it, probably," said Kathy. "My guess is that they've got more than a couple offshore accounts and some way they're laundering the money. They may even be living high on the hog someplace else, and that's where they're taking their cash to get it out of the country."

Sid shook his head. "This is a long-running operation, and they must have heard the rumors that their protection is getting fed up. Why haven't these guys run like hell?"

"I would," said Esther. She thought. "I wonder if I can find something in their bank records."

"That's an illegal search," said Kathy.

I sighed. "We're not necessarily trying to build a court case."

"On the other hand," said Sid. "If we can find a way to cut them off from their money, that might be a way to put them out of action."

"And chasing down the money will keep us invisible for the time being," Kathy said.

"We do need at least one of you for an operation Monday night," Sid said, and explained what we needed. Kathy volunteered for it since Esther was going to be looking for the money.

We left soon after that, and Sid and I headed home.

To Breanna, 9/10/00
Today's Topic: My First Car

Since we've been looking for a car for you, I can't help thinking about my first car. I'll show you the picture again if you want. But you agreed it was pretty damned ugly, and you were right.

See, the thing was, both Mom and I kind of thought Dad was taking revenge on me. I'd wrecked my mom's Datsun pickup the spring before, and Dad was really, really pissed. So, naturally, there was a story behind it.

Mom didn't have a car for a long time after Dad hired her because she'd sold the one she'd had that year she was out of work. She got around on the bus, and sometimes Dad loaned her his. Then, the winter before I met Dad and Mom, Mom had been driving Dad's 450SL on an errand and got rear-ended. It's how she got her bad back, too.

Dad, she told me, was seriously upset and put his foot down and told her she would buy a car, or he'd buy one for her. So, they looked and looked and looked, and Mom couldn't find anything that felt right. Her friends, the MacArthurs, had to sell their Datsun pickup, and Mom knew that second that was the perfect car for her. It weirded Dad out because that was not what he saw for her, only he knew it was the perfect car for her. It was the one aligned with who she was as a person, at least, as she was when she'd bought it.

It turns out that was why Dad bought the 450SL. When he first got his money, he was pretty much thrown for a loop. He was just getting his head together about who he was after coming home from the Vietnam War, when suddenly, he didn't have to think about making a living. So, after getting a vasectomy and contact lenses, he decided he'd buy a car, and it couldn't be just any car. He bought one of the first Mercedes 450SLs that came to the States. It was the car that aligned with who he was. So, he'd totally understood where Mom had been coming from when she bought the Datsun.

Then, when I wrecked the Datsun, Dad didn't really say so, but it was kind of like I'd whacked Mom but good. I mean, he knew I hadn't and that I felt really bad. But he still felt it. Which is why Mom and I used to tease him about wanting revenge on me when he got me the car he did. He did have a good reason for it, though, and you know what? He was right.

When I pulled into the garage that afternoon, I must admit, my curiosity was at full peak. I hadn't seen Nick's car yet. Sid had met me in the driveway when I picked him up for lunch. But as I got out of my car and before closing the garage door, I saw the car and went over to look.

My jaw dropped. "Sid, that thing is the ugliest car I have ever seen. What did you do?"

"I got him a Volvo, only one of the safest cars made."

I looked at him, but for once, could not get a read on what was going on with him. He wasn't angry, and he wasn't upset or sad. But he wasn't happy, either. [Yeah, it was that whole not quite ready to let go, but knowing I had to thing. - SEH]

"It's not even new."

"It's only two years old."

"Sid..."

"Honey, it's not his car in the sense that it reflects who he is. But he is not going to have to worry about scratching it. Or door dings. Or whacking a fender. He's a new driver, and he's already had one accident. I don't know how I got away with the dents and scratches I put on my friends' cars back when I was a teen. I didn't have my 450SL two weeks before I scraped the front fender on a cement light post.

I nearly lost it. My identity car and I'd already banged it." Sid shuddered. "It was not a good time."

"You're right." I looked at the car. "That poor kid. He's going to think you're out for revenge on the Datsun."

Sid shrugged. "There may be a little of that, but I don't think so. I just want him to be safe and not stressing out because his beloved car got a dent."

When Nick got home and saw the almost brown, boxy Volvo sedan, his eyes welled up.

"You don't have to take it," said Sid. "But it does have four wheels, an engine, and it runs."

"It does," said Nick with a sad swallow.

Darby laughed loudly. "That thing is butt-ugly! And I thought my dad's Toyota was bad. Dude! No girl is going to want to ride in that."

Sid glared at him. "Not necessarily a bad thing."

Darby suddenly looked nervous and swallowed. "Well, maybe it's not that bad."

Nick turned on his father. "You're still mad at me about the Datsun, aren't you?"

Sid glanced at me. "No. I'm not mad. I am concerned for your safety, and Volvos are very safe. You could roll that sucker over and still walk away from it."

"I'm not that bad a driver!" Nick yelped.

"You don't have to be for stuff to happen," Sid snapped. Okay, he didn't say stuff. "Do you want it or not?"

Nick looked at the Volvo, then looked at me, then looked at Sid. "Yes, sir. Thank you."

Sid gave him the keys. "It's a manual transmission, which should be a little fun. Why don't you take it for a spin?"

"Sure." Nick looked over at his cousin. "You mind being seen with me in this thing?"

Darby shrugged. "What the hell. I'm cool enough to handle it." His eyes lit up. "Let's go get Josh and get dinner."

Nick looked at me. "Can I, Mom?"

I glanced at Sid, then smiled. "Sure. But, Darby, remember you promised your mother that you'd be home tonight."

"I will." Darby got into the front passenger seat. "Hey, Nick, you got a cell phone!"

"Any calls that do not go to our numbers or emergency services, you pay for," Sid said.

"Fair enough." Nick went over and hugged his dad. "Thanks, Dad."

We watched, holding our breath, as Nick got buckled in and adjusted the mirrors. He took another minute to look over the dashboard. The engine started with a vroom. Nick smiled, then turned and looked over his right shoulder. The Volvo backed slowly down the driveway. As Nick drove onto the street, Sid looked at me.

"Why does he always ask you for permission?"

I shrugged. "You have been asking me that for how many years? I have no idea. He just does."

Sid went back to work on the sauce for the timbalos he was going to make the next day, somehow getting around Conchetta, who let him without much scowling, for a change. Then he and I ate dinner early because we had mass for the Feast of the Immaculate Conception. It's a Holy Day of Obligation, in that you're supposed to treat it as a Sunday. Our pastor at the parish, and our good friend, Father John Reynolds, presided at mass, then went out with Sid, me, Frank, and Esther afterward to our favorite bar to kick back and just chat. John and Sid have gotten close over the years, and Sid is decidedly bemused that one of his best friends is a priest.

The next morning, Sid let Nick and me sleep in before running. Neither he nor Nick, however, was particularly enthused when I plopped the boxes of Christmas cards on the breakfast room table before we ate breakfast.

"But, Mom, we've got, like, a bazillion people on the list," Nick groaned.

"Which is why we need to start work on this now before the O'Malleys get here," I said. "If we don't start now, we'll never get it done, let alone by Christmas."

Sid let out one of his sighs that means he's going to support me come hell or high water, no matter how nuts he thinks I am.

"Where's the address box?" he asked.

I put the box of three-by-five cards in front of him. "I've already checked off everyone who's already sent us a card and verified the return addresses."

I also got out each of our favorite fountain pens and an extra bottle of ink, and we got to work. I was impressed. We finished by three o'clock, and that included personal notes inside each card, signed by each of us, fully addressed, and stamped.

"I don't see why we can't use computer labels and our names printed inside," Nick grumbled as we finished.

"Ick." I made a face. "I hate that. Nothing personal about it."

Nick looked at his father, who shrugged. He had already taken one break to get all the pasta made for the timbalos he'd promised to make for Mae and Neil's open house, and another to pull together one of the fillings. Sid left for the kitchen to start rolling the pasta out and getting all the layers together.

Mae and family showed up at five, right after Sy and Stella did, and it was a lovely night.

The next day, Sid, Nick, and I headed out to Pasadena shortly after mass. The open house didn't start until two, but Sid wanted to be sure the timbalos would get into the oven at Mae's properly.

There's a reason the open house is such a favorite event in our family. There's a goodly chunk of Mae's friends who are also my friends, thanks to the Ladies' Night Out monthly poker party. Others are also friends because we see them at the open house every year. The kids all know each other, which means there will be some mischief, but it's not usually too serious. Okay, there was the time someone's shoe landed on the other side of the back fence, and the whole troop of them went around the block to talk to the neighbor involved. As far as I know, the shoe got returned.

My father oversees the penny-ante poker game in Neil's den. He loves playing poker. There are only six seats at the table, and it's surprising how often there's a line to get a seat.

And there is music and singing in the front room. Sid and Stella take turns playing the upright piano. Sy usually has his violin and sometimes his lute, which he did this year, and it's always hysterical. Frank brings both his flute and his guitar (he and Esther come because Esther's part of the Ladies Night Out group, and Frank and Darby are close).

Finally, there is food and lots of it. Cookies, casseroles, meatballs in crockpots, the timbalos, cheeses, breads, salads, and the occasional fancy canape (which almost always gets sucked up in minutes).

That year was pretty typical. The big thing was when Darby got a large group singing and dancing to The Time Warp. I knew the tune but had never seen The Rocky Horror Picture Show. [An appalling deficit in your education that has yet to be remedied. - SEH] Nick and Darby had seen the movie on video, and I'd seen the clip somewhere. Anyway, it was a lot of fun.

The afternoon wore into the evening, and finally, only the poker ladies and what husbands and boyfriends they had were left. Kathy called a brief meeting since we would not be playing poker that month, and we wanted to finalize our January retreat. Okay, it was technically a trip to Las Vegas, but most of us spent some time praying and not just to fill out a straight or keep from busting at Blackjack. Sid and Frank were able to lean on Dan Williams hard enough to get him to consent to his wife, Sarah, going for the first time. Tina Thibodeaux and Elena Herrera, who had started out as friends of Mae's from their church, would also be first-timers.

Finally, around nine, the only people left at Mae's were family. Sid and Mae chivvied the kids into helping clean up, then Mae and I headed out to the back yard and Neil's workshop behind the garage to pull in whatever glassware and paper plates had been left behind.

As we got close to the workshop, Nick's voice floated out of the door.

"Dude, are you serious? That's three girls, and you only lost it last weekend."

"So what?" Darby demanded. "It's cool, and it feels good."

Mae and I looked at each other, our hearts in our throats.

"Yeah, but three?"

"You might try it yourself before getting all weirded out."

"I don't have to try it to know you're begging for trouble. Please tell me you're using a condom when you do."

"Duh. I'm not stupid."

"You wouldn't know it from the way you're acting."

Darby cursed and rushed out of the workshop only to see Mae and me in the light over the door. He swallowed, knowing we'd heard, and ran to the house. Nick ran into the doorway and saw us and cursed under his breath.

"It's alright, Nick," I said softly. "You're just worried about him."

Nick ran for the house. Mae glared at me.

"It's your fault," she snarled.

"What?"

"He's just like you. He eats like you. He acts like just you did in high school."

"I didn't sleep around!"

Mae blinked back tears. "But it's always been about your stupid passions. Literature. Food. Even sex. Especially since you and Sid got together."

"We've been telling Darby that it's better with commitment. Nick understands that."

Mae just rushed into the house. I followed behind her.

The younger children had gone upstairs. Sid stood in the kitchen doorway, patting Nick's shoulder. He looked at me.

"Time to head home?"

I looked at my parents, Sy and Stella, and Mae and Neil. "Mae..." I said.

"It's alright, Lisa." She squeezed her eyes shut. "It's not really your fault."

Sid went over to her. "Mae, if anybody, it's my fault."

"No. Sid, you're probably the best example he has." Mae swallowed as Neil held her. "He knows what you were like before. And he knows how much happier you are now. Honestly, I don't know what's upsetting me more. That he's sleeping around or that he's not happy about it."

"Either is enough to worry about," said Sid.

Sy stepped up and put his hand on Mae's back. "I am so sorry, Mae. You and I both knew this was possible. As much as I hate to see it happening, I am confident that he will get through it. You and Neil love him too much for him not to. We all do. It is not going to be easy, but we will get him through this phase, and he will be the better for it."

Mae nodded and hugged Sy.

Stella rolled her eyes. "Maybe if we just recognized it as norm—"

"Not the time, Stella," Sid growled.

She huffed, but let it go. Mama buried her face in Daddy's chest.

I looked at my parents. "Um, Mama, Daddy, do you still want to come over to our place tonight?"

"I'm staying here," said Mama. "Mae and Neil need the support."

Mae shrugged, and Neil nodded. I figured Neil could keep Mae and Mama from killing each other.

Sy and Stella left at the same time Sid, Nick, and I did.

"Are you okay, Nick?" I asked as we headed for the freeway.

In the back seat of Sid's Beemer, Nick shrugged dismally.

"I hope he knows that I'm just worried about him," Nick said. "I mean, I don't blame him for being mad."

Sid sighed. "I suspect he'll figure that out. How quickly, I don't know."

It was a long, sad ride home and a miserable end to a day we normally loved. Sid was extra sweet to me that night, and it was very, very good. I just couldn't help wondering if my passions had led Darby to act out as he had.

December 11, 1989

It almost felt a little strange not having Darby at the breakfast table that morning. Or maybe the three of us were just feeling the events of the night before. Nonetheless, Nick headed out for school in good time, and Sid and I were left to look at each other.

"Which section do you want?" Sid asked as he folded up the front section of the newspaper and grabbed the second.

"It doesn't matter," I said. "I'm too worried about Darby to care."

He sighed. "The problem is it's his choice. However you, or even I, may feel about the morality of it, it is his choice."

"You're right. That doesn't mean I like it."

"That, sadly, doesn't matter."

Later that morning, Angelique called me.

"We had a great time yesterday, as always."

"Yeah." I sighed deeply. "It didn't end that well on the family side. Nothing I want to talk about."

"Ouch. Okay. I've got something for you, though. Can we do lunch?"

I sighed. "Sure. Why not?"

What Ange had was the police report on Stan Ford's accident and death. She understood when I wanted to get back home to go over it with Sid. She had to get back to work quickly, anyway. It was Monday and her busy day.

At the house, Sid and I took turns reading the report as we sat in the office. The brakes on Stan's car had been tampered with sometime between five o'clock, when Stan had left the car dealership where he'd worked, and ten o'clock, when he'd left the bar, then had the accident. He was over the legal limit on alcohol and had been speeding when the brakes failed.

"Sid, did you see this?" I turned the file on the crack between our desks so that Sid could see it right side up and pointed to the spot. "Special Agent Peter Venkt was on the scene and told the investigating officer to not only check for tampering but suggested that Louis Renfrew might have had reason to kill Ford."

"Huh. It was getting close to seven when Loser showed that night, and according to this, the bar was not that far away from the airport. It's just barely possible Loser did."

"Not unless he's developed a transporter beam," I said. "Nick and I saw him around five-thirty, quarter to six. Well, he saw us and thought Nick was you, at first."

"Which means Cobb and pals didn't know that Loser was meeting us that evening, and yet by last Monday, we all had recon vehicles watching us." Sid glared at the report. "And why kill Stan? It seems like they were trying to set Loser up for it, but why didn't they make sure Loser was in the Bay Area before they did it that way?"

"How did they even find out about us?" I asked. "Unless Louis is walking the fence."

In other words, acting as a double agent.

"Well, that office had been broken into before we got to it." Sid sighed and made a face. "And we know Cobb and his pals were watching it somehow because they harassed Frank and Esther."

We looked at each other, utterly puzzled. Then Mae called.

"Mama and I are going over to the Glendale Galleria," she said. "Do you want to come?"

I looked at my watch. "I'd like to, but can't. I've got a meeting tonight at seven and I'm behind on my reading. How are you doing?"

Mae sighed. "Fine, I guess. Neil had a little talk with Darby last night. Mama's surprisingly okay. She agrees with Sy that this sort of thing is to be expected, especially given the pressure Darby's been getting. We're just going to have to brace ourselves after Thursday's concert. I think Darby gets it that we're worried about him getting hurt. Anyway, since sitting around brooding about it won't help, Mama wants to go to the Beverly Center sometime. You know, as a distraction. Are you done with classes yet?"

"Finished last week. We can go tomorrow, maybe have the rest of the crew meet us there?"

"Sounds good. We can meet for lunch."

"Sure." I named a restaurant, and Mae agreed. "When are Mama and Daddy coming over here?"

"After the concert on Thursday. Is that okay?"

I made a face. Sid, sitting across from me at his desk, lifted an eyebrow.

"Thursday?" I said. Sid shrugged and gestured to indicate my parents might as well come that day as any. "That should be okay."

I hung up and looked at Sid. "This is not a good time for them to be staying here."

"We've had to juggle it before."

Nick showed up at three, grinning like Alfred E. Neuman.

"Good day, honey?" I asked as he came into the office and kissed me, then kissed the top of Sid's head.

"Yep." He stopped. "Um, Darby and I patched things up, too. He's got a lot bothering him."

"We know, son," said Sid.

"Anyway, he wants to come over after lessons today and practice with you for Thursday." Nick smiled weakly. "Is that okay?"

Sid smiled. "Of course, it is, and he can stay over, too, if he wants."

"Cool. I think I'm going to drive us tomorrow. Car-pooling is better for the environment, you know."

"Better get on your homework," I said, pulling Quack-enbush open. "Oh, and there's a trip to Beverly Center in the works for tomorrow."

"Okay. I'll call Darby at the music school." Nick left the office.

Darby showed up at five-thirty reasonably contrite. I lit the second candle on the Advent wreath, we ate dinner, and opened Christmas cards. Sid told the boys that he and Tom were going out that night. I reminded them that I had a liturgy meeting and would probably go out with Frank and Esther afterward. The only problem was that Nick noticed that I was wearing my black break-in pants and a light pink Oxford shirt.

I got up to go at twenty to seven, hurrying to the office to get my purse, and put into it a disassembled high-powered rifle, an automatic .45mm pistol, and plenty of ammo. Nick caught me.

"You're working tonight?" he asked.

I sighed. "Yes, but that's what we do, sweetie." I slung the purse over my shoulder, then went over and put my hand on his cheek. "It will be alright."

"Is Dad working, too?"

I smiled. "Yeah. I'll buzz you when we get in, but it will probably be late. Why don't you get back on your reading?"

He made a face. I went out to the garage. I hated it when Nick worried about us, but there wasn't any way around it. As Nick often reminded us, he'd rather be with us and worried than living with one of his rather odious relatives on his mother's side. We'd had the occasional interaction with them over the years, but the visits only reconfirmed that there was a reason why Rachel Flaherty, his birth mother, had been such a witch.

Sid and I sometimes toyed with the idea of leaving our side business, but there were three problems. One was that retiring was seldom an option in our biz. Once you were in, you were in for life, one of the reasons we'd been training Nick. The other was that Sid and I didn't want to leave the business. And, finally, we were beginning to get the impression that Nick was going to worry no matter what we did. Nick just seemed to worry a lot, and our leaving the business wasn't going to change that.

The liturgy meeting went by quickly. It was mostly about getting the church changed over from Advent decorations for the morning masses on Christmas Eve to the Christmas decorations for midnight mass that night. Esther headed home to meet Kathy and Jesse and take care of Keshon while Kathy and Jesse helped me. Frank came with me to act as look-out in the industrial park where the warehouse was. I parked a ways down, quickly assembled my rifle, and pulled it over my shoulder. Frank stayed near my car. It was getting perilously close to nine-thirty. Kathy was waiting for me in the bushes. Jesse was already on the roof. We looked in through the glass front door. The building was in darkness.

I knew Louis and the guys would be going in the back. Kathy silently and quickly got the lock picked on the front door, and we slid inside the building. A dark hallway led between several blackened offices into the cavernous space beyond. In the dim light, I could see the four walls lined with shelves and several pallets of wire-bound boxes scattered around the floor in the center of the room. In my ear, I heard shushing and whispers. The guys had arrived.

"Little Red, Red Sky," said Jesse's voice. "I'm in position on the roof. Big Red and company are entering the building."

Kathy and I moved quietly and slowly, but we saw movement at the back of the warehouse just as the door started to open. We ducked behind the nearest pallet. I gestured her over to the next pallet over, and she ran.

I could see the silhouettes of Tom, Sid, and Wallace against the light over the door outside. Sid dove first, and the others scrambled for a couple of pallets just as the flare and cracks of gunshots went off. I could see three men in the far corner across from the door. I let off a couple shots from the rifle, then ducked.

"Where's Loser?" Tom yelped.

I wanted to know that, too. The lights burst on, and the men in the corner recoiled. They were all wearing night vision goggles.

Tom gasped. "Let's get out of here!"

Wallace raised a handgun and fired at the pallet in the corner, then shot toward me and Kathy. Sid yanked him down.

"Big Red," I muttered. "You're a little too cool. This is supposedly the first time you've been under fire in twenty years."

The guys scrambled out of the warehouse, but the lights situation left Kathy and me in a bit of a pickle. I started firing at the far corner as Kathy ran for the front of the building. I saw one of the guys there fall over. It looked like Venkt, and he had a wound in his shoulder.

"Red Sky, Red Dawn, Little Red," said Frank. "It sounds like we've got company coming."

"They were waiting for us!" Sid was yelling, liberally adding curse words. "Loser, what did you get us into?"

Kathy angled into the doorway and took up firing with her pistol as I ran in that direction. We slammed the doorway shut and ran for the office and out of the building. I ditched the rifle in the front office. I always wear gloves in that kind of situation, so that wasn't going to be an issue.

Kathy scrambled out the front door, and we slid through the bushes to where my car was.

"Red Team," I gasped. "Red Sky and I are clear. Evacuate now!"

"Red Team," came Jesse's voice. "I am at the rendezvous and leaving."

"Company coming in from Laurel Canyon to the south, Red Dawn," said Frank. "Come get me and we'll head out."

I nodded at Kathy, and we took off our masks and gloves, then opened our black hooded sweatshirts. It was getting chilly, so we thought it would look more conspicuous if we took them off. We both had light-colored shirts on underneath, so we didn't look like we'd been breaking in anywhere.

I wasn't sure where Sid and the guys had gotten off to, but didn't hear anything from Sid to indicate that they'd been held up by the cops. Kathy and I somehow avoided the parade of police cars whizzing into the industrial park, lights flaring. We could still hear Sid and Tom yelling at Louis, but couldn't tell what they were saying.

"Good job, Red Team," I said, hoping that Frank could hear me. "Let's rendezvous at the Gate."

Or Frank and Esther's duplex in West Hollywood. Esther's code name was Red Gate, and Frank's was Red Door.

Esther was not thrilled to hear what had happened.

"It's a good thing we were there, though," I said. "It was clearly a trap. The question is, who set it?"

"I don't have anything yet," said Kathy. "Although Esther did get me some of the bank files."

She picked up her sleeping son, and I couldn't help smiling.

"He looks so cute that way," I said.

Kathy smiled at the toddler. "He is a good boy. Okay, full of himself, yes. But he'll settle down. Jesse did, according to his mother."

Jesse rolled his eyes but kissed Kathy on the side of her head. "Come on. We'd better get home before he wakes up."

Sid's Voice -

Lisa generally calls it Divine Intervention. I was not up to calling it that, but I was so glad when I saw that faint glint in the far corner of the warehouse.

We'd ridden over there in two cars, Wallace's and Tom's. Ange got left in Tom's car to monitor the conversation we were hoping to have. I was wired, but not on the same frequency as Ange, and it didn't show through my sweater and sport coat. I could hear Lisa and Kathy getting into position at the front of the warehouse.

Wallace was sweating like a horse. The beads on his forehead glinted in the dim light as we walked to the warehouse's back door. It didn't make sense right away. It was chilly that night. I figured he was nervous and couldn't blame him. Tom was calm, though I do not know why.

The plan was that Loser and I were supposed to go in last. Loser got the door open, and I got pushed in ahead of everyone. Wallace and Tom came after, and that's when I caught that tiny glint of something moving in a place where it wasn't supposed to be. I didn't wait. I dove for cover, and it's a good thing I did because the firing started quickly.

Then the lights went on. I couldn't believe it when Wallace got up and started firing back. I yanked him down when he got off a shot toward Lisa and Kathy. Then Lisa reminded me that this was not a normal event. It was a good reminder because I looked a lot cooler than I felt.

Lisa and Kathy returned fire on the guys in the corner, and Venkt went down with a hole in his shoulder. That had to have been Lisa. She usually aims for the shoulder and gets it.

Frank's voice broke in that the cops were coming, and I got out of there as fast as I could, as did the others. When I ran into Loser outside the warehouse, I let him have it.

"It wasn't me!" Loser yelled back. "If anyone, it was you."

"Shit," Tom gasped. "Let's get out of here."

We ran for Tom's car.

"Where's Wallace?" I asked as Loser and I got into the back seat.

"He ran off," said Tom. "Like we should have."

Tom drove slowly out of the industrial park as several police cars blazed in. I thought I saw Jesse driving Frank out, too.

"So, what happened?" Angelique asked, her face white. "All I heard was gunfire."

"Damn it," I groaned. "It was a trap. They were waiting for us."

"I know," Loser snapped and turned on me. "So, when did you tell the Feds about it?"

"I didn't!"

"He didn't, Loser," Tom yelled from the front. "It doesn't even make sense that he would."

"Unless he wanted to sell me out to those bastards." Loser folded his arms across his chest, then looked at me. "The first thing you did was dive for cover. It was as if you knew they were going to be there."

"I saw something reflecting." I swallowed and tried to remember how Lisa acted scared. Oh, yeah, she let herself be scared. I took a couple of breaths and let myself feel the fear. "I didn't know what it was, but it shouldn't have been there. And then the shooting started."

"Shit," Tom said. "You panicked, didn't you?"

"I didn't panic!" I glared at him, then shut my eyes. "Look. It's been twenty years. It's taken that long to get used to the idea that people aren't shooting at me all the time. And then this happens, and I didn't have my sidearm. I didn't have a rifle. Fuck. I don't want to carry again."

Loser looked at me speculatively, then glared out the window. "You might want to start. All of you might want to." He looked at Ange. "Is it possible that you let it out about tonight's operation?"

Ange turned and glared at him. "You don't know what I know, shithead, but I will tell you right now, one thing I do know is how to keep a secret. And who's to say you didn't set this up? Maybe you're the bad guy here."

"It wasn't my idea to bring you guys into this." Loser stopped suddenly.

"Fuck," I muttered. "I know who set us up. I don't think he wanted to. But he was expecting trouble."

Tom glanced at me in the rearview mirror. "Wallace?"

"Why would he do that?" Loser asked.

"If what's-his-name and his pals leaned on him," I said. "Maybe he got scared. You know, he did suggest that we try to be nice to them."

"So," said Tom. "Do we trust him again or not?"

"Why not?" I said. "We're trusting Loser."

"I take exception to that," Loser grumbled.

"And I don't give a fuck," I said. "There is nothing that has gone right since you showed up. Stan got murdered and the cops wanted to know about you."

"I was being set up."

I glared at him. "And how do we know that?"

"We do know that." Ange stared straight out the front window of the car. "I have a copy of the police report on Stan's accident. Louis is solidly alibied for the sabotage on the car. But Peter Venkt was on the scene, talking to the cops."

Which I, of course, already knew, and I suspected Tom did, too.

Loser shook his head. "Fuck. They're onto me."

"No shit." I looked at him. "How could that possibly be a surprise?"

Loser didn't answer, which was probably just as well. By that point, I was ready to take his head off and didn't have to pretend.

When we got back to Tom and Ange's place in Culver City, Loser headed out.

"You okay, Sid?" Tom asked. The good thing about Tom being in recovery is that he gets the whole past trauma thing.

"I don't know," I said, being honest.

I said the same thing to Lisa when I got home that night, and she asked me the same question.

"I just seem to be getting more and more pissed at the bastard every time I come up against him," I told her as I took my contacts out for the night.

"I don't think tonight was his fault," she said, smiling weakly. "I mean, it was a mess."

"It was a clusterfuck. No two ways about it. Those guys were waiting for us. I'm just glad you and Kathy were there to distract them."

"Someone on your side was shooting, too. Was it Louis?"

"No. Wallace. Who knew he carries?"

"He's not very good."

I couldn't help chuckling. My sweet, sweet Lisa is an incredible dead shot.

"Oh, Ange called just before you got home," she said. "Peter Venkt is in the hospital, but likely to live. The other two flashed their badges and weren't arrested, even though the warehouse is, apparently, stacked to the brim with evidence in various cases."

"Or evidence that's been skimmed from other cases and is being sold."

She nodded. "Probably."

I took a deep breath and let it go.

"My beloved and darling Lisapet." I turned to her, feeling myself leap to life as I did. "I just want to put tonight out of my mind for the time being and remind myself what is truly important to me, which is you, and why the only thing I want to do right now is make intense, passionate love with you."

She smiled and walked up to me, then kissed the inside of my left wrist. Oh, shit, that still gets to me. She didn't say anything more until we were both spent and sleepy, and then she thanked me as she always does after lovemaking, and I thanked her.

Loser, that fuck, had no idea just how lucky he was that she was in my life.

December 12 – 13, 1989

Lisa's Voice

That morning, at breakfast, we were interrupted by loud honking from the driveway. Sid looked worried for a second, then realized it was the Twelfth of December. Nick, Darby, and I hurried out to the front of the house, where Josh Sandoval stood outside his car. Sid followed us. As soon as the four of us were gathered outside, Josh sang Las Mañanitas loudly, and Nick, Darby, and I sort of joined in. Well, Nick and Darby did okay. My Spanish pretty much sucks.

The Twelfth is the Feast of Our Lady of Guadalupe, and singing Las Mañanitas, even though it is generally a birthday song, is part of the festivities. I went over to Josh and gave him a big hug and kiss on the side of his head.

"Hey, sweetie, I'll call your mom, but would you give her a heads up that there's a family trip to Beverly Center happening today?" I grinned at him.

Josh's eyes lit up. "Beverly Center? Hell, yeah."

"Thank you," I told him. "Hopefully, we'll see you this afternoon."

I was looking forward to seeing Lety and Reuben later that day. Lety is part of the poker group and a wonderful friend. Reuben and Sid have bonded as well. And Josh, Nick, and Darby are all best friends.

I called Lety a little bit later. She wanted to meet Mae, Mama, and me around two that afternoon. She would try to get her husband, Reuben, and Josh's younger brothers to join us around four-thirty or five, especially since they'd have to leave at six-thirty to go to Lety's mother's house for the last night of the Novena to the Virgin and party. While Justin and Kyle hate shopping, they do like arcades and malls, and anything connected to Sid's and my families.

So, I was in a nice, contented place when I got to the office, pulled open Quackenbush, and dove in. Until the phone rang again. It was Sid's morning for the phone, so I ignored it until he cursed.

"What?" I asked, almost silently.

Sid waved me off for the moment.

"Uh-huh… That doesn't make any sense… Alright. Thanks for letting us know… Don't worry about that part. We're on high alert here… Okay. Thanks. We'll talk to you later."

He hung up.

"What's going on?" I asked even as the receiver hit the phone base.

"That was Angelique." Sid took a deep breath. "Peter Venkt was found smothered in his bed at the hospital this morning."

"What?" I almost leaped out of my desk chair. "Could it have been Louis?"

"I wouldn't put it past him, but Ange doesn't think so. Harlan Cobb was seen at the hospital around four-thirty that morning, although it doesn't make sense that he'd have killed his partner."

"Unless Venkt was trying to get out without sharing their loot."

Sid shrugged. "That may be."

I sat back as another thought hit me. "I know I didn't kill him, but I feel as though I set Venkt up to be killed."

"I'm not surprised." Sid got up and came around to my desk, and pulled me into his arms. "You stopped him without killing him. That's a lot, sweetheart, and we know plenty of people who would have killed him without blinking."

"I know." I swallowed as my eyes filled. "And there's no way I could have foreseen someone smothering him in his hospital bed. Still, it just feels awful."

"Of course it does. That's because you are a good person and you care, and that's one of many reasons why I love you so much."

I pressed my lips together, then undid his belt buckle.

Sid squeezed me gently, then so softly, tenderly, pressed his lips to the old knife scar I had on my forehead, just below my hairline.

"I'll shut the door," he said. "Do you want a glass of water?"

I nodded, and he got it from the office bathroom.

Sid and I do come in for a fair amount of justified teasing because we really love having sex together, and we can be pretty uninhibited, let alone noisy. But there are times when our lovemaking is not about the joy, but about the violence we encounter. Making love is our antidote to that violence. As Dr. Heilland explained it some years before, making love, for us, is the most life-giving thing we do. So, loving each other physically helps counteract that horrible feeling when someone dies because of our actions.

Earlier that year, I had killed somebody. It was one of those situations where there was no time to aim, let alone think. Sid and I were up all that night, making love over and over again.

Fortunately, I wasn't in quite that bad a shape that morning. After all, I hadn't killed Venkt. As Sid had pointed out, I had actively avoided it. But it was bad enough and close enough to that last incident that my stomach was still roiling a little as we cleaned up. Sid offered to let me go with him to his appointment with Dr. Heilland.

"I'll be okay," I said. "I've got lunch and then shopping with Mama and Mae. That's life-giving, too. See you at the Beverly Center food court at six-thirty?"

Sid thought. "I should be able to make it then. I'll see if Stella and Sy want to come, too."

"That sounds like fun."

Sid headed off to the psychologist's office, and I did some reading before I had to leave to meet Mae and Mama.

Mae noticed right away that I was off and asked about it as we perused the menus at the restaurant. It was one of those oak and brass places that featured overpriced drinks and the same dishes everyone else did.

"Uh, someone I know died," I said. "No one close. It's just sad, is all."

"It's always sad when someone dies during the holidays," Mama said, then patted my hand. "I know you're feeling bad, but maybe a little distraction will help. Do we want to have some of those baked potato skins as an appetizer?"

"Sounds terrific." I put on a grin.

Mae's eyes lingered on me for a second before she agreed.

It was a lovely afternoon and evening. Mama made a point of getting new Christmas pajamas for all the kids, since they'd all grown out of the ones Grandma Caulfield had gotten everyone the year before. Lety caught up with us at two, and by three, Nick, Darby, and Josh had joined us. Around five-thirty, Reuben and Josh's brothers met us at the food court, and we began staking out a group of tables, just in time for Neil and the rest of his kids and Daddy to arrive. Sid had Sy and Stella with him when he showed at six-thirty. Lissy saw her uncle and ran to him.

"Unka Sid! Unka Sid!"

"Hey, Lissy." Laughing, Sid scooped her into his arms and picked her up.

He gave my niece Janey a quick one-armed hug and kiss, bussed me, then stood chatting with Reuben as Lissy snuggled into him.

"Oh, my god!" screeched a female voice. "Is that you, Sid Hackbirn?"

Sid's smile got rather tight as two women with high-lighted and gelled hair, designer handbags, and faux jeweled belts holding in their full tops, came walking up.

"Hey, ladies."

"It is you, Sid. Can you believe it, Sherry?"

Sherry's chuckle was significantly deeper than her friend's voice. "Look at you. With a baby, of all things."

Lissy buried her face into Sid's shoulder.

"She's my niece," Sid said.

The first woman looked over our group, not only missing me, but somehow not seeing Nick or Stella, either.

"Still," the first woman said. "What did that woman do to you?"

"What woman?" Sid looked puzzled.

"That little ice cube you married."

"Ice cube?" Neil sniggered, and Mae backhanded him.

"Or did we get lucky and that ended?"

Sid rolled his eyes. "It's not going to end." He looked over at me. "What she did to me was make me deliriously happy for the first time in my life." He smiled at the ladies as if to suggest that they'd done anything but.

"Come on, Sherry."

The two stalked off.

"Sorry about that," Sid said, shifting Lissy.

"Apart from your former bad taste, I see nothing to be sorry for," said Stella.

"It's like you've always said, Sid, honey," Mama said. "You gave up sleeping around because it wasn't doing anything for you. And I can see why now."

I was a little surprised by Mama. She usually pretended that Sid had been as pure as I was when I'd met him. But then I saw the thoughtful look on Darby's face and suddenly got it.

Josh, however, was glaring at his mother.

"Do I have to go?" he asked.

"Reuben, we've got to leave," Lety said. "Mamí will be mad if we're late."

"What about Josh?" Reuben asked. He's as tall as his wife is short, as calm as she's constantly in motion.

Lety turned to her son. "Your abuelita. She wants to see you."

"But Tío Alfonso will be there." Josh looked miserable.

Josh's uncle was determined to make Josh a real man. Now, Josh could and usually did act straight, especially at the all-boys high school he went to. But it was tiring for him, and around his family, he sometimes relaxed, and Alfonso was horrified.

Reuben looked at Lety. "Let him off the hook this time. He and Alfonso can beat each other up on Christmas Day."

"Alright." Lety hugged her son. "Justin, Kyle, come on."

The younger boys shuffled off.

Reuben and Lety are very supportive of Josh. So, it might seem odd that they'd sent their probably gay son to an all-boys high school. But Reuben says that Josh is going to have to learn how to function in that kind of world, anyway, and Josh wanted to go where Nick was going. What sold the school, though, was the spring before the boys graduated from middle school, Sid got both Josh and Darby enrolled at the martial arts dojo where we go to learn how to defend themselves. So, while all three of our boys do get some teasing, between Darby's violin, Josh's love of acting, and Nick being a dyed-in-the-wool nerd, they haven't gotten beaten up because the first time a group tried, the attackers were soundly thrashed.

The evening was very relaxing and did a lot to help me get over my morning's angst. Which was why we felt utterly blindsided when we got home to a ringing telephone, and it was Kathy.

She was in tears.

"It's Jesse," she told us over the speakerphone in the office. "He was coming home this afternoon from his grandma's place and got pulled over on Wilshire. The cops found four ounces of cocaine in the trunk of his car."

"Oh, my god," I gasped.

"Has he been booked?" Sid asked.

"No. They're holding him for questioning," Kathy said. "At least, that's what the lawyer I got says. Jesse won't talk without the lawyer there, but the cops are saying that they have to wait for some FBI agents who want to talk to him."

Even I cursed. "At least, they're just holding him for questioning."

"It's L.A.P.D." Kathy snarled.

She had a point. The thing is, if you're White in this area, stuff does not happen to you. If you're Black, it happens all the time. Worse yet, there were decent odds Jesse had already gotten knocked around.

"Better start hoping they keep holding him for questioning," Sid said. "If they run fingerprints on him, his cover is blown as an operative. The cops generally keep that stuff quiet, but with the Feds we're dealing with…"

Kathy cursed.

"I need to make a couple of phone calls," Sid said. "Who's the lawyer you got?"

Kathy told him, and Sid said there might be a better option, but that he'd see to it that whoever would work with the lawyer Kathy had.

"Kathy, do you want me or Sid to go over there?" I asked.

She sighed. "No. I'm not even at home. I'm at Estelle's." Estelle is Kathy's sister.

"Do you want us to take Keshon?"

"Oh, God, have mercy, no. I need my baby." Kathy's voice trembled, and it was so very frightening.

"Look, we know the coke wasn't Jesse's," I said. "We'll try to figure out how it got into his car. Okay? It's going to be fine."

Kathy took a deep breath. "I know, Lisa. I'm just glad we got you guys."

"Just be glad you guys are part of our operation," Sid growled. "That will save his ass, if nothing else."

We hung up after I reminded Kathy that I'd be praying for her and Jesse. Sid called Lillian and even called Dale O'Connor, which is saying a lot because Sid does not like Dale.

"Dale says it's on ice." Sid frowned as he hung up the phone.

"But why did they target Jesse?" I asked. "That doesn't make sense."

Sid's mind was somewhere else. "I may not know why, but I'm willing to bet I know when."

"What do you mean?"

Sid went to one of our file cabinets, unlocked it, and pulled out a file.

"This." He tossed the file of photos onto my desk, then sorted through the pictures. "Here it is. I wasn't sure what to make of it when I first saw it, but now I do."

The photo was of Special Agent Bruce Whitemore standing next to Jesse's car.

"I don't know why he stashed the drugs in Jesse's car," Sid said. "But I'll put up some serious money that he did for some reason."

"Why not?" I asked. "He'd have to figure that Jesse would get pulled over at some point. But why attack Jesse? He and Kathy arrived with a freaking toddler in tow. Why would they think Jesse was up to something?"

Alas, we found out why the next day, but not before we found we had a similar problem.

The thing is, we have a great drug-sniffing dog. Not Bowser. Bowser isn't good for much besides looking cute and helping you feel good because you're petting his belly.

Motley, on the other hand, had been trained to find cocaine by his previous owner. About a year and a half ago, Sid and I worked a case where several illegal substances turned up. Motley had gotten a workout but proved he had not lost his drug-sniffing skills one iota.

That Wednesday morning, as the four of us humans and two dogs left the house to go running, Motley whined and ran up to Darby's car in the driveway. We called him off and did our run. But when we came back, Sid glanced at me and chivvied Nick and Darby into the house with Bowser on their heels. Motley ran up to Darby's car, sniffed it, then whined and pawed at the back driver's side door. I winced. I didn't have any lockpicks on me.

I went inside, got Sid on the intercom, and asked him to get breakfast ready. The lockpicks I retrieved from the office. I was in and out of Darby's car in an instant, with a small plastic bag of some white powder in my hand.

"What the..." Sid groaned when he saw it.

The boys had been sent safely (we hoped) off to school in their individual cars since Darby would be at Stella's and Sy's music school after school, and Nick would (again, hopefully) return to the house.

"They're targeting us," I said. "Which makes a little bit of sense. They knew that Louis was connecting with his old friends."

"But how?" Sid looked at the plastic bag with horror.

"Honey, if I knew that, we'd have the case broken."

"I know." Sid groaned. "This is ridiculous. What can they think is to be gotten from chasing down Loser's friends?"

"Apart from setting Louis up?" I did add a bit of emphasis to Louis' name. Sid did not, alas, notice.

Sid shook his head. "Even odds Loser is setting those bastards up to serve his own purposes."

"And, as you have pointed out to me more than once, does it make that much of a difference?"

The doorbell rang. I did not recognize the man on the doorstep that our video camera showed us, but Sid did. He was a tall man with full shoulders and an attitude.

Sid let him in and started the conversation in the hall, presumably with whatever codewords were appropriate.

"Well?" Sid asked as he led our visitor into the office.

"You've obviously guessed I'm not just a former Special Forces guy," said the man. He had medium brown hair and was wearing an expensive suit. He reached out to shake Sid's hand, and I saw a tattoo on the back of his wrist.

"And you've figured out I'm not just a freelance writer and veteran." Sid smiled at him.

"But my name really is Zack Peters." The man laughed. "Your crew member has been safely sprung from jail with no charges. There were threats of a suit for false arrest. Neither Cobb nor Whitemore came in to question him, so I'm guessing they hung him out to dry just for the fun of it."

"What do you mean?" I asked.

"Those bastards do it all the time." Peters rolled his eyes. "They see a Black guy someplace they don't think he should be, they plant some drugs in his car, and just wait. He's Black, he'll get pulled over sooner or later, and usually searched, legally or not. If Cobb had been trying to bring your friend down for some reason, they'd have put an APB out on the car. The only reason L.A.P.D. knew to hold him for questioning was that Whitemore usually likes to know when one of his victims has been brought in."

I groaned. "That is disgusting."

Sadly, however, it was not that surprising. Sid and I live in Beverly Hills, and our stupid neighbors are so prone to calling the cops when Jesse and Kathy come to visit that Beverly Hills P.D. knows them and knows to leave them alone.

Sid looked Peters over. "And how do you know all this?"

"A mutual friend of ours." Peters chuckled. "He and I have been trying to get these guys since Vietnam. We've had to tread pretty damn softly. Cobb's connections are significant."

"So, why now?" I asked. "You've had almost twenty years since the war ended."

"Yeah. Twenty years for the resentment to build. Twenty years to piss off a lot of people." Peters grinned. "Eventually, that sort of thing is going to come back and bite you in the ass."

Sid shrugged. "We've been told that the people who have been protecting them are getting fed up."

"And how." Peters' eyes swept over the office. "Besides, they've almost disrupted one of our operations. I don't know why our mutual friend thinks you guys are so damned important, but he is not happy."

"I'm told we get the job done," I said.

"Yeah." Peters' grin seemed jovial, but something was just a hair off being sincere.

"Which mutual friend?" Sid's smile was also jovial, but also a couple hairs off sincere, although I suspect I was about the only person who would have noticed.

"I believe you knew him as Colonel Landry."

I couldn't help wondering if Peters knew Landry's real name, and if he did, why wasn't he using it? Sid and I did know Landry's real name, which was Congressman Dale O'Connor. There's a reason why Sid has a serious grudge against him, and it's not just because O'Connor is a full-of-himself, sexist asshole. O'Connor blackmailed Sid into intelligence work back when Sid was in boot camp. Then, when Sid was discharged from the Army, O'Connor sucked him right back into intelligence work, this time as part of Quickline. Both times, O'Connor used the alias Colonel Landry. Sid didn't find out his real name until 1985, when we were working on another case that O'Connor was part of.

"I do know him," Sid said.

Okay, both of us had our best poker faces on and were watching even the least tic in Peters' face. That Sid had used the present tense did not get past Peters.

I smiled. "Look, if we're all trying to achieve the same end, maybe we should share information."

Sid looked at Peters. "What gets me is why these guys didn't cut bait and run like hell weeks ago. They have to have known their protection was weakening."

"That's a good question." Peters sighed. "There's no question that Cobb has gotten cocky. Twenty-plus years of getting away with murder can do that to you. On the other hand, I think that's why Cobb iced Venkt. He didn't want to take a chance on Venkt talking."

"Venkt wasn't under arrest," I said. "As I understand it, the police thought Cobb and Whitemore were legit and that the warehouse was part of regular FBI operations."

Peters shrugged. "Maybe Venkt was waffling. Maybe Cobb doesn't want to share. Does it really matter?"

"It might," said Sid. "Especially if you want to pin Venkt's murder on the right person."

Peters' eyes narrowed as he looked at Sid. "If you're worried about your buddy Renfrew, I have no idea how he got involved in all this, but I have evidence that he was solidly alibied for Venkt. He's one lucky SOB that way. Trust me, I was looking at him for that one."

"That's good to know," said Sid. "So, how do we stay in touch with you? To share information and all that."

"I'll be around," Peters said. "But there's always our mutual friend."

"Okay. Well, you know where to find us." Sid smiled.

He escorted Peters out of the house. I looked at Sid as he came back into the office.

"Do you trust him?" I asked.

"About as far as I can throw him."

I winced. "That's probably pretty far."

Sid looked at me, then laughed. "How about as far as I trust Loser."

"In other words, not very far at all."

"No."

December 14 - 17, 1989

Lisa's Voice

Kathy and Jesse celebrated his release with his family. That next morning, however, found them in Sid's and my office. They were not happy to hear what Zack had to say about the arrest.

"Pure racist bullshit," Jesse growled, pacing the office. "It's going to take videotape of them whaling on us before White people get it."

[Ironic as hell that even the videotape didn't help us White people get it. - SEH]

"At least, we have reason to believe that it wasn't our operation that was threatened," Sid said, holding and jiggling Keshon. "Small comfort, I know, but I'm looking for anything right now."

"They've also targeted my nephew's car," I said. "I found drugs yesterday in the back seat."

"Why not Nick's or yours?" Kathy asked.

"They're in the garage," I said. "Darby's car is out and vulnerable in the driveway."

Sid sighed. "I know what I need to do." He winced. "I don't want to get rid of you, but it would be a lot better if you weren't around for this next part."

Kathy and Jesse agreed. Kathy took Keshon from Sid only to have the child split our eardrums with his screams.

"At least, he likes you," Jesse said, smiling weakly.

Sid's Voice –

I got Loser to meet me at the end of the Santa Monica Pier right before noon. The sky was clouded over and threatening, but I knew there was a bar nearby if it started to rain before we were done.

He was waiting for me, hunkered down in a jacket that was about the same size and style as a windbreaker, but heavier than that.

"Hey, Sid," he said as I walked up.

I looked out over the whitecaps on the ocean in front of us. "What the hell is going on? First, you damned near get us killed. Then my good friend is targeted, and even my nephew."

"What do you mean?"

"Both of them had drugs planted in their cars."

Loser shook his head. "You sure they're not using?"

"Jesse? Hell, no." I stopped. Darby had been off but wasn't showing the signs of coke use. "My nephew neither. Look, I get that you need help, but you've been lying to us. I need to get these bastards off our ass. I don't give a fuck about you. Trust me. But this is affecting my family and my friends. Do me a favor and be straight with me for a change."

"What makes you think I'm not?"

"Getting shot at in a warehouse. And the more I think about it, the more I realize that you couldn't possibly expect Angelique to do much about these fucks. Come on. She's great, but she isn't an agent. And if these guys have such great protection, what is she going to do about it?"

Loser sighed. Even odds it was genuine. "I was hoping you guys could protect me. Part of the whole hiding in plain sight thing."

"Uh-huh."

"If you're not going to believe me, then why are you here?"

I shook my head. "I don't know. I've got to do something." I sighed. "They're hurting my family. That may not be something you understand, but it's real for me."

Loser snorted. "I get it better than you think." He looked at me. "Sid, I don't want to hurt you or your family. It's true that I'm probably in too deep to get out of this on my own. I don't know what to tell you." He swallowed.

Damn, I wished Lisa were with me. There's a reason she's so good at poker. She can spot those tiny little signs that tell when someone is lying.

Loser looked around the pier. "I do have some evidence on these guys. Do you mind holding it for me?"

"What do you mean?"

Loser pulled a floppy disk from his jacket pocket. "Dates and shit. At some point, I'll have to go public. But if you and Tom have this information, it will back me up. You know I need it. They're special agents. Who's going to believe me when I'm up against them?"

I took the disk. "This is the best you can do?"

"Right now, yeah."

"Fuck you. Fuck you and the horse you rode in on."

Loser laughed. "Fuck you, too."

He turned away and walked up the pier to the street. A huge wave broke on the end of the pier, sending spray into the mist. My breath blew out in a little cloud, and I realized the mist was coalescing into tiny raindrops.

Lisa's Voice

When Sid got home, he was not in a good mood. He went straight to the office without a word. I grabbed the remains of the chicken salad that Conchetta had made for lunch and brought it to him.

We have four computers at home, which seems like a lot. Okay, it is a lot. Sid and I each have one for our respective writing work and have had for several years. Nick has one for his schoolwork. But then there is the fourth computer. It's supposedly a portable, and it is easier to move it from place to place than our Macintoshes. But it doesn't work with either of the Macintoshes. Esther says it has a different operating system, whatever that is.

It did work with the floppy disk that Sid had brought home. However, what was on the disk was pretty much useless.

"We have this already," Sid groaned, adding a few other curse words.

"Does he know that?" I asked.

Sid shut his eyes. "Possibly." He groaned loudly. "That's the problem. I have no idea how much of what he's told me is the truth. Lisa, he's done nothing but lie to us."

I sighed. "You're right. But we've gotten enough from other sources to know that some of it must be true."

"But what parts?" Sid shook his head. "Damn it, they targeted Darby's car. And what they did to Jesse."

"I know, lover. That worries me, too. At least, we don't have to think about it until tomorrow."

Sid looked up at me, worried. "What the hell do you mean?"

"Tonight is Darby's spotlight concert. We just have to get him through that, then we can think about other things over the weekend. By the way, it's starting to rain."

Sid looked out the front window of the office and cursed. "You're right."

"I've already called Mae. If there's powder, they're all up for it."

Sid laughed. "It will get them out of town tomorrow."

"Mm-hm." I smiled back but knew darned well it was the lure of fresh powder as much as it was keeping my family safe.

You see, when it rains in our part of Los Angeles at this time of year, it generally means it's snowing in the mountains that surround us. Which means a ski trip. Having grown up in South Lake Tahoe, Mae and I love skiing. Sid loves to ski, too, and none of us likes the weekend crowds. A Friday is pushing it, but we do recognize that we can't really control the weather.

Sid immediately called his contact and secured lift tickets. Neil and Mae love skiing enough that they don't mind Sid paying for it. I called Mae to let her know that the kids would be out of school the next day. She was ecstatic.

Well, she was about the ski trip the next day. She was not so happy about that night.

"Did Darby eat anything this morning?" she asked.

I made a face. "Not much. He's feeling it."

"Shavings. He's worrying, isn't he?"

"He's been pretty nervy since he got back from the rehearsal with the orchestra yesterday." I sighed. "Sy says it's normal and he should be."

"Probably." Mae groaned. "This sucks, Lisa. I know Sy is right, but it's so damned hard to watch. I just want to pull Darby into my arms and not let go until he's fifty."

I laughed sadly. "I know what you mean. Darby will be okay. We love him. He knows it. He'll be fine. We just have to trust that God will have His hand on him."

"You're right." Mae swallowed audibly. "See you tonight."

When the boys pulled up after school that afternoon in Darby's car, I had Motley check it. It was still misting pretty heavily, but we were between downpours.

"What's going on?" Darby growled.

"Somebody's been playing some nasty pranks," I told him.

Darby looked at Motley, and his face went pale. "You're checking me for drugs, aren't you? I remember Motley does that."

"Darby, I know you're not using drugs. There are some guys who are harassing us, and they planted some cocaine in one of our friends' cars."

"Oh, bull-puckey." That was the term he used. Darby will not swear in front of me or Mae. "You don't trust me!"

He stormed off into the house.

Nick just shook his head. "He's been a mess all day."

Motley sniffed all around the car, then quickly lost interest.

"At least, Darby's clear." I started up the front walk. "He does seem more nervous than usual."

Nick followed me inside the house. "I think it's that stupid agent, Crispin."

Darby stormed through the hall to the front of the house, his overnight case and violin case in hand.

"I've gotta go home," he announced, glowering. "I'll see you guys tonight."

The front door slammed behind him.

"So, what's with the agent?" I looked at Nick. "I know he's been putting some pressure on."

"He keeps telling Darby that his parents are holding him back and that he'll miss his big chance if he doesn't sign with him now."

"That's nonsense."

Nick sighed. "But Darby doesn't know that. The scary thing is that Aunt Mae and Uncle Neil don't know the classical music business, and Crispin keeps pushing the idea that Sy and Stella haven't kept up to date with it."

"Hm."

Sid got home early from the music school, and the three of us hurried to a restaurant not far from the theater where the concert was being held. Mae and Neil were already there with Janey and Ellen, and my parents. The twins were a little too antsy, and Lissy was way too young to spend an evening listening to classical music, so they were at home with a babysitter. Sy and Stella were also at the table. Darby was already at the theater.

"I am so glad, too," Mae sighed as I slid into a chair between her and Sy. "Even Mama was having a hard time with him."

"Young artist," said Sy.

"And apparently that agent Crispin," I grumbled and told them what Nick had told me.

Sy sighed deeply. "Then we will get someone to talk to him who is currently in the business and doing very well at that. She's coming to the concert tonight, so that should help. When can we set up a more formal meeting?"

Mae and I dove for our organizers.

"We've got the choir party on Sunday," I said, flipping pages. "But the just usual stuff after that."

"Monday would work for us," Mae said. "You guys want to eat dinner at our place?"

"I think so," I said.

Mae and I checked with our respective spouses and Mama and Daddy, while Sy whispered something to Stella, and it was agreed we'd spend Monday evening with Mae and family, although we decided to have dinner and the meeting at Sid's and my place.

Having the meeting planned helped all of us to relax, and we lingered over dinner until it was time to go over to the theater for the concert. I was so glad the twins had stayed home. Darby was on last, and Marty and Mitch would never have made it.

Ah, but Darby played so beautifully. It was the Bach Violin Concerto in A Minor. Both Mae and I couldn't help sniffling. He's so serious when he plays, and yet there's such a glow about him, you can tell he is in utter bliss at the same time. Sy nodded, smiling. Darby's newly gained ego may have been causing other trouble, but one lesson that had stuck solidly was that when he played for others, he was to give it his all or not bother.

After the concert, we headed backstage. Darby, still in his rented tux, was accepting congratulations from the conductor. Sy's eyes narrowed as one small fellow with dark hair, gelled and sticking up, approached Darby.

"Good evening, Mr. Crispin," Sy said loudly.

The man turned. "Oh, hello, Dr. Flournoy. You've chosen quite the protégé."

"As I well know." Sy looked up. "Ah. And here's Ms. Stein. Thank you so much for coming, Roxanna."

She was about my height, with light brown hair piled on top of her head. She wore a royal blue jacket and straight skirt with a white blouse coming untucked, and glasses dangling from a chain around her neck. She walked up and gave Sy a kiss on the cheek.

"It's good to see you, Sy." She turned and smiled at Darby. "So, you're the young man."

"Yeah," said Darby with a grin.

Her lips pursed a little. "Sy was right. Nice job, by the way." She turned and saw Crispin. "Alex, darling, why don't we stop harassing innocent little artists and go get a cup of coffee?"

Crispin reluctantly left with Ms. Stein.

"Man, I'm starved," Darby sighed loudly. "I gotta get something to eat."

"In good time, young man," Sy said. "Where's your bag?"

"In the dressing room." Darby started to put away his violin. "Ellen, go get it."

"No, she won't," Mae said. "You go get it. In fact, go get changed pronto, then neatly hang up your tux, and we'll go."

"But I'm hungry now!"

Mae got a solid grip on her son's arm and marched him into the dressing room.

"If you ever treat one of your siblings or anyone else as your personal servant again, I swear, Darby, I will break your hands."

"And I will help," said Sy.

Darby looked terrified.

"Yes, you are very talented, my son." Mae was shaking. "But that does not entitle you to act like a little shit. Do you understand?"

Darby swallowed. "Yes, ma'am."

"Alright. The sooner you change, the sooner we'll get you something to eat."

There wasn't much open at that hour, so we found a McDonald's. Darby ate two Big Macs, two large fries, and a chocolate shake. He had barely finished slurping down the last of the shake when he started blinking and yawned. He and his family went out to their van, and Janey told me the next day that Darby had fallen asleep even before Neil had the engine started. Mama and Daddy followed Sid, Nick, and me home.

Sid, Nick, and I did not go running the next morning. It was still raining, but that didn't matter. We were all up by five-thirty. Sid and Daddy got the ski rack onto the top of Sid's Beemer and locked down five sets of skis and poles. Mama made a full pot of hot coffee while I ran hot water into the two insulated bottles. Nick got the toast going. There was plenty of fresh powder in the mountains, and the slopes were calling.

It was one of those great days that remind me why I love being with my family so much. It was Lissy's first time on skis, too, and everyone took turns teaching her how to stop and glide, and she really took to it. Daddy even said she picked it up faster than I had. Sadly, though, I couldn't convince anybody to race me. Well, I am the fastest skier in the family.

Darby and I got a chance to talk, too, sitting next to each other on the chair lift.

"I'm sorry about yesterday," he said.

"I accept your apology. And it really was about those guys harassing our friend."

"I know." He smiled and ducked his head. "Sy wouldn't tell me how I did last night."

"It was gorgeous." I slung my arm across his shoulders. "You are so talented. But that does come with a certain amount of responsibility."

He sighed. "Just call me Peter Parker."

"Huh?"

"Spider-Man. With great power comes great responsibility. Peter's uncle keeps lecturing him that way."

"Oh."

"Aunt Lisa, was I really that bad last night?"

It was my turn to sigh. "Yes and no. But it would be all too easy for you to get worse, and none of us wants that for you. I mean, do you want to be a jerk?"

"No." Darby shook his head.

"You'll be fine, then. Just take us seriously when we call you on it."

"Okay."

"Wanna race me?" I nudged him playfully.

"No."

It was an altogether satisfying day, but by the end of it, I was also reminded why I don't like spending time with my family.

"I think I need some time to myself," I told Sid as we got into bed that night.

"Well, the plan is to go to the Third Street Promenade tomorrow."

"We've been there."

The city of Santa Monica had newly refurbished their big, closed-street walkway, and it had opened the previous September.

"Everyone else hasn't," Sid said. "Why don't you stay home?"

"I think I will. Now, how do I thank you for being so sensitive to my needs?" I grinned.

Sid just chuckled lecherously.

Saturday was sheer heaven. I mostly stayed in bed all day, read a silly murder mystery, dozed, and didn't think once about grammar and rhetoric and how to teach it, or federal agents, or much of anything except how lovely and quiet it was.

Sunday provided another all-too-brief lull in the craziness, only it wasn't entirely a lull. It was time to get the Christmas tree. Two years before, our parish's school decided to have a Christmas tree lot for a fundraiser. It's been darned successful. After mass, I sent Mama, Daddy, and Sid on home to get the space in front of the living room niche window ready while Nick and I picked the actual tree out. We'd pre-ordered an eight- to nine-foot tree. All I had to do was look at the ones they had, pick it out, and get it onto the top of Sid's Beemer.

It wasn't even twelve-thirty by the time we rolled up the driveway.

"I did it again!" I hollered into the front as I opened the double doors. "It's absolutely gorgeous."

"You always do, dearest," Sid said, laughing.

And I had done it again. The tree was exactly five inches too tall.

"That's a nine-foot tree!" I moaned. "That's a ten-foot ceiling."

Daddy and Sid cut down the bottom, as usual, then once it was in the stand and anchored to the wall, Mama gathered Daddy and Nick, and they went out somewhere. I took a deep breath of one of my favorite scents in the world - that of a Douglas fir in my house.

"I'd better get going, too," Sid said with a sigh. "We're just meeting down at the Plaza. I'll be back within an hour."

"Okay. I'll get the lights checked for dead bulbs."

Sid's Voice -

I hadn't wanted to put off the tree decorating. It's something that I truly enjoy doing with Lisa. However, Wallace was worried, and I couldn't blame him. He'd found drugs in his car and had gotten rid of them just in time before a couple of cops served a search warrant on him. It had scared the shit out of his wife, too. So, he arranged to take the family shopping at the Century Plaza mall, which was the closest one to us, and meet me at one at a restaurant there.

I wasn't in a good mood, as it was, but having to listen to him complain about Lottie annoyed the spit out of me.

"Why do you keep putting your wife down?" I snarled at him.

Wallace sat there for a minute, shifting awkwardly. "What do you mean?"

"Just now. You rolled your eyes because she was scared by cops serving a search warrant on you, then said she was being a ninny because she wanted you to call her when you got to work the next day." I shook my head. "How is it being a ninny to want to know that your husband got to work safely after an experience like that? You do it all the time when you talk about her. Is your marriage that bad?"

"No. I guess." Wallace sighed. "It's how all the guys at work talk, the old ball and chain, stuff like that."

"That doesn't mean you have to."

"I suppose." Wallace thought it over for a minute. "But why do you care?"

I frowned. "This project I was working on a couple, three years back. It was the same thing, a bunch of guys running their wives down right and left, then bitching because they didn't get enough sex."

Wallace chuckled sardonically. "Yeah, well, being married with kids makes it really hard to have sex with any regularity."

"That has not been my experience."

We fell into silence.

Wallace looked at me, pondering. "Sid, do you ever ask yourself what you want out of life?"

"What do you mean?"

"I don't know. It's just that I used to think I knew what I wanted. A good job, a wife, being a better dad to my kids than my dad was to me. Only I'm turning into him. That's what gets Lottie. She says I don't talk to her anymore. I don't spend time with the kids. It's just like my dad was. Problem is, I don't know what to talk to them about."

"Huh. Don't know what to tell you. Lisa, Nick, and I, we talk all the time about our lives, what we think about things."

"So, what did you want out of life when we were kids?"

I shrugged and shifted. "I had no idea. Honestly, pretty much everything I have now just happened to me. My money. Nick. When I met Lisa, I was looking for a secretary. In fact, what made her so good that way was that there was no sex going on. We could just work together and be friends. Then we fell in love. Her family adopted me. Nick showed up. The next thing I knew, we were getting married, and I was playing the organ for church services. I have a family now. I like having a family. I like being married and having my son. I'm so proud of that kid. And proud of my wife, too. Lisa is an amazing woman, and I don't mind saying so."

"Huh." Wallace sighed. "So, what are we going to do about these Feds?"

"I have no idea." And even if I had, I wasn't going to tell him.

"Can we set up a meeting? Please?"

I looked at him. "Sure. I'll see what we can do."

"Wednesday night, okay?"

"Sounds okay. I'll check with Lisa, though, and get back to you."

"Why do you have to check with your wife?"

I rolled my eyes. "Because A- she keeps the family schedule, and B- it's a basic courtesy. She checks with me before making any commitments."

"That's weird."

I got up and slapped his upper arm. "Maybe. But keep in mind, I'm the one getting more sex now than I did before I got married. And I got a lot of sex before I got married."

I left the table just as two kids, a young teen girl and a pre-teen boy, came running up.

"Dad!" the boy yelled. "See what I got Grandma!"

Wallace awkwardly hugged his son and daughter.

I left, shaking my head. Back home, Lisa had all the boxes out with the ornaments and garlands and lights. I couldn't help giving her an extra warm kiss before we went to work. We had a new star for the top of the tree that year. The previous topper, an angel, had fallen off the tree and shattered the year before, when Bowser almost knocked the tree over. Bowser and Motley were curled up on the living room floor. Fritz, who was inside for a change, dozed on the big sofa, while Blueberry slept on the floor underneath. Long John sat on the piano bench and glared with her one eye.

Lisa and I got the lights on the tree, and they twinkled individually, making it hard to see where they were even and where they weren't. Then the garlands. I opened the first ornament box and almost choked.

"Are you okay?" Lisa put her hand on my arm.

"Great, actually." I chuckled. "I was just remembering when you bought all this stuff, that first Christmas."

She had been so passionate and joyful that it infected me. Oh, I'd wanted to make love to her then, and at the same time, it was so much fun just being with her. I had no idea then what that special closeness we were building would lead to. I couldn't have imagined it.

And the memories continued. One of our little traditions, in addition to decorating the tree just the two of us, is that we each buy one or two ornaments to reflect the previous year. I swallowed as I hung the miniature Arc de Triomphe that Lisa had bought for Christmas, 1983, to signify the incredible trip we'd taken to find out who was leaking about Quickline, only to fall in love with each other. She sniffled as she gazed at the little comedy and tragedy mask ornament I'd bought in 1987 in memory of a play she and Nick had done during that case.

We had just finished and were happily necking in front of the tree. I loved the feel of her hands on my ass and how her ass felt under my hand. My other hand slid up her torso, and my thumb softly stroked the side of her breast.

"What time is it?" she asked, grinning.

"Mom! Dad! We're home!" Nick yelled from the doorway.

"That time," I whispered.

"Oh. There you are." Nick laughed.

"It looks beautiful, Lisle," Mama said.

"Yeah," I said, checking my pocket watch. "It's almost five. We'd better get these boxes put away and get the dining room ready for the choir party."

The choir party is a potluck, so there wasn't much to be done. And sure enough, Frank and Esther were the first ones there, right at five-thirty.

It was crazy. It was even chaotic. But I swear, it made me happier than I'd ever been. I had to figure that was why I didn't want to run Lisa down or complain about being a family man. I'd never wanted to be one, never expected it to happen. Yet, it had, and I was having a blast.

December 18 – 19, 1989

Lisa's Voice

Conchetta Ramirez is a saint. There is no other way to describe her. When she first signed on to work for Sid, long before I came along, she was just cleaning and cooking for a single guy who occasionally had a girlfriend to stay for two weeks at the most. Then the single guy had me move in with him. Conchetta took that in stride, then Nick's arrival. Then my whole family moving in and out of our quiet existence. Not to mention, the dogs and the cats.

As I have noted, things are pretty fluid in December, especially, with either last-minute guests or sudden decisions to go out for dinner or lunch. Conchetta, bless her, takes it all in stride and even seems to enjoy the challenge of our crazy life. Which is why Sid generally cedes control of the kitchen to her. As much as he likes to cook, he does not like doing it day in and day out and is perfectly happy to let Conchetta do it for us.

There is one small fly in the ointment, however. Conchetta does not like sharing the kitchen with Sid. She has to let him use it when he wants. It is, after all, our house, and we are her employer. That doesn't mean she's happy about it when Sid wants to start a cooking project while she's still working.

That Monday, Roxanna Stein was coming to our place, along with Mae, Neil, and Darby. Sy and Stella were also coming, of course, and my parents were already there. Sid had started marinating some chicken to make coq au vin the day before and was putting everything together when Conchetta arrived at ten that morning.

"What are you doing?" she demanded as she hung her raincoat on the hook on the pantry door. It being winter, she was wearing a long-sleeved t-shirt over her jeans rather than the usual short-sleeved one. That day's shirt featured Motley Crue.

"We're having guests tonight," Sid said. "I'm making coq au vin."

"Why? You think I couldn't have done it?"

"Of course, you could, Conchetta. I just have a specific plan in mind."

Conchetta rolled her eyes. "That's fine on a weekend. But it's Monday."

"It's a two-day process, and I want to see it through. It'll be in the crockpot all day, and I'll be out of here just as soon as I clean up."

"And I'll have to try and find where you put everything."

Sid and Conchetta have very different ideas on how a kitchen should be organized, and I'm pretty sure Conchetta was still miffed about earlier that fall, when Sid had the pantry rebuilt to include a wine fridge. That was a nasty fight. [It was our house. I still do not understand what part of that she didn't get. – SEH]

I think that's when Mama and I left the house. Mama wanted to go Christmas shopping. I had another errand to run, this time to the copier store.

I had finished Quackenbush the week before (I have no idea how), and needed to copy all the parts of it that I might need for my dissertation, and even a few parts that I was pretty sure I wouldn't need, and, dang it, there was the probability that I was not going to copy something that I would, in fact, need later, and I couldn't really copy the whole damned thing, or could I? I did. Needless to say, it took a while and repeated trips to the store's registers so that I could buy more change for their copy machines.

When I finally got back home, Sid had Bob Kinney on the speaker phone in the office. It might be an understatement to say that Bob was freaking out.

"Sid, they served warrants on both my office and my house!" he screamed.

"They didn't find anything, did they?" Sid said.

"Would I be calling you if they had?" Bob screamed even louder.

"I don't know," said Sid. He looked at me and rolled his eyes. "Bob, I understand it's upsetting, but why are you talking to me about it? Why aren't you calling Tom? Or Loser?"

"I can't get a hold of Loser, and Tom's not home right now."

"And I can't do anything about this," Sid said.

Bob swore. "What the hell else am I supposed to do? I can't afford a bad rep. The worst of it is, Sid." He lowered his voice. "They may have something on me. I do like a little bit of pot now and again. I mean, come on. Who doesn't?"

I flushed. I don't like smoking pot, but it helps my back pain just enough, and that is the only reason I will occasionally smoke it.

"I understand that," Sid said, holding onto his patience with both hands. "But that doesn't change anything. I can't do anything about this."

"Just listen," I mouthed to him.

He shrugged.

"What the hell did that bastard do?" Bob went on. "I know he wanted to come back as himself. But he's got Federal Agents out to get him and now me."

"We're getting harassed, too," Sid said.

"But we didn't do anything! All we did is meet with the asshole. One time. You didn't even stick around."

"I know." Sid looked at me again, and I shrugged. "Um. Do you want to talk to him again?"

"I want to wring his scrawny neck."

Sid smiled. "That does sound like fun. Too bad it would get us into worse trouble. Look, Bob, here's an idea. Loser said he would come to a party at my place this Saturday. Stella's going to be there."

"Stella? Really?"

"Any way you can come down here this weekend? I know Stella would love to see you."

"I'd really like to see her. Yeah, sure. I'll be there."

Sid gave him the details on the party and hung up shortly after.

Esther came by shortly after that, with another floppy disk in her hands.

"I got a line on where Cobb has stashed his money." She put the floppy on my desk. "Actually, Venkt's and Whitemore's money, too."

"That's good news," said Sid. "Any way we can freeze their assets?"

"It's already done," said Esther. "I don't know how, but nobody can get that money."

"Wouldn't they each have more than one account, though?" I asked.

"Of course," Esther said. "I found several, all frozen."

Sid got up and started pacing. "That might explain the harassment, though. If their accounts are frozen, and they think Loser is behind it, then harassing Loser's friends might just put enough pressure on Loser to let the money go."

I looked at him. "So, what do we do about it?"

"Set up another meeting with Loser, I think." He smiled at Esther. "Thanks for bringing this by."

"No problem."

She left, and I'd barely shut the front door when our pagers went off. I went back to the office.

"It's Lillian," Sid said, looking at his pager.

He dialed the call and put it on the speakerphone. Lillian wanted to set up a meeting with us and Dale O'Connor. Sid was not thrilled, but arranged for us to meet Dale for dinner at a chain restaurant near us the next night. He also invited Lillian to the Then-Some party for our friends on Saturday. Lillian begged off. She had family obligations. Dale wouldn't come to the party even if asked because my parents would be there. Dale is the congressman for the district where my parents live. He also tried using my father's business for one of his operations, and Daddy did not take kindly to it. Okay, he threatened to shoot Dale, and I have to concede that I wish Daddy had.

That evening, Mae and Neil arrived by five-thirty. Darby showed shortly after six with Stella and Sy right behind. Sid got out a cheese plate with bread rounds and put it on the tall, but narrow, antique dresser we have in the dining room on the wall next to the living room. He added a stack of small plates. We don't put food on any of the end tables in the living room. Even Motley, who is very well-behaved as a general rule, can only resist temptation so long, and Bowser is surprisingly agile when it comes to reaching the top of the dining room table. As Sid opened two bottles of Chablis, I got out the wine glasses and the larger ice bucket for the Chablis and sparkling water.

It was past six-thirty when Roxanna Stein showed up. She was wearing a dark blue suit that, but for the color, looked remarkably like the one she'd worn the Thursday before. Her blouse was a silk ivory, and there was a small, dark stain down the front. She petted the dogs and cooed at the cats. Sy introduced her all around again, pointing out to Darby that Stein represented some significant musicians, names that Darby recognized and gulped at.

Stein took some cheese and a glass of wine and asked Darby how long he'd been playing, if he had any favorite composers, the usual sort of chatter.

"How do you know Sy?" Mae asked casually. Sort of.

"Several of my clients were his proteges at one time or another," Stein said with a smile. "Our world is a fairly small one, so that's no surprise. Besides, Sy would blush to say so, but he is pretty big potatoes in our business."

Which he is. Frank had told me that his textbooks are required reading at a lot of colleges, let alone the sheer number of violinists he has taught over the years.

"Big enough," said Sy, patting his ample tummy.

"Well, is it time for dinner?" Sid asked.

Everyone agreed, and while Sid worked out the seating arrangements, Mama and I brought in the salads on the serving cart. Sid and I sat at the ends of the table. Mama and Daddy sat on either side of me. Neil sat next to Mama, with Mae next to him, and Stein next to her, and Sid at the end. Darby sat next to Sid and across from Stein, with Sy, then Nick, then Stella, and Daddy. Stein looked at me curiously as I lit the third, pink, candle on the Advent wreath in the center of the table.

Sid passed the bottles of Chablis around. Nick looked at his father, hopefully. Stein saw the look on Nick's face. Darby was also looking hopeful, too.

"Are you a wine drinker?" she asked.

"Just a little at dinner," said Nick. "It's so I don't go hog-wild."

"I wish more parents were that sensible," Stein said, laughing.

"Yeah!" yelped Darby.

"Just a little," said Mae.

Stein, who also knew Stella fairly well, asked about the music school, and Stella mentioned that Sid was teaching and had a very promising student in Alicia Mendoza. Stein looked over at Sid.

"I'm a pianist, also," Sid said. "I'm just not a performer."

As soon as the salads were done, Sid put the dishes on the serving cart, took them to the kitchen, and then returned with the big tureen of coq au vin. Daddy saw to opening two bottles of Burgundy (the real stuff from France) and getting the wine poured. Stein was favorably impressed and said so. But then we finished eating. Mama and I cleared the dishes from the table and returned.

Stein got a leather-padded notebook from her briefcase and perched her glasses on the middle of her nose.

"I think the first thing you folks need to understand is that I do not take kids on as clients." Stein folded her hands on top of the notebook. "I don't touch anybody who is not out of college and with an established career."

Darby looked crestfallen.

"In other words," said Mae, glancing at Sy. "You have nothing to gain or lose by talking to us."

"Exactly." Stein looked at Darby. "I know Alex Crispin has been courting you pretty heavily, Darby, and after last Thursday, I know why. He's not a bad agent, but he's not the best."

"He says I should be touring now," Darby said. "That being the new whiz kid will get me places."

"Actually, I agree with him," Stein said.

"You do?" Darby's mouth hung open.

Mae and Neil looked worried.

Stein held up her finger. "With one important caveat. Only a few dates."

"But Crispin says I need to be out there, doing as many dates as I can."

"Well, that's where we beg to differ," Stein said, smiling. "Darby, when I saw you Thursday after the concert, you looked pretty tired."

"I was mostly hungry." Darby winced. "It's kind of hard to eat before I play."

"And you almost passed out in your food," Mae said.

Darby laughed. "I fell asleep really fast."

"That's actually a good sign," Stein said with a smile. "It means you're putting your all into your performance. But do you want to feel that way every night, week after week, no weekends off, only a couple weeknights, but on and off planes so fast you can barely keep track of where you are, let alone see anything?"

Darby gulped.

"That's what Crispin is offering you," Stein said. "And why we tend to disagree. He overbooks his artists, and at your age, that can be dangerous. You will make some significant money with him. But to be honest, you can get a better agent than him, make almost as much money, and not put your health at risk."

"You really think so?" Darby asked.

Stein stared him down. "I know so. I took the liberty of contacting a couple of my colleagues in New York. Sy was good enough to overnight them a recording you'd made with Stella this fall. Both are very interested and will be happy to fly out here after the New Year to talk to you and your parents." She looked over at Mae and Neil. "Seriously, there is no reason not to let Darby do a little touring, principally during the summer when it's not going to affect his education. It will be good exposure for him and help him to see what he's getting into with a concert career." She handed Mae a couple of business cards. "These guys handle young artists. They are focused on growing an artist into his career, not just exploiting him."

"Do we just send him off with the agent?" Mae looked worried as she glanced at the cards.

"Oh, no. One of you will have to go with him, and it needs to be a parent. However, both of these guys will help you with the ins and outs, and please feel free to call me with any questions you have." She looked over at Darby again. "You are an exceptionally talented young man. But

more than that. You are insanely lucky. You are surround-
ed by a family that loves you deeply enough not to let you
get away with crap and to protect you from the sharks out
there. A lot of kids, their parents get blinded by the money
and the fame. Or get taken in, themselves, not intending
to hurt their kids, but not knowing any better. That's one
of the reasons I do not deal with young artists. I refuse.
It's too heartbreaking to see yet another kid with amazing
potential go down in the worst of flames, and it happens
all too damned often. Now, I know Crispin's putting on
the pressure, and he does have a point about you needing
some more exposure. But be careful with him. You can do
better."

Darby swallowed and nodded.

"Thank you, Roxanna," Mae said.

Stein left shortly after, thanking Sid for the lovely dinner
and giving Sy and Stella each warm hugs.

I was glad that Darby chose to follow his parents home
that night. I was not so happy to see him the next afternoon, right before dinner time, mostly because Mae had
called me that morning. There had been a nasty fight after
they'd gotten home that spilled over into the morning.
Mae and Neil saw no reason to talk to Alex Crispin. Darby
wanted them to give him a chance.

Darby, however, was not going to talk to us about it.
Nick had said that Darby had gone out with some girls
that afternoon. Darby was not going to talk to us about
that, either. Nor was there much Sid and I could do about
it because we had our meeting with Sid's least favorite
person.

"I think I'm in a perfect mood for talking to Dale," Sid said to me as he drove us over to the restaurant in Brentwood.

"May I beg to differ?" I sighed, looking out at the gaily decorated street. "He pushes all our buttons when things are going great. Now, it will be just that much harder not to smash his face in."

"At least, he's not going to ruin a good mood."

I sighed. "I don't know why Darby's listening to that Crispin."

"Crispin obviously knows how to run a con." Sid shook his head. "He's a lot like Loser that way."

"So, what do we do?"

"There's not much we can do. If Mae and Neil don't want to talk to Crispin, that's their choice."

"They probably should. We don't know for sure what he's telling Darby, so we can't counteract it effectively." I glanced at Sid. "Think we could talk to Crispin with Darby?"

"We'll see. It's going to be dicey. Darby's got rehearsal all week with the youth orchestra starting tomorrow. We've got this case to deal with and slide past your folks. I still have choir practice and lessons to teach. Plus, we have our party on Saturday to get ready for."

"You know, you'd think I'd be used to being this busy all the time."

Sid chuckled as he pulled up to the restaurant's valet parking.

Dale O'Connor is in his sixties, I think. He's tall, with broad shoulders, light gray hair around a bald spot that seems to grow every time I see him. His posture is ramrod erect, betraying his earlier career in Army Intelligence. He was all smiles when he saw us, jovially shaking Sid's hand and kissing my cheek before I could pull away.

"Good to see you guys," he said. He waved at the waiter and got us seated right away.

"Did Adrienne come down with you?" Sid asked as we looked at our menus. Adrienne is Dale's wife.

"Hell, no!" Dale laughed with gusto. "Are you kidding? This time of year, and all the malls down here? I'd be broke in a New York second."

Which was absolute nonsense. Adrienne did love to shop, but Dale not only had plenty of resources to fund it, he took an odd sort of pride in how much she bought, no matter how much he complained about how much it cost him. [Furthermore, we later found out that Adrienne had plenty of her own resources to fund her shopping habit. – SEH]

I pressed my lips together. The waiter arrived. Sid and I each ordered a glass of white wine, while Dale requested a scotch and water, and a plate of mixed appetizers.

"So, why are we here, O'Connor?" Sid asked. "I'm reasonably certain it has nothing to do with the joy of sharing potato skins."

Dale shrugged and grinned. "May as well make the most of it."

Dale's big fantasy was that we were all bosom buddies, the best of friends. Never mind that Sid and I routinely pissed him off. I might also add that Sid does not like potato skins, at least as they are generally prepared in trendy restaurants. He seldom eats potatoes, in general, although he is not averse to eating the skin. But he does have a point that most potato skin appetizers are about the load of sour cream and less about the bits of bacon and cheddar cheese.

When the plate of appetizers arrived, I let Dale and Sid fill their plates first. Dale knew why and piled more food on his plate than he would have usually. He won't admit it, but my appetite does scare him. I still got the lion's share of the platter.

Dale continued to evade Sid's attempts to get the meeting ball rolling until we'd all been served our dinners. Dale had a full rack of ribs. I knew darned well the barbecue was not likely to be that good, and opted for prime rib, which they did rather nicely at that particular chain. Sid got the roasted chicken.

"Okay," Dale finally said as he gnawed on a rib bone. "The first thing you two are going to want to know is that Peter Venkt very probably killed Stanley Ford. Our guys found recon photos of Ford in Venkt's place, along with photos of the accident itself that do not match the crime scene photos."

"Fine," said Sid. "Venkt's dead. What good does knowing that do us?"

"It tells you that your friend Louis was right about Cobb and his pals."

Sid rolled his eyes. "A- we already knew that, and B- how does that help us get Cobb?"

Dale shifted. "Okay. Maybe it doesn't, except that Venkt was one of his pals.

"Big fat, hairy deal," said Sid. "I get that we're not going after a court case here."

"No, we're not." Dale glared at us. "We're looking at disposal. The good news is you two don't have to worry about that part."

"Just setting him up." I glared back at him.

"As usual, you two don't get it." Dale tried to suck the meat off another rib bone. "The guys that have been protecting these bozos are now pretty high up in the Federal government, and I mean next to the Oval Office. That may be why they're feeling they can take Cobb and Whitemore on. I don't know. I do know that your friend Renfrew has gotten a copy of their dirt file. Even more significant, in the last few days, Cobb has contacted a couple of his protectors and let them know that if something isn't done soon, he will unload the dirt."

"Again, big, fat, hairy deal," said Sid.

Dale shrugged. "It means Cobb made a backup or two."

"Duh," I said. "Are we looking at getting Cobb's dirt file or taking Cobb down?"

Dale shook his head. "There's more to it."

I glanced at Sid. "Like the fact that Cobb's overseas assets are frozen? As are Venkt's and Whitemore's?"

Sid shot me a proud grin.

Dale gasped and cursed. "How did you know that?"

Sid grinned. "You asked us to investigate. We did. What we don't know is who froze those assets and how."

"You don't have Need to Know. I said close to the Oval. You can skip the snooping around there."

"Come off it, Dale," Sid snarled. "That's the whole reason you got us involved in the first place."

He sighed. "That, and your buddy Renfrew." Dale shrugged. "He's been doing me some favors for a while now. Frankly, I was hoping to keep the two of you apart for the rest of your lives. But things happen."

"Like what?" asked Sid.

"Renfrew wanted help. I told him to ask his old high school buddies."

Sid looked like he was about to strangle Dale. "What?"

Dale blinked. "I may have hinted that one of my guys was part of that group."

"So, you risk blowing our cover just to nail some pain in the ass?" Sid was darned near beside himself.

"It's a chance I'm willing to take." Dale glared at Sid. "I've been after these bastards since... Well, a hell of a long time. Before the war ended. They were and are a stain upon the honor of the U.S. military and are a stain upon our federal law enforcement. You saw what they did to your friend just because he happens to be Black. I'm guessing you've run into more of their harassment. I'll do whatever it takes to nail them. Yeah, your cover is important. But you and Renfrew also have the best chance to get those guys in the crosshairs."

Sid shook his head and let out a little groan. "Dale, I do not care about your revenge. Yeah, these guys need taking down. I won't argue that. But it really pisses me off that you keep thinking that you have to play these petty games to get us to cooperate. Just be straight with us, asshole. Okay, so we're not interested in killing people. You knew that from the beginning. But there are other ways of dealing with this kind of stuff, and we are damned good at it. As long as we know what the hell is going on."

"That's why you're here." Dale grinned at us.

I have to confess, I came very close to smashing Dale's face into his plate at that moment. I like to think I am a better person than that, and I usually succeed in not resorting to violence. I did that night. But not by much.

"Is there anything else you're going to tell us?" Sid asked.

"You don't need to know anything else."

"We'll see about that." Sid got up. "I think it's time for us to leave. Thanks for dinner, Dale."

Dale did have the decency not to yell after us. I was pretty annoyed that I didn't get to finish my prime rib, but I totally loved sticking Dale with the bill.

December 20 -21, 1989

Sid's Voice

That Wednesday did not start well, nor did it get any better. Lisa was still annoyed with Dale and that she hadn't gotten to finish her prime rib. I couldn't blame her for either issue. Dale was a pain in the ass, and she loves prime rib and seldom gets it. At least, she wasn't annoyed with me.

Darby was sullen and bordering on snotty during our run, then was almost late to school thanks to taking his time getting dressed. I called Sy from the office soon after that and asked about talking to Alex Crispin.

"If the crux of Darby's argument is that his parents aren't giving the guy a fair shake, then maybe we should check him out," I said.

"I have checked him out," Sy growled.

"Maybe we can find out what he's telling Darby."

Sy snorted. "I have already tried. Furthermore, yesterday, I learned something that Roxanna was, unfortunately, unaware of on Monday, which has led me to believe that Mae is utterly correct in her instincts to avoid the fellow."

"What?"

"A young woman has come forward accusing Alex Crispin of sexually abusing her while she was a minor and a client of his. A civil case has been filed, and she is looking for other clients who experienced the same thing. Which also means that Mr. Crispin is facing the loss of his business, whether he is guilty or not."

"And that means he's getting desperate." I rubbed my forehead.

"Indeed. It does not mean he would abuse Darby similarly. But Crispin needs the boy and sooner rather than later. The problem we now have is that if we present this information to Darby, it will appear as an attempt to unfairly wrest him away from Crispin and whatever inducements the foul weasel is offering him."

"Shit. Now, what do we do?" I glared out the office window.

"I have no idea beyond seeking aid from the Divine, but that department belongs to neither of us."

I sighed. "I'm afraid not. Well, thanks, Sy. Have you told Mae about Crispin's troubles yet?"

"Not yet, but I will shortly."

As we hung up, the phone rang again. It was Tom. He had talked to Wallace, and while I wasn't thrilled with what he proposed, I decided to go along with it.

I checked my pocket watch, smiling at the soft melody as it tinkled out. Lisa had given the watch to me for my birthday that first year she was with me. That night was probably when I first started falling in love with her.

I shut the watch and went to find Lisa. She was sitting in the library in the bay window's seat with her feet up. It was one of her favorite places to read, with the right kind of cushions for her back and a nice view of the front yard's rose garden. There was a little table next to the window, and Lisa had two dishes on it, one with several apples, the other with a core. Motley and Bowser hovered nearby in the vain hope of snagging a core or two. Lisa's colored file cards, highlighters, pencil case, and a notebook were scattered to her side in front of the window, and she munched on an apple as she read.

I just watched for a minute, enjoying looking at her, but then she looked up and smiled at me.

"Phones are busy today," she said. "Any acceptances?"

I winced. "No, just bad news." I told her about the planned lunch with Wallace, Tom, and Loser, then the call with Sy.

She shifted. "We can't not tell Darby. What if he falls for the guy and it's a disaster? He'll be upset that we didn't warn him and justifiably so."

"Let me think about it, okay?" I sighed. "I'd better get going."

"I'll be here."

I kissed her goodbye.

I met the guys at a coffee shop near Tom's school. He had an extended lunch break that day, but still couldn't stay too long. He was already at the table with Loser, and Wallace hurried in.

"Guys," Wallace said as he sat down. "We've got to do something about these Feds. One of them followed us as I took the kids to school yesterday. Another's been hanging around my wife's office."

"Now, we've got to stop them," I grumbled. "What makes you think we're going to help you after you set us up?"

"Fuck." Wallace almost broke down.

"It was you," Loser said.

"They leaned on me." Wallace looked at Loser. "They came in with their badges and told me that you were the bad guy, that I could help them. So, I told them what you guys were planning. I didn't know they'd have another shooter there. I didn't know they'd start shooting. Then I go and draw on them. God, what was I thinking?" Wallace blinked. "Then they served that warrant on me, and now my kids. And my wife."

Tom sighed. "Wallace, you'd better scram."

"What?"

"We have no good reason to trust you." Tom glared at him. "So, get the fuck out of here and let us figure it out."

Wallace took off. Loser sat back in his seat and shook his head.

"I gotta hand it to you, Sid. You were right about him."

I shifted in my seat as the waitress came over to take our orders.

When she was done, Loser leaned forward. "Alright, I've got a way to get Cobb and Whitemore to a rendezvous, and I may have some help for us. But Cobb's not going to show up for me. I need one of you two guys to set it up, then be there so that we can draw them out."

"Why do I feel like we're being set up for target practice?" I asked.

"You're not," Loser said. "You'll be covered."

Tom snorted. "Loser, you're about as trustworthy as Wallace."

"Fine. Let these bastards keep harassing you." Loser shrugged. "They're only going to keep it up."

"Why?" asked Tom.

The waitress brought our food, and we waited until she was gone.

Loser dug into his burger and fries. "They might be thinking that you've got something they need."

"You didn't." I was ready to pound the living daylights out of him.

"I didn't tell them anything. But I do have something they need, and it's possible that since I've suddenly renewed our acquaintance, they think you guys have it. And they're not going to give up until they get what they want."

Tom frowned. "Okay. That would explain the search warrants on Wallace and Bob. But why haven't Sid or I been served?"

"Can't say." Loser shrugged, shoving fries in his mouth. "Maybe they weren't able to secure warrants on you guys. Or maybe they couldn't get the drugs planted. I mean, Tom, I know you've got some good security on your place. What about you, Sid?"

"It's pretty tight."

Loser held out his hands. "There you have it." He smiled and took another big bite of his hamburger, then talked as he chewed. "So, basically, one of you gives Whitemore a call. Tell him you've found something that I left behind. Set it up for some park or someplace outside, but not too crowded. They're not going to show up if there are too many people around."

"But who's going to arrest Whitemore?" I asked.

"Someone's coming to help with that. We'll see to getting him cuffed and taken care of."

"I'll set it up," Tom grumbled.

Loser nodded. "Great. You carry any heat, Tom?" He looked over at me and chuckled. "I know you're carrying, Sid."

I shifted my shoulder holster. "Not because I want to."

"Angelique taught me how to shoot," Tom said softly.

"Why don't both you guys go?" Loser used his last few fries to wipe up the burger juice on his plate. "We'll set it for tomorrow night, say, around nine."

"Fine," said Tom.

"Alright." I sighed.

Loser got up, tossed a ten-dollar bill onto the table. "Okay. See you then."

As Loser left, I looked at Tom in mild shock.

"You know," I said. "He's done nothing but lie to us."

"I know." Tom fidgeted with one of his French fries. "He's a fucking con man and always has been. That's what we liked about him, remember?"

I rolled my eyes and worked on finishing my salad as Tom finished his French dip.

Lisa's Voice -

Sid was in one lousy mood when he got home from his meeting. He told me what had happened, then went to sulk in the office. My back was getting a little stiff from sitting all day, so I took a walk outside. By the time dinner rolled around, Darby was not there. At least, he called to let us know that he was going to get dinner with a friend from the orchestra. I could hear the giggles in the background, but decided not to question it. I just told him to be home before nine. His tone was a touch surly, but he agreed.

Sid went off to choir practice and didn't come back until after nine-thirty, which was a good thing. Darby had arrived home in a somewhat better mood. But as he kissed me good night, I could smell it. He'd had sex, presumably with the young thing I'd heard giggling on the phone.

That night, Sid had two nightmares, which did not make getting up that next morning any easier.

It only got worse. I was beginning to despair of having a good holiday. Sid was still in a lousy mood about the setup that night and was sleepy to boot, thanks to the nightmares. Darby had gone back to acting snotty, and Mama gave him what for as he ran off to school.

Fortunately, Mama and Daddy left to meet Mae for some last-minute Christmas shopping and wouldn't be home for dinner. I was settling in for some more reading (which was boring me to tears) when Sid called me into the office.

"What's up?" I asked.

"About that meeting tonight, we've got it set up for a park in the Valley."

I sighed. "What time?"

"Nine-thirty, but do you mind staying here and keeping your parents distracted when they get back? I'd ask Nick, but we need him to keep an eye on Darby."

"Okay."

The phone rang and I picked it up. It was Sy and I put it on the speakerphone.

"I have come up with a plan to inform Darby of the allegations against Mr. Crispin, hopefully, in a way that will not only expose the bastard but will not make Darby feel as though we're trying to get the fellow." Sy's voice, as usual, was utterly sonorous. "We will give Darby what he wants.

We will set up a meeting with his parents and Mr. Crispin, and ask about his current client list, which is a perfectly legitimate question, then perhaps, in a roundabout way, express our concerns about the over-booking and then the allegations."

"That sounds like it could work," I said.

Sid smiled. "I agree. Have you talked to Mae about it?"

"She's out, I believe," I said. "I'll call this evening. Shall we set it up for tomorrow night? At the place of their choosing?"

"Sounds good," said Sid.

We hung up, then ate lunch. Soon, Sid had to go teach, and I tried not to read the same paragraph over and over.

Darby came home for dinner. Sid stayed out because of his meeting.

"He's working, isn't he?" Nick asked me softly as Darby changed clothes from his school uniform.

"I'm afraid so. But you know he's good." I hugged Nick, feeling almost as worried about Sid, myself.

Which may be why Darby and I had such a big fight after dinner. Mama and Daddy had come home for dinner, after all, but they and Nick had excused themselves from the table already, Mama and Daddy to watch TV in the rumpus room, Nick to his room to work on his homework.

"I'm going out," Darby announced as he finished eating.

"What about your homework?"

He shrugged. "It's no big deal."

"Yes, it is." I glared at him. "How much homework do you have?"

Darby squirmed. I could tell he didn't want to lie to me.

"Not that much."

"How much is not that much?"

"Just some math, and, um, history questions, and a lab to write up."

I stared him down. "We'll talk about you going out when you get all that done."

"Aw, come on!"

"Come on, what? You know darned well one of the conditions of staying here is that you keep up on your homework."

"I don't have to stay here." Darby was on his feet.

I was on mine. "I know you don't, but your parents aren't going to let up on the homework, either. I didn't say anything about going out last night, and I know damned well what you were up to."

"Yeah? How?"

"I could smell it. You think I don't know what sex smells like?"

"It's my choice!"

"I didn't say it wasn't. But I'll be damned before I make it any easier for you to do something stupid like sleep around."

"Aren't you the hypocrite? You married a guy that slept around."

"He'd stopped before I agreed to, and you know it."

"Yeah, well, you guys didn't wait to get married to do it."

"What we did involved two adults in a committed relationship, neither of which is your situation. And just so you know, we weren't having sex. We couldn't. We had to wait because your uncle was afraid he'd been exposed to AIDS and was terrified that he was going to give it to me. Which, by the way, is why he doesn't want you sleeping around. We don't want you getting AIDS, and it is in the straight population."

Darby suddenly sniffed. "I know what I'm doing! I'm keeping covered."

"Thank God, you're doing that."

We stared at each other, both trembling.

I closed my eyes, then took a deep breath. "Darby, please. Just do your homework tonight."

He nodded and went to his room. And stayed there.

Sid's Voice -

It had turned cold that night. The air was dry, but the wind blew in off the desert with an icy chill. Loser and I waited in the front seat of his car, watching the orange glow of the park lights on the path. It was one of those long swathes of green that follow a cemented-in gully along Laurel Canyon Boulevard. Tom had taken up a position near the restroom, but Whitemore had said he'd meet him on the path around eight. It was not even seven-thirty.

"Not unlike 'Nam," Loser said after an extended silence.

"How would you know?" I glared at him. "You didn't stay that long."

"Long enough." Loser shuddered. After a minute, he sighed. "Look, I understand why you're mad at me."

"You do?" I seriously doubted that.

"It sucks that you didn't get the chance I did to swap dog tags, but it's not my fault."

"Like hell, it isn't." I shook my head to clear it. "And that's not why I am mad at you. I am mad because I have spent almost twenty years feeling like absolute shit because I came back, and you didn't. Absolute shit."

"Ah. Survivor guilt. That's a bitch. I know."

As if he did. At that point, I realized I didn't care. It had felt bad enough thinking about all the other guys I'd known who didn't make it back. That Loser hadn't been one of them after all, didn't really make any difference.

"I am also pissed about all the lies and shit you've been pulling, putting my family in the crosshairs."

"Yeah. Sorry about that." He looked at me and sighed. "You weren't supposed to get sucked into it. Turns out somebody didn't make contact like he was supposed to. Or maybe he has a reason for laying low. Or somebody else may have lied to me, and God knows, he would have."

I chose not to respond.

A lone man came walking down the path. It looked like what I remembered of Whitemore's relatively heavy profile. Loser quietly got out of the car.

"It's time," he said. "You stay put here unless it looks like Tom needs the help."

"Right."

I would have loved to have been wired. I would have loved to have had Lisa there, waiting on the restroom roof, her rifle in hand.

Tom left the shadows of the restroom and approached Whitemore. He was about fifty paces away when I saw the flare of a gun blast in the parking lot, then heard the crack. Tom fell. I slid out of the car, my automatic in hand, looking for the source of the fire.

There was a dark figure crouched about three cars down from me. Crouching low myself, I slid in that direction. More shots were fired, this time aimed toward the dark figure behind the cars. I ducked again. I couldn't see Loser. Tom remained face down on the walk.

Whitemore had sought cover behind a tree that was far too small to cover him. The dark figure popped up from behind the car long enough for me to see his face. It was Harlan Cobb. I couldn't figure out why he was shooting at his partner. I debated aiming for him, but realized that I wasn't covered from Whitemore and would only give away my position.

Cobb suddenly ducked without firing. I looked over toward Whitemore. Loser and another larger form I vaguely recognized slammed into the crooked Fed in a squeeze play. Whitemore tried to break free. The larger man punched Whitemore, and Whitemore fell, but didn't entirely stop struggling. Loser got his knee on Whitemore's back and pressed the nose of his automatic behind Whitemore's ear.

"You're dead if you move, Whitemore," the other man yelled, and I suddenly realized it was Zack Peters.

He roughly handcuffed Whitemore, then, laughing, he and Loser yanked Whitemore to his feet. A second later, Cobb popped up from behind the car and fired twice, both times landing in Whitemore's chest. I tried to draw a bead on Cobb, but he was off and running. I fired anyway. He was gone.

I ran over to where Tom was on the sidewalk. He was still breathing. I grunted as I rolled him over.

Tom opened his eyes. "Are we clear?"

"Yeah. It's all over. Where'd you get hit?"

Tom laughed. "I didn't. I just got down and stayed down."

"Oh, thanks be." I sat back on my heels. "Fuck, Freeman, you scared the living shit out of me!"

"Better than getting hit and both of us having to explain it to Angelique." Tom grunted a little as he sat up. "Where's Loser?"

"Right here." Loser walked up, with Peters behind him. "Looks like you're okay, Freeman."

"Not a scratch. You guys?" Tom stopped as he looked at Peters. "Who are you?"

"Some help that showed." Loser shrugged. "He'll take care of Whitemore and the cops."

"And if you guys don't want to be around for that, I figure you've got about five minutes," Peters said.

I followed Tom to his car. Tom drove me to where I'd parked mine at an all-night diner on Ventura Boulevard. A half hour later, I was not surprised to see Peters waiting for me as I pulled into my driveway. I parked outside and went to talk to him in his car.

"I thought you were working this by yourself."

"I thought I was, too." Peters shrugged. "But our mutual friend had other ideas."

"What the fuck?"

"He'd already set Renfrew up as part of this." Peters made a face. "I don't know why he thinks involving civilians is such a good idea."

"Good thing I was told to help. What's going on with Whitemore?"

Peters shrugged. "He's dead. Don't know who shot him, though."

"It was Cobb. I saw him do it. And he aimed right at Whitemore. He wasn't trying to hit you two."

"That's an interesting twist."

"Isn't it, though?"

Peters let out his breath, and it fogged in the night's chill. "Well. Time to call it a night."

I went back up the driveway, got my car running and into the garage. Only to find Lisa and her mother were fighting with each other. I didn't need that and decided to find Daddy, who was wisely staying out of it.

The two women patched it up shortly after ten, for which I was grateful. Apparently, the gist of the fight was that Lisa had gotten a little too frank with Darby about our sex life before the wedding, such as it was. Lisa was also upset about the fight with Darby, but put that aside to ask about my night.

I told her what had happened, and neither of us could come to any real conclusion. Then I asked what had happened with Darby, and there were no conclusions to come to there, either.

"It's, like, this will be the worst Christmas ever!" Lisa groaned as we held each other in our bed.

"It may be," I sighed. "But you know, it's still better than anything else I've ever experienced."

She sighed. "You're right. And there's still time for things to get better."

My hand slid down onto her sweet, sweet breasts. She chuckled.

"Honestly?" she asked.

I blinked. "I'd like to get some sleep tonight."

We don't sleep very well when we don't make love. So, we pretty much make love every night. I was (and still am) getting more sex than I ever did before. Who knew?

December 22, 1989

Sid's Voice

It is amazing what a good night's sleep will do for your perspective. Lisa still grumbled about getting up to go running. She always does. But I felt I had a handle on my life again.

Darby was less enthused. He wasn't angry. Just... Upset, I guess. As we came back from our run, he held me back before we went inside the house.

"Uncle Sid, can we talk?" he asked.

"Sure, but now?"

He winced. "Maybe after breakfast? I know I've got to go to school, but..."

That he was asking was enough for me at that point. And there was something in his eyes.

"I'll write you a note excusing you," I said. "Just, please, be on time for breakfast, and ready to go."

"Yes, sir."

He ran into the house. It was my turn for the first shower, and Lisa was already in the kitchen. I could hear Mama talking to her, but not what she said, as I went upstairs.

Breakfast was relatively quiet. It always is. Lisa and Nick are not morning people, and I respect that. Besides, it's nice to be able to read the newspaper in peace, speaking only to share the different sections. Nick didn't question it when I told him to drive himself to school. Mama looked like she was about to, but I shook my head.

I sent Darby to the office and asked if Lisa needed anything out of there right away.

"No. What's going on?" she asked.

"I'll tell you when I know," I said.

In the office, Darby sat on the couch, staring at the floor. I would have sat down next to him, but even five years after the molestation, he was still a little awkward about me touching him. So, I avoided it and sat down in my desk chair.

Darby swallowed. "Aunt Lisa got mad at me because I'm sleeping around."

"She told me."

"I kinda dumped on her about you and her not waiting for the wedding." He looked at me. "She said you did."

"Well, in terms of traditional full intercourse, yeah, we did. She say why?"

Darby nodded.

"You understand that's why I'm worried about you sleeping around." But even as I said it, I wondered how honest I was being. "It is seriously dangerous in a way that wasn't when I was your age."

"I get that." Darby shrugged. "I mean, I'm using condoms, okay?"

"That's good. However, you know they are not foolproof. I was using one when Nick was conceived."

Darby laughed. He knew that story. Then his eyes filled, and he blinked it away.

"Okay," I said. "Maybe I'm also a little worried that you're not happy about your sex life right now."

"It's okay." Darby swallowed and blinked again. "It's not that. Or maybe it is. I don't know. I mean, it's fun, but it's not all that great." He took a couple of deep breaths. "Uncle Sid, I'm still scared of it. I mean, that's why I did it. I don't want to be scared of sex. And you and Dad keep saying the best way to deal with your fears is to face them head-on."

I sighed. "That can also mean just talking about it, you know."

"I guess." He frowned. "Crispin says that I'll be able to get any girl I want."

I couldn't help chuckling. "That is and isn't true. Darby, I suspect that with time, you'll be a pretty decent lover. But even if you aren't, there will always be girls and women who won't mind about that because they got a piece of you. And I don't care how good a lover you become, there will always be some women, some of them very desirable, who will never sleep with you. That I got your aunt to eventually sleep with me? Well, you know what I gave up. Happily, I might add. She wasn't going to take me any other way. But the thing is, getting sex is easy. Being in love isn't, and being in love is what makes the sex really good. So if you're still scared, it may be because the real love isn't there."

Darby's brows knitted together. "You think so?"

I frowned. "Yeah. I do. I might not have before, but I do now. I am crazy in love with your aunt. It makes a huge difference."

"I'm not really hurting anybody."

"That used to be my justification. But I have since found out that, yeah, I did hurt quite a few women, some of whom were good friends. I also hurt your Aunt Lisa. And as your mother once told me, I hurt myself by cheating myself out of a full, rich relationship with your aunt because I was too busy giving bits of myself away to every woman that came along."

Darby nodded, then sighed. "The funny thing is, Crispin thinks I should be sleeping around. That I deserve it."

I tried not to laugh. "Crispin is telling you a lot of interesting things, isn't he?"

"Yeah." Darby winced. "But, Uncle Sid, I'm not a little kid anymore. I've got to figure out these things for myself. I mean, at some point, I have to stand on my own two feet and decide for myself. Right?"

"Absolutely." I couldn't help chuckling. "But that doesn't mean you're not going to fuck it up occasionally. Nor does it mean you're being a little kid if you listen to the older and wiser shit and realize that, hey, maybe they've got something. Seriously. The only advantage I have on you right now is that I've been alive longer, and a lot of the shit you're dealing with, I've already dealt with. Whether you and I come to the same truth at the end of the process, I don't know. But I do know that when I pulled my head out of my ass long enough to listen to the older and wiser shit, I was usually better off."

"But you didn't have to think about touring and your career and all that."

"No. You're right. I didn't. I had to worry about a war and getting drafted. I had to worry about what career I wanted. I'm not saying you and I have the exact same challenges. You wonder if you're doing the right thing by listening to your parents. I worried about the same thing. I blew mine off and ended up in Vietnam."

"Oh. Yeah."

"Exactly." I waited for a minute, then smiled at him. "You're a good man, Darby. You've got a good head on your shoulders. The big difference between you and most kids your age is that you've got a lot of shit being thrown at you right now because of your talent that a lot of adults don't deal with well. What you need to hold onto is that you've got a whole crew of people who love you. We're the ones who don't care about the quick score because we need the cash. We're the ones who want to see you grow into a successful career and who don't want to see you crash and burn because you tried to do too much too soon. You need to hang onto the people who love you, not the people who want to use you or need you to cover their asses. Sometimes it's hard to tell who's who. But the people who love you will tell you the truth, whether you want to hear it or not."

"You know. That's what Crispin says."

My stomach turned, but I covered and shrugged. "Sometimes, even assholes get it right."

"You don't like him?" Darby looked at me.

"I don't know him, so I don't know. I don't like how you've been reacting to him, though. You may be right, but you don't seem happy, and that's what bothers me."

"Oh." Darby looked at the floor again.

I could see him struggling with something, but did not want to press it. In the end, he chose not to tell me, and I had to honor that. Shit, I hate being honorable sometimes. I wrote Darby his note excusing him from being tardy.

Mae already had Lisa and me set up at the school for that sort of thing. We'd set up Mae and Neil for similar for Nick, so that wasn't any big deal.

I sent Darby off. Mama wanted to know what we'd talked about, but fortunately, the phone rang at that moment, and I was able to hold her off. It was Loser.

"Yeah. What do you want?" I asked him.

"I, eh, want to apologize for last night."

"What?"

Loser coughed. "I didn't mean to put you in the crosshairs again."

"Oh, please. How could you not have expected people shooting? Especially after that last time."

"Look, I'm going to tell you the truth. I was hired by one of the guys protecting Cobb to get the dirt on him and take him out."

"I see. So, why are you telling me this, and why are you telling me now?"

"It's a long story."

I waited. "What are you looking for, Loser? Absolution? Fine. You've got it."

His chuckle was deeply sardonic. "You know, that's one thing I really like about Angelique and your wife. They keep calling me Louis."

"I didn't know you didn't like being called L— your nickname."

"I didn't know any better until people started calling me by my real name."

"Oh." I sighed. "Then I guess I owe you an apology."

"How the hell were you going to know? My mother fucking called me that." He sighed. "Look, I just want you to know that things are going to back off for the time being. We have to lay low because of the holiday."

"Very well." I paused. "Are you coming to the party tomorrow? Stella would like to see you."

Admittedly, I think Stella wanted to give him a piece of her mind, but she did want to see him.

"Yeah. I'll swing by. Looking forward to it."

Lisa's Voice -

The incredibly annoying thing about this stage in my dissertation process was that I had to read. And read. And read some more. Don't get me wrong. I adore reading. I even enjoy reading scholarly treatises on subjects I'm interested in. But doing it as a full-time job was insane. Ashton and Scoresby were beyond mind-numbing, yet there were those in my field who considered them the ultimate word. By Friday afternoon, my eyes were watering, and I was seriously looking for ways to debunk them. At least, I'd been able to buy the book and could mark it up at will.

The only thing that saved my backside was that my wonderful boy came running into the house from the garage.

"I'm in the library," I called when he hollered that he was home.

Mama and Daddy were in the living room. Sid was in the office. Nick came to me.

"Hey, sweetie," I said as he came in and hugged me. "What's up?"

"Two weeks off from school." Nick laughed. He looked at my book. "What's that?"

"Ghastly stuff, but I have to read it." I checked my watch. "At least, we'll be heading to Pasadena in a few."

"What's up?"

"The big meeting with the nasty agent." I looked at Nick. "Have you met this Crispin guy?"

Nick shook his head. "No. Darby won't let me near him."

"Hm. That speaks volumes."

"I suppose."

Darby had chosen to go to his home straight from school that day. Sid and I packed Nick, Mama, and Daddy into Sid's Beemer and headed there just after four-thirty. Traffic was pretty nasty, but we got to the O'Malley house by quarter 'til six. Sy and Stella were just behind us. Mae had dinner ready. She told us that Crispin had been invited to dinner but had refused. I'm not sure how Darby had reacted to the news, but the rest of us knew that did not bode well.

Crispin showed up on time at eight o'clock. The thing that annoyed me was that his entire manner was as greasy as his gelled hair, which stood up all over the crown of his head. We gathered in the living room. Sy forbore asking questions, leaving that to Darby, Mae, and Neil. The younger children were upstairs, but I was willing to bet they were listening at the stairwell, except for Lissy, who was in bed at that point.

So, Mae and Neil asked. They asked about his client list. Crispin claimed it was confidential, which seemed a little odd since Roxanna Stein had been happy to let us know who she represented. They asked about the overbooking. Crispin said that he only wanted his clients to get as much exposure as possible and smiled at Mae and Neil rather condescendingly. Then they asked about the rumors of sexual abuse. Crispin smiled.

"Oh, please. There is so much jealousy in this business." He rolled his eyes. "It's no wonder that some of my less successful colleagues would want to libel me this way."

"Libel or is it slander?" Mae pulled out some legal-sized papers. "They're not the same thing. Either way, is it slander if there's a court case against you?"

Well, Mae is a librarian, and if there's one thing she knows, it's research. And she'd clearly gone down to the court offices. Darby gulped but didn't say anything. Crispin winced, then smiled.

"Anybody can sue. It's proving it that's the issue."

"Funny thing is, when I called the New York city courts, they promised to send me at least two other cases," said Mae.

Crispin laughed. "Again, it's about proving it."

Mae and I both looked at Darby. He was breathing heavily, but didn't seem quite ready to give in.

"The thing is," Crispin continued. "It doesn't matter what you think. It's what Darby thinks."

"He can't sign a contract," said Neil. "He's too young."

"Not if he's emancipated through the courts." Crispin grinned. "And I've got the papers right here."

Darby had the grace to look insanely guilty. Mae looked at Neil and swallowed, then looked at her son.

"Darby, do you really want this?"

Darby looked at all of us. "I need to stand on my own two feet."

Crispin smiled. "Come on, Darby. Why don't we finalize this outside?"

The two went out to the front drive. The rest of us waited. It took every bit of self-control I had not to sneak out and listen in. I looked at Sid. He was thinking the same thing.

"No!" Darby suddenly yelled. "Get away from me! Get the fuck away from me!"

"Shavings," Mae sighed.

We heard the back gate open and slam closed. Then we waited.

And waited.

Finally, the back door opened. Darby walked into the living room. He swallowed and looked at Mae and Neil.

"I owe you guys an apology," he said slowly, then looked at Sid, me, Mama, Daddy, Sy, and Stella. "I owe all of you an apology. I've been a real shit lately."

"Darby," Mama started, but Daddy squeezed her arm.

"I'm sorry," Darby continued. "Everything just happened so fast. I didn't want to be afraid anymore. You know, about sex and being a soloist, or not getting a career because I waited too long. I'm sorry."

Mae went over to her son and pulled him into her arms.

"My darling, darling boy." She kissed the side of his head. "I forgive you."

"Come here, son." Neil held his arms out from where he sat in the chair next to the couch. "I forgive you, too."

Darby held his father for a minute, then slid down next to Mae on the couch.

"Darby," Neil said. "You are supposed to be asking us what we thought and felt when we first saw you, right?"

"Yeah."

"When I first saw you," Neil continued. "The doctor was holding you upside down, and you were screaming, the umbilical cord still attached to your little tummy. And I was terrified. I was responsible for you and for your mother. And at the same time, I loved you so much. Just like I love your mother. And as time passed, that love only grew to include Janey and Ellen, Mitch and Marty, and Lissy. I loved you then, and I love you now. You are my precious son, in whom I am well pleased."

Mae put her arm around Darby's shoulders. "My sweet boy. That night you were born, I was exhausted and barely conscious. Then they put you in my arms, and I had to tell you your name, Darby William O'Malley. I wanted so much for you to know in those first minutes of your life who you were and how much I loved you. And I still love you, my darling boy. You are so talented, and I am so proud of you. But at the same time, it worries me. There are so many people out there who will think they love you but won't know you or really care about you because they just want to be part of your talent. Or worse, pretend to love you because they want to exploit it. It's going to be hard sometimes to tell the difference. That's why I want you to know what real love is. And when it comes to sex, I don't want you to be afraid of it. But when the love is real, I firmly believe you won't be afraid. In fact, that's how you'll know it is real love."

"I hope so," Darby muttered. "I just feel like sh— I mean, not good right now."

"Oh, honey," said Mama. "That's okay. That's how you know you're going to get better. Can you give me a hug?"

Darby pulled himself up off the couch and went over to where Mama stood and hugged her. Then he hugged Daddy. He hugged me next.

"I'm sorry I yelled at you last night, Aunt Lisa."

"I forgive you, sweetheart."

He hugged Nick next, then Stella, then he went up to Sid and hugged him. Sid's eyes were wet. It was the first time Darby had touched Sid since Darby had been molested by the neighbor five years before. The poor kid hadn't been able to touch any males except his father and younger brothers since then.

Finally, Darby went up to Sy. They'd had the same problem. But Darby hugged Sy hard.

"Are you okay?" Sy asked, holding him close.

"Yeah."

"Why?"

Darby smiled. "Because I know you love me."

Sy nodded. "Indeed, I do."

December 23 – 24, 1989

Today's Topic: Spending the Holidays Together (cont.)

As for the concept of Then-Somes. It's part of the larger term for the Whole Fam-Damily, as in the Whole Fam-Damily and Then Some. Darby came up with the term when he was fourteen and thought he was really getting away with something. But then it caught on. The Then-Somes are the people we're close to who are not part of our actual family and have families of their own to celebrate with, whether it's Christmas or other holidays or life events.

Kathy Deiner and Jesse White, and their kids are Then-Somes. So are Frank Lonnergan and Esther Nguyen, and Flora. Mom's poker friends are part of it, including the Sandoval family. Aunt Mae's friend, Loretta Tsing, is one, and the Thibodeauxs and the Herreras. The Mendozas were, but they're pretty much family now. Father John Reynolds (have you met him yet?), Tom Freeman and Angelique Carter. Sarah Williams and her daughters.

The Then-Somes party just happened the Christmas before Mom and Dad got married and kind of kept happening, always on the Sunday before Christmas. We do invite other friends, too, and nobody is concerned about who is really a Then-Some and who isn't.

You and your mom are like the Mendozas, not technically family yet, but getting there.

Because Sunday was Christmas Eve that year, which meant the Then-Somes had other obligations, we decided to have that party on Saturday.

Thanks to Conchetta, Sid and I do not have a lot to do in terms of getting the house ready. It's always immaculate. The Christmas decorations had been put up at the end of Thanksgiving weekend. That year, I made sure the fourth candle on the Advent wreath was lit, even though technically Christmas Eve was the fourth Sunday of Advent. Conchetta had also made two large pans of enchiladas and a smaller pan of her wonderful chiles rellenos. The enchiladas are a big favorite. The chiles are only for those of us who love eating fire. They are really spicy.

Sid had spent the better part of Friday working around Conchetta to make another two timbalos and a massive mound of cole slaw. Mae brought two huge cheese trays. There's an Italian deli not far from where they live, and the cheese they have is amazing.

We'd bought a case of Champagne, another case of chardonnay, this time from Napa, and a case of cabernet sauvignon from the Santa Ynez Valley. There were also a couple of bottles of good bourbon that Sid hid in the antique breakfront in the dining room. Most of our friends weren't going to abuse it, but Sid knew his old high school buddies and didn't trust them except for Tom.

That Saturday morning, Mama and I shredded another couple heads of lettuce while Sid chopped tomatoes and cucumbers, grated carrots, chopped broccoli, and put sunflower seeds into a bowl. This was our salad bar. Mama had baked dozens of cookies the week before in the evenings so that she didn't bother Conchetta.

By eleven, everything was ready, and by noon, the house was full. Kathy and Jesse arrived first with Keshon. Several choir members came with their families. Sarah and Dan Williams were there, with Sandra, who was Lissy's age, and Susannah, who was a year old. All the little ones were put in the rumpus room, and the child gate was spread across the archway inside to hopefully keep them in there. Mama volunteered to stay in the rumpus room. Carl and Erin MacArthur's youngest landed there, as well, as did anyone four years of age and younger. The school-age kids pretty much ran about at will, some roughhousing. Others just playing.

The Mertons arrived just after the Sandovals did. Stella got up from the couch and gave Wallace a long hug, and introduced him around.

Terri Merton, the fourteen-year-old girl, somehow connected with Janey, and the two spent most of the party in the library playing poker with Daddy. Terri's younger brother, Tyler, spent the party running around with Justin and Kyle Sandoval, and Mitch and Marty, Motley and Bowser on their heels. Our cats just hid, as they always did during larger gatherings.

Frank and Esther were there. Father John Reynolds, our parish pastor, showed up in his civvies. He and Sid have gotten really close over the past few years. John sat down with Stella in the living room, and the two chatted, which is always slightly amazing given Stella's antipathy toward the Catholic Church and priests, especially.

My cousin Maggie showed up and introduced her new boyfriend around, then promptly left. That she showed up at all was kind of amazing. She and Mae had never gotten along, which was part of why Maggie hadn't been at Mae's open house. The other part is that Maggie can't stand small children, and even though the twins were nine, that was close enough. She and I had been working on mending our formerly lousy relationship, and it was getting better, which is why she came by to say hello.

One rather notable absence was our good friend Henry James. He'd been our supervisor for the side business until about three years before, when he'd retired from the FBI. In fact, Angelique had part of his previous job as our co-ordinator for equipment and liaisons with the visible FBI. Sid and I had gotten the job of supervising our line for the courier part of our business. Henry, who had also lost his wife, Lydia, to cancer barely weeks after he officially retired, turned around and went back into undercover work in the field.

Sy tuned his cello as Bob Kinney came in. Bob went right up to Stella and gave her a big hug, then John made room on the couch so that Bob and Wallace could talk with Stella. Tom joined the group shortly afterward. Ange and I sat in the conversation group closest to the front door and watched.

Sid came in with a freshly opened bottle of Chardonnay and poured, then set the bottle on an end table and sat down on the piano bench to talk to his old buddies and Stella.

Screams erupted from the back of the house, and Mae wandered in.

"That was me," she said apologetically. "Your cat Fritz brought a dead mouse into the sun porch, and startled me, Erin MacArthur, and Leslie." (Leslie Bowman was my best friend in high school and one of the poker friends.) Mae shuddered. "Nick and Ellen decided they want to dissect it, and Esther wants to watch."

I sighed. "As long as they want to keep it in the lab, I don't care."

"They're dissecting a mouse?" Tyler Merton said, grinning. "I wanna see that."

Lottie Merton plopped down next to Ange and me.

"Oh my god, you've got a lively crew," she giggled.

"At least, they're not blowing anything up," I said. [Remember the first time Max Beard and Fran Mercer visited? That was some blast, in the literal sense. - SEH]

The doorbell rang, and I got up to get it. Louis Renfrew was at the door. As I admitted him to the living room, silence fell on the group around Stella.

"Well, Mr. Renfrew," Stella said sternly. "Alive and well, I see."

"Yeah. I'm afraid so." He chuckled lightly, then went over and kissed her cheek. "I apologize for any grief I may have caused you."

"And dragging my boy into trouble again." Stella shook her head. "I assume you again expect him to save your ass."

"I don't expect him to do anything, Stella." Louis laughed. "It's really good to see you. In some ways, you were the mom I never had."

Stella shook her head as Bob and Wallace echoed the sentiment.

Sid, who had gone into the dining room, came out just then with a glass for Louis and another bottle of Chardonnay. I smiled and watched the guys talking to Stella and her smiling at them, then went over to Sid and hugged him.

He laughed quietly and whispered in my ear. "You know, it's the weirdest thing. Of all our mothers, it turns out mine was the most functional."

"It doesn't surprise me." I gave him a quick squeeze. "You're pretty functional, yourself. It had to come from somewhere."

"I suppose."

The guys suddenly roared with laughter.

"So, what was it, Tom?" Bob demanded. "I mean, Liz was Most Likely To dot, dot, dot. That was an easy one to guess."

[Which said a lot about why Liz wasn't there. – SEH]

Tom, who had been on the yearbook their senior year, had put Liz Warner and Sid in as Most Likely to... because the class had voted another pair as Most Likely to Succeed. The idea was to fill in the ellipse. It was completely unfair to Liz because, even as loose as she'd been, she was one of the brightest kids at the school. I was kind of sad that she hadn't made the party, but she does not like being reminded of her high school years.

"I don't remember what it was supposed to be for either of them," Tom sighed. "It just sounded funny."

Wallace guffawed. "I thought Sid's was Most Likely to Get His Ass Shot by an Angry Father."

Sid sighed as Ange and I burst into laughter. I couldn't help it. I squeezed his left cheek and the scar there. Stella saw us and looked at Sid.

"Sid," she said. "Is that scar on your ass from a bullet hole?"

Sid put on his best grin, but I knew he was a little embarrassed.

"I'm afraid so, and I'm not saying how I got it." He moved away from me toward the dining room. The guys laughed loudly, and Mae yipped.

Ange tugged the sleeve of my newest Christmas sweater. "He told me it was a jealous husband."

"None of the above," I whispered back. "But I can't tell you how."

That was because Sid had gotten shot while detaining a suspect.

Esther showed up in the arch between the living room and dining room.

"I heard someone say that hole in Sid's ass was from a bullet," she said loudly.

Daddy came in from the library. "I just want to say officially, it was not me."

He and Sid get along really well. It's just that they didn't always, and still joke about it. Daddy didn't get along for a long time with Neil, either. Daddy always has been very protective of Mae and me.

"You really got a bullet in the ass?" Bob asked, laughing.

"What's the big deal?" Sid asked. "You want to see it?"

"No!" Mae yelped.

"Come on, Mae," Esther said. "I think you and your mom and the kids are the only people in this house that haven't seen Sid naked."

"Some of the kids, too," I said. "There was that pool party at the Sandovals' last summer. And Nick and Darby have."

Mae gulped. "What about Erin and Leslie?"

"They were at the pool party," Esther said.

"And there's Daddy and Neil."

"Nope," said Sid. "Remember that hotel in Seattle? We were all sharing changing quarters."

"John!" Mae all but leaped on him.

John shrugged. "I see his ass all the time at the gym. The guy does not put on a towel to get to the showers."

"And we've all seen it," said Tom. "Just not recently."

Sid laughed and held out his hands. "Anytime you want, Mae."

Mae shuddered. "No!"

"I do not understand all this fear and shame over the human body," said Stella. "Our natural state is simply our natural state. There is no reason to be embarrassed by it."

"Tell that to Lety Sandoval," I said, giggling.

"Tell me what?" Lety asked, coming into the room.

"The pool party last summer."

Lety gasped, and while it was in Spanish, I'm pretty sure that what came out of her mouth was obscene.

"I will never forgive Frank!"

John laughed.

"What happened?" asked Lottie. "And you have to count me as someone who hasn't had the chance to see Sid naked."

Esther laughed. "My husband, Frank, and Lety's husband, Reuben, last summer were playing some stupid game with Sid, where if you lost a point, you had to take on a dare. So, Sid lost a round and Frank dared him to go skinny dipping, which was really stupid because everybody knew Sid would do it. But then Sid dared Reuben and Frank to do it, too. And they did."

"And they were sober!" Lety cried. "I have never been so embarrassed!"

"We're close friends," said Sid, unabashed. "What can I say?"

Kathy wandered into the room. "What's going on?"

Mae pounced on her. "Kathy, please tell me you've never seen Sid naked."

"Of course, I have," Kathy said. "That pool party at the Sandovals' last summer. Why weren't you there?"

"We must have been in Nebraska to see Neil's family."

"You know," Kathy thought. "There was also the sunbathing incident a couple years ago in Cancun."

"I forgot about that," Esther guffawed.

"So, I don't believe in tan lines," said Sid.

"Hey, Sid," announced Frank, coming into the room holding a guitar and a flute. "It's time to get that bullet-riddled ass of yours onto the piano bench and get some music going!"

"Thanks be," Sid muttered, sliding onto the bench.

"I am tuned," said Sy, settling his cello between his knees. "Perhaps we should start with some Beatles in honor of your old friends? Ah, I know. Eleanor Rigby. Who wants to sing lead?"

"Mae and I can," I said.

And we did. We did that and Yesterday, which also has a really great cello part, then worked our way through most of the Sergeant Pepper's album. And it went on from there. Stella and Sy played a sonata for piano and cello, then Sid and Stella played the Brahms Waltzes for Two Pianos that they'd been practicing all month. Nick came in and sang Everybody Wants to Rule the World playing his electric guitar. Darby played guitar, too.

Bob sang surprisingly well. Louis just hung back and watched, something going on behind his smile.

We ate. Wallace almost cried when he tried the chiles rellenos after he saw me wolfing one down without blinking.

Mama came out to eat but hurried back to the rumpus room just in time to catch Lissy and Keshon decorating the one clear wall with some crayons somebody had left behind.

"Another mural," I told Sid, and he laughed.

And slowly, the house emptied. Mama made sure that everyone knew that Darby would be on the local public TV station the next day with the Youth Orchestra, which didn't do much for Darby's nerves. At least, he was still eating.

Sid and I walked out with Wallace and Lottie and the kids as they left, the setting sun turning the driveway orange. The kids ran ahead to their car.

Sid shook Wallace's hand as Lottie hugged me.

"I had so much fun," Lottie said.

"You've got a good life here, Sid." Wallace looked bemused. "Terri wants to play poker with me, and Tyler wants to set up a lab at our house."

Lottie looked fondly at her husband as she took his arm.

"You do that, then," said Sid. "But I highly recommend two hoses for the lab."

We laughed and headed back inside. In the library, Bob was getting cleaned out of all his change by my father and Janey. Esther looked at her hand and cursed as she always did, whether she had something or not. Mama came in and kissed Daddy on the head. My father chuckled and squeezed her butt.

"Bill, you are just terrible!" Mama said. But she was laughing as if she'd enjoyed it.

The interesting thing was the way Bob watched my parents.

Louis had disappeared sometime before. Kathy and Mae were already bringing abandoned dishes into the kitchen from around the place. Sid gave me a lazy kiss, then went to help. Stella, Sy, and Tom were having some debate or another while Ange chatted with Esther and Frank.

Keshon and Lissy both shrieked, and I went into the rumpus room to find out what was up. They were the last two little ones left, and both were pretty worn out by the day's festivities. Thinking about Sarah and Dan got me wondering if they'd seen Sid... Of course, they had. They'd been at the pool party, too. Dan had not been amused.

I called Marty and Mitch in to watch Keshon and Lissy, then went after Nick, Darby, and Ellen to get them to help clean up. Sid nearly tripped on Bowser again, and we almost lost a full tray of dirty wine glasses. Mae and Neil and the kids stayed at the house, as they usually did.

It was an altogether satisfactory day.

Sid's Voice -

We'd done the Christmas Eve presentation at the Music Center before, so we knew what we were up against. Since the program was free, one generally had to stand in line for the better part of the morning to get tickets. However, Darby had been able to get six tickets for us. We all debated whether it was worth standing in line to see if the rest of us could get in, but then decided that only some of us would go, which meant Mae and Neil, Lisa and me, and Sy and Stella. Mama and Daddy elected to watch it on TV and babysit Darby's siblings. Nick and Josh decided to stand in line. Darby needed to be at the Music Center hours before things began, so he asked if he could ride with them. He hadn't brought his car, and Mae and Neil were parked on the street.

Since Mama and Daddy had been staying with us, we'd let them park their rental car in the garage. Given all the sabotage and what Darby had found in his car, the last thing we wanted was for Lisa's parents to get pulled over and searched for drugs. Nick parked in the driveway, and we let Motley check the car every day. So far, there hadn't been any trouble.

Christmas Eve morning, though, Motley went nuts, whining and yelping. Lisa got her parents distracted while I searched the Volvo, and, yes, there was a nice, small packet of what we later tested and discovered was cocaine. Motley and I also checked Mae and Neil's van, and it was clean.

Nick and Darby headed out, but then Nick called around nine from his car. I answered in the office.

"Dad, I got pulled over," he said, his voice worried. "I didn't do anything, I swear I didn't. I was driving the speed limit. They said I made a bad lane change, but I wasn't even changing lanes. They searched the car, too."

"Did you get to the Music Center okay?"

"Yeah, and just in time."

"Did the cops have a warrant?" I glared at my desk.

He gasped. "I forgot to ask. They let us go, but f—, uh, man, they were scary."

"I'm sure they were," I growled. "On the way home, why don't we stay together? Okay?"

If Nick had gotten pulled over under those circumstances, then, based on what Zack Peters had told us the week before, Cobb had probably put an APB out. I called

Kathy and Jesse and made sure that they checked their car. Fortunately, it was clean, as was Frank and Esther's. I called Louis next and had to leave a message.

Janey wandered into the office. "Hey, Uncle Sid."

She's got brown hair and Lisa's big cow eyes, and at thirteen, was getting to be just as pretty as her aunt and was at least as astute.

"You look upset," she said, plopping onto the couch.

"I'm afraid I am." I leaned back in my desk chair and still found a way to smile at her.

"Oh. Is it about that friend of yours who swapped out his dog tags in the war, then pretended he was dead for, like, ever?"

I had to laugh. "And who told you about that?"

"That other friend, Mr. Kinney. He told Grandpa about it last night while we were playing poker. He's a lousy poker player."

"Janey, compared to you, your aunt, and your grandfather, just about everybody is a lousy poker player."

"Yeah, but he was really easy to read. And when Grandpa asked him how he knew you, he told Grandpa all about your six friends, and how one had died recently, and then about this guy named Loser." She made a face. "That's an awful name."

"I know."

"Uncle Sid, do you think about the war much, and being in it?"

I sighed. "I usually try not to. It was pretty terrible."

"I bet. Mom says you got stuck there an extra year."

"Two of the worst years of my life. Put me behind on my education. Lost my scholarship to University of San Francisco."

"But it put you at the same university where Nick's first mom was at the same time as her. So, you wouldn't have had Nick if you hadn't been in the war."

Okay, that one hit home in a really weird way. But Janey was like that.

"I mean," she continued. "The war was terrible, but some good stuff came out of it for you."

"Yeah. I guess it did."

She came over, gave me a quick hug, then ran off.

She was right again. If it hadn't been for the war and being blackmailed into intelligence work, I wouldn't have gotten a lot of what I did. It wasn't an easy thought to swallow.

Lisa put yet another oversized Christmas sweater on over her tight jeans that day, since it was a casual concert. Even Darby would be wearing a bright green shirt and dark slacks instead of a tuxedo.

We all arrived in good time, found Nick and Josh, and settled in for a couple of hours. Darby was smack in the middle of the hours-long program featuring music and arts groups from all over the county. The Youth Orchestra set up during a dance number from a local folklorico. When the curtain rose, the kids were in their chairs, and Darby stood to the side of the conductor.

It was a nice rendition of the first movement from Winter, by Antonio Vivaldi, part of the Four Seasons suite. I know how well Darby plays. I'd only been working with him since I'd known him. However, there remains a world of difference between knowing how well he plays, even when you hear him practicing on a regular basis, and seeing him in concert mode. It's mind-boggling. Even Sy got caught up, and he knew better than any of us just how good Darby is. In a way, I didn't blame Crispin for chasing the boy as hard as he had.

Lisa and Mae had tears in their eyes as the audience leapt to their feet at the end. I wasn't sure how, but he'd done even better than he had the week before, and Vivaldi is not easy.

We slid out of the row at the Chandler Pavilion and hurried backstage. A couple of reporters were there, taking pictures of Darby and the conductor. He saw us and his eyes lit up.

"Hey, Mom!" he called. "I'm hungry!"

We couldn't help laughing.

"Don't worry," said Mae. "Hurry and get your bag. Uncle Sid put your name on the rest of the timbalo."

Darby whooped with joy, then stopped. "Mom, can I ride back to Uncle Sid's with Nick and Josh?"

Mae smiled. "Sure, sweetheart. We'll see you there."

I glanced at Nick, and he nodded. We followed the Volvo home. Nick drove right at the speed limit, which about made me nuts, but it was more important to stay with him, and that he didn't speed. There would be time for that later.

What I hadn't told Darby was that another treat was ready for him. He shrieked when he saw the platter sitting next to the ice-cold shrimp and crab claws.

"Oysters!"

He fell asleep after sucking down about a dozen of the oysters, finishing off the third of a timbalo, and a quarter of the shrimp and crab claws. Which was fine. The rest of the family decided to settle in for naps, as well. Mama distributed that year's Christmas pajamas and nightgowns to howls of laughter when the family saw what she'd gotten me. That year, it was bouncing Santa heads on a neon green background. Mama always made a point of getting me the most garish, god-awful pajamas she could find simply because I refused to wear them. Then I went upstairs to our bedroom, where Lisa was waiting for me.

December 25, 1989

Sid's Voice -

There is something magical in the pre-dawn of Christmas morning. The Then-Somes party, and then the frenetic energy of Christmas Eve are wonderful. But Christmas Eve, in particular, involves wired kids of all ages. Plus, I was usually thinking about Midnight Mass and what I was going to be playing. But at five a.m. on Christmas morning, almost everyone is still asleep. Our family does not tend toward morning people, even in infants and toddlers.

Our tradition is that anyone under eighteen gets a present or two from Santa, which are left unwrapped and placed under the tree. Everyone gets a stocking, and it can be a bit of a trick putting in the stocking stuffers when the recipient is right there stuffing another stocking or two.

The Christmas of '89, I went right to bed after Mass. Lisa, Mae, and Neil took care of stuffing stockings, getting the Santa presents out, and assembling the tricycle for Lissy. Lisa and I had gotten our lovemaking in during nap time, so she didn't have to wake me when she finally got into bed that night.

No matter how little sleep I've gotten the night before, I'm almost always awake at five. If I'm really tired, I can roll over and go back to sleep until eight, which is not Lisa's idea of sleeping in at all. Five a.m. that day came too quickly, but there I was, wide-awake, Lisa next to me, her cute little whistling snore going. I rolled over, kissed her forehead, then got up. She was out cold and never noticed.

I put on sweatpants and a long-sleeved t-shirt that Lisa had bought me the year before. The shirt had one of those international symbols for "No," namely the big red circle with the diagonal line through it, overlaying a big green L. As in No L. It was as close to the whole Christmas kitsch as I was willing to get.

I checked to make sure the intercom was on so that Lisa would hear either Lissy's or the twins' shrieks of joy that Santa had come, then went downstairs to start breakfast. The kids are allowed to play with their Santa presents when they wake up, but we all wait until breakfast is ready to unwrap everything. Which means being late with breakfast is not popular. I turned on the oven to get it preheated, then went out into the hall.

The house was silent and dark. The younger kids were still fast asleep in the rumpus room. I breathed in the quiet with the faint hint of evergreen in the air. Back in the kitchen, I got the bread pudding I'd assembled the morning before from the fridge and slid it into the oven. I needed a cup of coffee, but with no one due to wake for at least another hour or so, I got the kettle going instead of the coffee maker and ground beans for the filter cone over the single cup.

"Uncle Sid?"

I turned and smiled. Janey wore a flannel nightgown with red stripes and tiny Christmas icons in between the stripes.

"Hey, Janey."

She's the only other member of the family who likes the early morning hours.

"Merry Christmas." She ran up and gave me a warm hug, and I hugged her back.

"Merry Christmas, kiddo. You want some coffee?"

She made a face. "No, thank you."

"What can I get you?"

"Is there any tea, please?"

"Yes, there is." I got the box of Assam down, glad that there was plenty of water in the kettle.

"Can I help you make breakfast?"

"You most certainly may." I chuckled. Janey and I had found many special times together, but as the years passed, early Christmas morning, before anyone else woke up, got to be our favorite.

"What have we got on the menu?" she asked.

"Well, I've got the bread pudding in the oven now, but it's going to take a good hour to finish. We can still put out some oatmeal, and you know your grandfather isn't going to be happy unless there's some bacon."

Janey laughed. "Or scrambled eggs. And Aunt Lisa wants bacon."

"The Whole Fam-Damily wants bacon."

Janey and I went to work. We nixed the oatmeal because we'd have the bread pudding. We got the chafing dishes ready on the dining room table, then took my coffee and her tea to the breakfast room table and sat down. We couldn't do anything about the bacon that early, let alone the eggs.

"So," I said. "How are things going with you?"

"Pretty good," she said, then frowned. "I mean, Gina Preston called me last week. She said her cousin Wyatt had seen my class photo and wanted to meet me." She rolled her eyes.

"You are pretty cute."

Janey snorted. "Yeah, but you know what he was interested in, and it wasn't me talking to him. If the only thing he sees in me is how I look, I'm not interested."

"And I'm glad you're not."

"Uncle Sid, why are boys only interested in what I look like?"

I shrugged. "I have no idea. Your aunt had a similar problem, she tells me. I just know that the women I liked the most had brains and were fun to talk to. That's part of what I love about your Aunt Lisa."

"She says it's primary socialization. That our culture encourages boys to only see women as objects for their gratification. You know. I think she's got a point."

"I agree."

Janey's big, round eyes pierced through me. "Did you use to see women that way?"

I shut my eyes and thought about how to phrase it. "I hope not. Before I knew Lisa, and even after for a while, it was about the sex. But I do hope it was truly reciprocal. Lisa once accused me of using women, and my response was that they were using me the same way, so it was fair."

"You know Darby..."

"Yeah, I know."

Janey shrugged. "He's going to do what he's going to do." She frowned. "Uncle Sid, what made you change your mind about sleeping around?"

Oh, yeah. That kid always asked the hard questions. A lot like her aunt did.

"Um. I got bored with it." I stopped and thought. "That wasn't entirely it, but it didn't help. I fell in love with your aunt. Granted, it took me a while, but I finally had to accept that what I felt for her was real love. After that, there was no reason to sleep around."

Janey nodded. "I thought so."

"You would."

"Uncle Sid, are you still thinking about the war?"

I took a deep breath. "I am."

"You know your friend, Mr. Renfew?"

"Yeah?"

Janey grinned. "He's a good person. I mean, I know he does bad things. I don't think anyone taught him how to be good. But he is, at heart."

"Really?" I snorted. "You do realize that he has done nothing but lie to me of late."

"So?" Janey shrugged. "He shouldn't. That's not good. I just don't think he knows how to do anything else. You know what I mean?"

"You may be right, Janey."

I had to laugh. As usual, Janey had put her laser beam on the essential issue.

"Okay. What time is it?" she asked. "I figure if we get the bacon in the second oven by seven, everything will be set by the time Lissy wakes up."

Yes, I have two ovens in my kitchen. As for breakfast, we did bacon in the oven because that was the only way to cook enough for the Whole Fam-Damily at one time. Janey and I took turns beating the eggs, then she laid out the bacon strips on three of my half-sheet pans.

Lisa's Voice -

Oh, I was exhausted when I crawled into bed the night before. Sid was chattering away in his sleep, so I kissed his forehead, not that he noticed, and rolled over myself.

It was about eight-fifteen when the twins began the shrieking. Marty was ecstatic that he had the new wood carving tools he'd been pining for. Mitch crowed over the new skateboard and helmet he had. Lissy started crying, but shrieked with joy when she saw her tricycle. Slowly, the rest of us emerged from our rooms, dodging Lissy as she pedaled her way through the halls surrounding the living and dining rooms.

The other kids took down their stockings and crowed over their gifts. Well, Janey was helping Sid with getting breakfast together. Nick had a roof rack for his Volvo, one that could carry either skis or a surfboard. He, Josh, and Darby had gotten hooked on surfing the summer before. Santa had brought Darby a new surfboard.

Thank God, Sid had made plenty of coffee. The whole house smelled of coffee, baking bread pudding, and Christmas tree. Oh, and bacon. Janey brought out the chafing dish filled with scrambled eggs smothered in cheddar cheese. The bread pudding wasn't quite done, but there was only so much Sid could do about that.

We looked at stockings and sipped coffee while Sid brewed another pot and Darby and Nick helped him get the turkey ready for roasting. Finally, the bread pudding was done, and pulled from the oven, and the turkey went in. Plates were distributed, and we all settled into the living room, with the dogs hovering nearby in the hopes of getting a treat. Sid got out a trash bag, and Mama took custody of it because Sid sometimes got a little overzealous when it came to clearing away the torn wrapping paper.

"Hey, remember when Uncle Sid threw out Aunt Lisa's earrings?" Marty said, laughing.

Sid sighed. "Uncle Sid remembers that one all too well."

Well, that Christmas (in 1984) had not been a particularly good time for Sid and me, although it wasn't bad enough to break us up.

[I'm amazed that the twins remember it. They were only four that year. Mitch told me recently that it's the first thing both he and Marty remember, although it's mostly the hullabaloo that happened when we discovered that the aquamarines had disappeared. It was Darby who told them when they were six or seven what the hullabaloo was about. And as difficult as things were that year, it was still better being with you than without. – SEH]

Daddy saw to distributing gifts, making sure each one was opened and duly appreciated before giving one of the twins the next gift to hand to its recipient. With our large family, this means unwrapping gifts takes a while. Sid took a break early on so that the rest of the adults and Nick and Darby could get more coffee.

One of the best moments was when Darby got a decent-sized box from his parents. Inside was a tuxedo.

"We'll have to get it tailored," Mae explained. "But I've got a strong feeling you're going to be needing one soon."

Darby looked up. "You mean...?"

Neil smiled. "We've talked to the two agents on the phone that Ms. Stein recommended, and the three of us will be meeting with them after the New Year to make the actual selection. But, yeah, looks like you're going on tour this summer."

Darby bounced up, almost knocking his plate onto the new tux, and hugged his parents.

Then I got a small flat box from Sid. Inside was the owner's manual to a small photocopier.

"Sid, what is this?" I looked up at him.

"Your new copy machine. I figure it will be cheaper than using the copy shop and save hours of time."

"Honey, these things aren't cheap."

Sid shrugged. "What do I care? The guys will be here to set it up after the holiday is over. Which means you will be forced to take a break this week."

I reached over and kissed him warmly.

The unwrapping went on. By the time we'd finished, the turkey was starting to smell divine. Darby and Sid retreated to the kitchen to finish cooking dinner, while Mama, Mae, and I took over straightening the living room, and Sy and Stella brought the breakfast dishes into the kitchen and cleaned them. Neil and Daddy tried to get Lissy to take a nap.

It was late afternoon when dinner was ready, and the great Boxing Day Excursion Debate began. The kids decided they wanted to go to Universal Studios. Sy and Stella were all for it. Mama and Daddy volunteered to stay back at Mae and Neil's to babysit Lissy, who was still too young for amusement parks. Sid and I looked at each other and wished we could have volunteered first. Mae and Neil were resigned.

Then, Darby and Nick asked the final question for their family history project: Describe your first faith experience. Sid just chuckled. Being an atheist, he had no faith experience, and none of us expected him to answer.

Mama answered first. "I've always believed. I can't remember a time when I didn't."

"Me, neither," said Mae with a bemused look on her face. "God has always been a part of my life, and praying is second nature to me."

Neil sighed and shook his head. "You know, I gotta say the same thing. Sorry, guys, but I've always believed in God and can't remember when I didn't, or when I wasn't committed to it."

Nick looked at me.

I thought. "Huh. I did have a faith experience apart from just believing. It was when I was in high school. I went to a teen retreat my sophomore year. It was part of Confirmation class. One of the leaders challenged us to make a conscious decision about whether or not we believed or wanted to believe. So, I really thought about it and prayed about it, and realized that, yeah, this was what I believed and that I wanted to make a commitment to the faith." I smiled. "It felt really good, and I think I've only gotten stronger in that faith as I've grown."

"What about you, Grandpa?" Nick asked.

Daddy looked at me and blinked a little. "I've always been Catholic, always went to church. But I wasn't always so sure about God. I mean, I just kind of took it as a given. But then, when your grandma was pregnant with Lisa, she went into labor two months too soon. We were so sure we were going to lose another one, and worse yet, after Althea had carried her for so long." He swallowed and shook his head. "You know how she kept having miscarriages before then. I was in the waiting room at the hospital, and Sister came out and asked me what the baby's name would be if it was a boy or if it was a girl. Althea was already unconscious. Women were knocked out for labor at that time. I forget what we were going to name a boy."

"It was David Lee, honey." Mama smiled at him.

"That's right." Daddy shrugged. "But we had decided on Lisa Jane for a girl. I asked Sister why she wanted to know the names, and she said, 'So that we can baptize the baby the second it's born.' Oh, that scared me like nothing else. If they were going to baptize a baby that fast, they were not optimistic about the odds of it surviving. And yet, when Sister came out to the waiting room again, she was smiling. The baby was a girl, and she was alive. It was still pretty touchy, though, and Sister took me to the nursery so that I could see her." He blinked. "She was so very tiny, and in that moment, I prayed like I had never prayed before, and somehow, I knew that she was going to be alright. That God was going to hear my prayers, and that's when I really became a believer. It was still scary for a while there. But she made it, and look at her now."

Daddy grinned at me.

"Wow," said Darby, laughing. "That's going to be great for the presentation, Nick."

"We have to do an oral report on our histories," Nick explained. "And Darby and I are going to do ours together because we're cousins."

"Oh, that sounds like fun," I said.

"Are you two going to ignore Sy and me?" Stella asked suddenly.

"But you guys don't believe in God," Nick said.

"I certainly don't," said Sy. "I went to church every Sunday until I left home, and never believed in any of it, and was thoroughly glad not to have to get up early on Sundays. Day of rest. Pshaw. If it was supposed to be restful, then why didn't they let us sleep in, for Heaven's sakes?"

"Stella, you don't believe in God, either," Darby said. "You're why Uncle Sid doesn't believe in God."

"True enough." Stella smiled at Sid, then looked at the boys. "But there was a time when I did believe. I remember my First Communion. I was seven years old and had a beautiful white dress and veil, and thought nothing could be better than taking that host on my tongue. I was even toying with the idea of becoming a nun. My father thought that was a fine idea, which may be why I didn't. Of course, he was why I stopped believing."

"Aunt Stella," Mitch said. "It's really sad that your father was so mean, but we love you."

Stella blinked and laughed. "And I love you all, too!"

By the end of dinner, Lissy was getting cranky, so Mae and Neil packed up their family. Darby stayed behind to help clean up, and Nick offered to drive him home and spend the night in Pasadena. Mama and Daddy decided to go over there as soon as the cleanup was finished. Sy and Stella left for their place right after Mama and Daddy left.

As we shut the front door, Sid and I looked at each other and grinned. The house was quiet, and we were finally alone. Then the phone rang. I went into the living room to put away the gifts that had been left out. Sid took the call in the library. When he came into the living room, his face was grim.

"Angelique was kidnapped just now," he told me.

December 25, 1989

Sid's Voice

Tom and Angelique were just coming home from Christmas with her brother and his family, when Tom dropped her off in front of their apartment building and went to park the car, their carport being quite a way off from the apartment itself. She wasn't in the apartment when he got there. He looked over the balcony and saw a gunman forcing her into a car with her hands cuffed behind her back. Tom thought the gunman looked like Cobb.

Why he called Louis first, I don't know. He mumbled something about since it was, essentially, a cop that had kidnapped her, it didn't seem likely the cops would be of much help. Anyway, Louis agreed that the cops shouldn't be involved and said he'd be right over. I agreed to get there as fast as I could, too.

I had to go upstairs and change first. I was still wearing sweatpants and that long-sleeved t-shirt. Lisa followed me up.

"I'll call the rest of the team and put them on alert," she said. "What do you think we'll need?"

"I have no idea. Could be a simple extraction, could be we'll need sniper fire." I stopped and looked at her. "Can you be ready for anything?"

"Of course." She bit her lip and frowned. "I'm not sure when Esther and Frank are leaving for Chicago."

Esther and Frank generally spend Christmas Day here in Los Angeles because of Frank's choir directing duties, and Esther's family is here. But they often leave Christmas night or the day after to go visit Frank's family in the Chicago area.

"They're leaving tomorrow," I said. "The bigger problem will be Kathy and Jesse if they can't get Estelle to sit with Keshon at the last second."

I got into a pair of jeans and a dress shirt, then slid on my shoulder holster, and grabbed the .45 automatic out of the locked dresser drawer. The good thing about unstructured jackets was that the gun didn't show as badly as it did in my Italian cut suits. I got a khaki jacket on and kissed Lisa. She handed me a box of ammo.

"You never know," she said.

"Thanks, Lover." I kissed her again and held her, then hurried out to the garage.

Tom was way past thinking clearly when I got there. He paced relentlessly in the living room while Louis peeked through the front window curtains.

"Damn," Louis said. "He probably saw you come in here."

"Who?" I asked.

"Cobb." Louis left the window. "He's sitting in a car across the street watching this place."

"Shit!" Tom yelped. He turned on me. "So, what are you going to do about this?"

"Me?" I stepped back. "I can't do anything."

"Then why do you have a gun on?"

I smiled weakly to buy a moment. "I've been carrying since we got shot at that first time. I've carried since I got back from 'Nam, until a few years ago."

"Bullshit!" Tom went back to pacing. "Ange works with agents on top-secret projects, all kinds of undercover people. I know god-damned well you're one of them!"

"What?" Louis asked, looking at me, then Tom.

I blinked. "What the hell are you talking about? Ange and I are friends. I'm friends with her former boss. We've been friends since before I knew Lisa."

"That doesn't mean you're not one of Ange's undercover guys." Tom glared at me.

"Fuck," said Louis. "Now, it makes sense."

"Huh?" At that point, I was genuinely bewildered and not just faking it to keep my cover.

"I don't know, Sid." Louis' grin was almost evil. "Does the name Colonel Niles Landry mean anything to you?"

Of course, it did. Landry was the alias that Dale O'Connor was using when he first blackmailed me into intelligence work, and then, after the war, to suck me back in again.

"You mean I was right?" Tom stopped pacing and gulped.

"Of course, you were right." Louis smiled. "I went to Landry a couple months ago because I needed help nailing Cobb and friends. I've been doing favors for Landry for years. He told me that one of my old high school buddies could help me." Louis frowned. "Landry is the kind of prick who would withhold a bit of critical information like exactly who, but it was almost like he couldn't remember the name. I thought it was you, Tom."

"Me?" Tom's face went white. "Why?"

"Girlfriend with the FBI? And you were the one guy who was willing to help." Louis jerked a thumb at me. "Not like this asshole, who had to be dragged along kicking and screaming. Not knowing who it was, I had to guess. So, that's why I got the four of you together. I'd already checked out Stan and knew damned well he wasn't the guy I needed."

I looked at him. "And now you're so sure I'm your guy."

"Yeah, Sid." Louis walked right up to me. "You're the only one who got drafted and the one who most likely had contact with Landry. Not to mention Bob's pot problem and Wallace being a weenie. There's also a scar on your ass that you don't want to talk about. And then there's your wife."

I'd seen Louis looking at Lisa here and there and wondering.

Louis laughed. "She only looks harmless, Sid."

I couldn't help it. I choked and laughed because I'd been saying the same thing about Lisa for years. But there was my cover. Looking at Tom, I realized that was blown and then some. I shrugged. Lisa is kind of my weak spot.

"She could kick your ass three times over, Louis." I looked at Tom. "This can't get out, you know. The only reason my family and I are safe is because no one knows about us."

"Except Colonel Landry," said Louis.

"That cocksucking bastard." I shut my eyes. "The next time I see that fuck, I am going to take him out."

"I'll help," said Louis.

"When did you run into him?" I asked.

"He showed up shortly after I pulled my tag switch. He helped me get away with it."

"I don't care about trips down Memory Lane right now!" Tom went back to pacing. "What are we going to do? Call the cops? Call the FBI? Come on. Ange is one of them."

I looked at Louis. "You seem to know a lot about Cobb. Come clean this time. What's his game?"

"The same as you've heard." Louis took a deep breath. "He has a dirt file. Names, dates, all sorts of stuff. A few years ago, I ran across some information that could have made a certain politician, well, uncomfortable. It was deeply buried and well worth burying. So, I blackmailed him. But see, the thing is, the way blackmailers get caught is that they get greedy, always wanting more from their victims. My dad told me that. I hit the politician once, made a genuinely nice score on it, and left it. So, suddenly, this guy gets a lot closer to the Oval Office than anybody would have expected, and last year, he's sweating a little. He contacts me and says he's got some guys who will mess me up unless I do him a favor. He also points out that I know one of his pals, Niles Landry. Well, Landry's been on my ass ever since the war. Yeah, I owed him, but the fuck is still collecting. Still not sure how this politician and him knew each other. Landry wants me to steal Cobb's dirt file and take him and the other two out, which, by the way, I was more than happy to do. Cobb knew I hadn't died."

I looked at him. "How did he know that?"

Louis winced. "Not sure. I've got a bad feeling it was that asshole Landry. Could have been something else. Anyway, I'd been doing odd jobs for Cobb, as well, for obvious reasons, and not liking it. So, I stole the dirt file. But see, here's the problem. Cobb is one mean son of a bitch, but he's not an idiot. He had a couple more copies. He may have more, but I got one more, and I think I know where a third one is."

"But why would he take Angelique?" Tom said. "And where's he keeping her? In that car outside?"

Louis went back to the window and peeked out. "He's still there, but I don't think he's got her with him. He'd have stashed her." He turned. "As for why, he needs a bargaining chip but bad. I'm not sure how, but all his assets and his friends' assets, including the foreign ones, are frozen. Even if he skips town, he has no money. His Fed pals aren't going to want it to get out that they've got a bad apple, nor that he got the drop on one of their own, even if she's technically a civilian."

"Any guesses as to where he stashed her?" I asked.

"Well, the Feds know about his warehouse, so I doubt he put her there." Louis shrugged. "Most likely spot is his house. It's in Encino."

I looked at him. "Do you have an address?"

"Yeah. But he's keeping an eye on this place. How are we going to leave without him spotting us?"

I grinned. "You have forgotten. I have my wife, and as you said, Lisa only looks harmless."

Lisa's Voice -

Sid called me at close to ten-thirty. We needed an extraction and search. That was no problem, but we didn't know how much time we had. I called Kathy and Esther. They were both ready to go. In fact, Kathy was already over at

Esther's place. I gave them the address, and they got to Encino before I did. Well, I probably shouldn't have taken Coldwater Canyon, but that's usually the fastest way to get to the San Fernando Valley. It was, however, Christmas night, and the 405 freeway was clear for a change.

I saw Esther's car as I pulled past the target house.

"Hey, Little Red," Kathy's voice rang in my ear. "We have eyes on you."

"Eyes on you, Red Sky and Red Gate. Meet you at the driveway."

I parked half a block down from the house. It was a ranch-style, probably built in the Sixties, with an automated gate across the driveway. There were lights on over most of the doors in the neighborhood, not to mention the yards. But the windows in the houses all around were dark. Some folks still had their Christmas lights on, even at that hour. The colored lights on one house winked out as the three of us crossed the street, our black, hooded sweatshirts open. Once we'd slipped into the shadows next to the gate, we zipped up and put on gloves and black, all-over ski masks.

Esther chuckled as she looked at the gate. "Piece of cake."

I'm not sure what she used to disable it, but she had it cracked open within seconds. We slid along the side yard to the house. Esther spotted something, again, I'm not sure what, but gestured that we should go around to the back. On the side of the house, she found something else she liked, fiddled with a metal box for a second, then laughed softly.

"That was too easy," she muttered happily. "If he weren't a bad guy, I'd be making a client call."

I heard Kathy's sigh, but we slid around to the back of the house. Kathy picked the lock on the back door, and we slid inside. I sent them to the front of the house to begin their search for the extra dirt files and went to the back to see if I could find Angelique. Ange was my target because she knew about me. She didn't know about Esther and Kathy. At least, I don't think she did, and I didn't want her to if she didn't. Ange was in the front side bedroom, blindfolded and handcuffed, sitting on the bed in there. I slid back into the hall.

"I have the extraction subject," I whispered. "Will remove ASAP. You stay on search."

"Copy," said Kathy's voice softly.

I slid back into the bedroom and hissed. Ange started.

"I'm here to get you to safety," I whispered.

"Who...?"

"Never mind."

I sat down next to her on the bed and got a lock pick out of one of the pockets on my break-in pants. I first slid the blindfold off her, then popped the cuffs relatively quickly. I nodded at her, and we slid out the back door and around the side of the house. I was able to crack the driveway gate open just enough for each of us to slide through, then pushed it back. I led Ange to my car. She gasped as she recognized it, but opened the passenger door and got in.

I slid behind the wheel and pulled off my mask and gloves.

"How...?"

"Come on, Ange. You know better than to ask."

She cursed.

"Little Red, we have paper and two floppies," said Esther.

I felt my pager buzz and looked at the readout. Sid had sent the signal.

"That will do. Perp is in motion. Evacuate now."

Another minute or so, I saw the two dark forms opening the driveway gate. I didn't wait but started my car and took off.

I parked out front of the apartment building in Culver City and walked Ange up to hers and Tom's place. Sid and Louis were there in the front room. Ange ran to Tom's arms, and I pulled the other two guys out of there pretty quickly.

"Got her out, huh?" Louis chuckled.

"It wasn't that hard," I snarled.

"Yeah, but he's got high-level security on his place."

I shrugged. "If you know what you're doing, it's no big deal."

"Oh, come on!" Louis laughed.

My left hand whipped out and yanked his face next to mine. "If you know what you're doing, it's no big deal."

Sid laughed loudly. "Like you said, Louis. She only looks harmless."

I shoved Louis into the wall of another apartment. "By the way, I'm right-handed."

"I'll, uh, remember that," Louis said softly.

Sid and I went down the stairs to the street.

"See you at home?" he asked, smiling.

"Yeah." I smiled at him and gave him a quick kiss before heading to my car. "Love you."

"Love you, too."

December 26 – 29, 1989

Lisa's Voice

I will confess that I really, really wanted an excuse to get out of going to Universal Studios that day. However, when Dale O'Connor showed up on our doorstep at seven that morning, I almost chose the theme park.

Sid let Dale in. "What's this about?"

"We've got a job to finish," Dale said.

"And we have things to do today," Sid said, leading him into the office.

"You bet we do." Dale laughed jovially.

Sid turned on him. "Stuff with our family. Not you."

Dale chuckled. "Oh. So, you don't mind Cobb planting drugs in your kid's car, then calling the cops on him."

I had no idea how Dale had found that out. He'd probably looked up some police report and put two and two together.

"It's Dale or Universal," I said, wincing.

"Normally, that's a pretty easy choice." Which was saying something because Sid seriously hates the theme park. Sid glared at Dale. "Except that you do have a point about Cobb. What do you want?"

"We're working on setting up a transfer. Cobb needs his dirt file and badly. Renfrew has agreed to sell it to him."

"So, what does that have to do with us?" Sid asked.

"Renfrew needs cover."

Sid shook his head. "And you can't do it."

"What good will I do?" Dale tried to look, oh, so innocent.

Sid cursed.

"We need at least one sniper." Dale looked at me, as well he should have, then at Sid. "And you're already up to your hips in this."

"What about Tom and Angelique?" Sid asked.

"They're being covered. One of her colleagues may have suggested that she and her lover boy might want to stay in their apartment today."

I took a deep breath. I so wanted to smash Dale's face into something.

"What's the plan?" Sid asked, sighing in resignation.

"We'll wait 'til Renfrew gets here."

Sid and I looked at each other and rolled our eyes.

"Does he know your real name?" Sid asked.

"No."

"And when were you going to tell us this?" Sid asked.

Dale laughed. "Sid, you are not bad at preempting me, so I thought I'd wing it."

"What the...?" Sid looked at me, then at Dale.

"Okay," Dale said. "I caught on to Cobb when I was checking out Renfrew." He smiled. "It was right around the time I was beginning to realize just what I had in you as an asset. Part of my checking around led me to your buddy Renfrew, which I did not need. If I was going to keep your cover intact, the last thing I needed was one of your friends hanging around. So, when that led to Cobb, I was pretty happy when your friend pulled his dog tag switch. I got his ass out of there, saw to it that Mikowski, the guy your friend had swapped with, was recovered, and sent home. Then, when the Wall happened, I made sure that Mikowski got his name on it. But before that, I still had Cobb to deal with and you to get off the front lines."

"I got myself off the front lines," Sid said. "Remember? I could type and got the clerk position in Saigon."

Dale blinked as if he hadn't remembered, then forced a laugh. "You just beat me to it, that's all. I would have found another way."

"I'm sure." Sid folded his arms across his chest. "So, now what?"

The doorbell rang. Dale grinned.

"I'm willing to bet that's Renfrew now."

I left Sid and Dale fake-smiling at each other and went to the door. Louis was there. I brought him into the office, but Sid sent us to the breakfast room.

"Lisa and I need to eat," Sid said. "You guys want some coffee?"

They both agreed, and Sid went ahead of us to get our breakfast. We offered both some of the fruit salad Sid had been making when Dale had arrived. Both Louis and Dale looked appalled. I went back to buttering toast. Louis wanted a couple of slices. Sid had his. I took the rest. I also got the lion's share of the fruit salad. Dale has seen me eat any number of times and knows what I can do. Louis looked a little afraid.

There's a waist-high breakfront in the breakfast room where we keep a lot of the dishes we have. But the break-front has one drawer that holds notepads, sheet paper, pens, and pencils. Sometimes we need that stuff at breakfast or lunch. I grabbed some blank typing paper and pencils right before I sat down to eat.

The plan was pretty straightforward. As soon as we were done, I called Mae to let her know that Sid was not feeling well and that we'd stay home so that he could get over it. I don't know if Mae believed me or not, but she went with it.

Dale took off, which was a good thing. Louis stayed. He toyed with his coffee cup as Sid cleared the table.

"More coffee?" Sid asked as he returned with a full pot.

"Definitely," I said, pushing my mug toward him.

"Yeah, thanks." Louis held out his as well.

I moodily stirred sugar and milk into mine. Sid hesitated, then poured himself a rare second cup. He used to have a bad caffeine addiction, but since being off the stuff for a lot of years, he can now drink coffee, which he loves, as long as he doesn't drink too much of it at one time.

Louis looked almost guilty as he looked at Sid. "I had to get out of there, you know."

Sid sighed. "I know how bad it was."

"Yeah, it was, but that's not why I did it." Louis looked at him. "This is the part I couldn't tell you last night because Tom was there. Cobb killed the guy I swapped tags with. Mikowski was about to blow the whistle on Cobb and his pals. Cobb didn't know that I saw him do it. But then, he knew he'd killed Mikowski, and after I disappeared and they all said Mikowski's stiff was mine, Cobb figured out what I'd done." Louis looked away and sighed. "I took Mikowski's orders and ran because I was next on Cobb's list. I knew too much."

The weird thing was, I got the feeling that, for once, Louis was telling the truth.

"Then why didn't he kill you later?" Sid asked, still reserved and pissed. "If you were working for him, he'd have had the chance."

"Cobb had something on me." Louis sank into himself. "That made me more useful to him alive than dead, and knowing him, it was also more fun to pull my strings. That's why I'm here now."

Sid shook his head. "You're here because we both got played by Landry. Several times over, I'd say." Sid sighed and looked at his coffee cup. "Let's just get this bastard, okay?"

Louis made the call from our house. The meeting was set up for that afternoon, which I was not thrilled about. It meant I had to be in position at least an hour and a half ahead of time, and hanging around on a rooftop waiting for bad guys to show is not my idea of a good time.

There's a section of downtown Los Angeles, just to the east of City Hall and Little Tokyo, that's pretty run-down and largely vacant, except for a few artists in lofts. Most of the buildings there have two stories, but a few have as many as four. I landed on top of a four-story building, wired, and bored out of my mind. For some reason, Cobb didn't want to trust Louis, so Louis agreed to send his civilian buddy, Sid, to meet with Cobb and hand over the paper file and floppy disks Louis had. Sid's job was to get close enough to Cobb to knock him out and get him cuffed so that Dale could file charges against him. My job was to convince Cobb that Sid had enough coverage that shooting him would not be a good idea.

Sid got into position about five minutes before Cobb was supposed to show. Louis, who was watching from a ground-level vantage point, let us know when Cobb approached the alley where Sid was hiding.

Cobb looked around and pulled his gun.

"I'm here!" his voice rang through my earpiece

"You've got a gun," Sid called, sounding nervous. He was getting so good at acting like he was scared.

"So what?" Cobb hollered, adding a curse word or two.

"Look, I just want to give you what you want and collect the cash. I don't want to end up dead."

I drew a bead on Cobb's shoulder with my high-powered rifle, just in case.

"Get your ass where I can see it," Cobb ordered.

It was the last thing he said. A second later, two shots rang out from the direction Louis had been hiding, and they caught Cobb in the torso, and he went down, falling onto his back. Louis walked out from his hiding place, his automatic in his hand. He stood over Cobb, then shot him in the face.

I turned away, trying not to wretch.

"That's for Don, you fuck," Louis said.

Sid and I pretty much spent the rest of the day making love, trying desperately to banish what we'd seen with our passion for each other. Louis called that evening. Sid took the call while I heated up turkey and gravy leftovers in the microwave. A few minutes later, Sid came into the kitchen.

"How do you feel about spending a few days in D.C.?" he asked.

"Fine, I guess." I looked at him. "What about the family?"

"We'll bring them with us. I'm pretty sure I can talk them into it."

"Okay."

Sid went back to the breakfast room to finish the call, then joined me in the kitchen.

"So, what's with D.C.?" I asked.

He sighed. "The Wall."

As in the Vietnam Veterans Memorial.

"Oh?"

"Louis hasn't seen it yet. We both decided we needed to take a look."

"Why?"

Sid smiled at me. "Don't know why for him. For me... You know, everything I have right now that I truly care about, I have because of that fucking war. Janey was right Christmas Eve. If I hadn't been drafted and spent those two years in 'Nam, I wouldn't have been at Stanford the same time as Rachel, and I wouldn't have Nick. That war gave me my life's work in intelligence. That intelligence work led me to you and kept me with you in spite of my complete inability to sustain a relationship. And because of you, I chose to get to know Nick when he showed up. Because of you, I have become a part of your family. Because of you, I reconciled with Stella, and not only do I have her, I have Sy, as well. And all of that was because of the worst two years of my life." He shrugged. "So, I'm going to the Wall with Louis." He paused. "But I do want to go wired. I may need you to keep me from strangling him."

I laughed. We ate turkey and gravy leftovers, then went back upstairs to give life to each other.

Three days later, I waited in the suite in Washington, D.C. Sy and Stella had corralled almost everybody for a walk on the mall, starting with the Lincoln Memorial. Sid had gone ahead. I was only waiting to give him a head start. I didn't realize that Mae and Darby had stayed behind until I heard violin music from the suite's living room. I slid out of my bedroom and smiled as Mae sat on the couch, her feet up and eyes closed, and Darby facing her, playing something very sweet and slow. I slipped out of the suite.

I tapped in a message on my transmitter when I got near the steps of the Lincoln Memorial. The ground was mostly white with snow, and the air was filled with the puffs of breath from the tourists. I heard Sid laugh and curse.

"There you are," Louis said.

"You ready?" Sid asked.

"Yeah, I guess so." Louis paused. "I'm told Mikowski's name is right next to mine."

"I don't know about that, but I know where yours is. Come on."

I watched as they walked to the section Sid wanted. There was one name that I thought Sid would go to first, and he did.

"Robinson?" Louis asked.

"Yeah. Buddy of mine."

Sid swallowed as he put his hand on Arlen Robinson's name. He still felt guilty about his friend's death, partly because he hadn't been able to prevent it, and partly because he had killed the sniper who had killed Robinson, and it was the first time Sid had killed somebody.

Then Sid pointed to a panel a little below Robinson's. "There you are, and there's Mikowski."

Louis sighed. "Well, there's some justice, at least." He paused, and the two men stood looking at the names silently for a few minutes. "So, this is supposed to help us come to terms with the war."

"I don't want to come to terms with it," said Sid. "This war was wrong, hideous, utterly inhumane. Why would I want to come to terms with that? It also gave me a lot. I'm not sure what to think about that, but it's true."

Louis sighed. "Come on. Let's go over to the Lincoln Memorial. I've got somebody I want you to meet."

They started for the stairs to the huge white building. Janey and Lissy saw them coming, and Lissy broke away from her older sister, running to their uncle.

"Unka Sid!" Lissy screamed.

Sid laughed and scooped her up as Janey ran up to hug him. "You found us."

"Hi, Mr. Renfrew," Janey said.

I hurried down the steps of the Memorial, turning off my transmitter. Another woman, blond and close to Louis' size, walked beside me, although she didn't know me any more than I knew her. A young boy, about nine, with light blond hair, ran ahead, two younger girls following him.

"Hey, honey," said Louis to the woman. "Sid, this is my wife, Nancy. Nance, my buddy from high school, Sid Hackbirn."

"Nice to meet you, Sid," Nancy said.

"Nice to meet you." Sid reached out to me with his free arm. "Hey, Lover. Uh, Nancy, this is my wife, Lisa Wycherly. These are our nieces, Lissy and Janey."

"My step-son Todd, and our daughters, Karen and Stacey." Louis gasped a little as the three children plowed into him. "Nancy is the only woman I never lie to."

"Bullshit," Nancy said with a smile. "You lie to me all the time. I just know when you do."

Sid looked down at Janey. "So, where's everybody else?"

"Over there, waiting for you." Janey pointed at the steps to the Lincoln Memorial.

Sid looked up and smiled. "It's been good to see you, Louis."

"Good to see you, too, Sid."

The two men shook hands, and our respective groups moved away from each other.

"Who was that little boy with your friend?" Mama asked Sid as we walked up.

"Louis' son," said Sid. "Why?"

"You know who he looks like."

We looked back. Louis and his family were making their way toward the Washington Monument. Louis had said he'd gotten some information about a certain politician that had stayed buried, but not how he'd gotten it. Funny thing was, Mama had a real point about that boy.

12:45 a.m., 3/6/21

Coming Soon

Believe it or not, **Necessary Chances** is the last Quickline novel. Don't panic. Sid and Lisa and the whole crew will be back with a new assignment. Eventually. In the meantime, book six in the Old Los Angeles series will come out in late spring of 2026 -

DEATH OF A PROPER BOSTONIAN

A deadly homecoming

It's August 1873, and at last, physician and winemaker Maddie Franklin Wilcox makes the long journey home to her beloved native Boston. Her business is to deliver her ward and apprentice, Elena Ortiz, to the local women's medical school, and to visit her father, and her sister and family.

But at a dinner with the family of Maddie's late and very much unlamented husband (at least, on her part), young John Wilcox, a cousin there to entertain the guests with his nature talk, is shot. Then the next morning, the eldest of the Wilcox brothers is found shot in his bed. Maddie quickly concludes that the shooting of the oh, so charming naturalist was but a distraction for the shooting of her former brother-in-law.

Chased by a corrupt Boston police officer, confronted again and again by the relentless prejudice of the city's medical practitioners, and in danger of losing her heart to young John Wilcox (who had plenty of reasons to want his cousin dead), Maddie's happy homecoming becomes a morass of suspicion with someone willing to kill her and the people she loves.

Thank You for Reading

I do hope you enjoyed the book.

If you can do me one small favor, please. Can you go to one of the social media/retail profiles below and leave a short review? It doesn't need to be a lot, just honest.

a amazon.com/Paths-Taken-Operation-Quickline-Book-ebook/dp/B0DGMYM7GB

BB bookbub.com/books/paths-not-taken-by-anne-louise-bannon

f facebook.com/robingoodfellowent

g goodreads.com/book/show/218688480-paths-not-taken?from_search=true&from_srp=true&qid=eCL2BChH7v&rank=1

Other books by Anne Louise Bannon

I'm so glad you liked this book! Check out my other novels, available in print or ebook at your favorite retailer:

Old Los Angeles Series:
Death of the Zanjero
Death of the City Marshal
Death of the Chinese Field Hands
Death of an Heiress
Death of the Drunkard

Operation Quickline Series:
That Old Cloak and Dagger Routine
Stopleak
Deceptive Appearances
Fugue in a Minor Key
Sad Lisa
These Hallowed Halls
My Sweet Lisa
A Little Family Business
Just Because You're Paranoid
From This Day Forward
Silence in the Tortured Soul

Amateur Theatricals
Paths Not Taken
The Room Where it Happened
Necessary Chances

Freddie and Kathy Series:
Fascinating Rhythm
Bring Into Bondage
The Last Witnesses
Blood Red

Daria Barnes:
Rage Issues

Mrs. Sperling:
A Nose for a Niedeman

Brenda Finnegan:
Tyger, Tyger

Romantic Fiction:
White House Rhapsody

Fantasy and Science Fiction:
A Ring for a Second Chance
But World Enough and Time
Time Enough
And I would be honored if you left a review for this and
any of my books on the below sites. It really helps.

BB bookbub.com/profile/anne-louise-bannon

goodreads.com/author/show/513383.Anne_Louise_Bannon

facebook.com/RobinGoodfellowEnt/

amazon.com/stores/author/B00JCRXST2?ingress=0&visitId=bfadb491-d1ac-4575-84da-bb4f7d325ad9&store_ref=ap_rdr&ref_=ap_rdr

pinterest.com/AnneLouiseBannon

instagram.com/annelouisebannon4/

Connect with Anne Louise Bannon

Thank you for sticking it out this long! Please join my newsletter. It's the best way to stay up-to-date on my upcoming projects, blog posts and even the occasional game and giveaway.

You can sign up for my newsletter on Substack, Substack.com/@annelouisebannon. or by visiting my website, annelouisebannon.com

And don't forget to connect with me on your favorite social media platforms:

BB bookbub.com/profile/anne-louise-bannon

g goodreads.com/author/show/513383.Anne_Louise_Bannon

f facebook.com/RobinGoodfellowEnt/

a amazon.com/stores/author/B00JCRXST2?ingress=0&visitId=bfadb491-d1ac-4575-84da-bb4f7d325ad9&store_ref=ap_rdr&ref_=ap_rdr

P pinterest.com/AnneLouiseBannon

instagram.com/annelouisebannon4/

About Anne Louise Bannon

Anne Louise Bannon is an author and journalist who wrote her first novel at age 15. Her journalistic work has appeared in Ladies' Home Journal, the Los Angeles Times, Wines and Vines, and in newspapers across the country. She was a TV critic for over 10 years, founded the YourFamilyViewer blog, and created the OddBallGrape.com wine education blog with her husband, Michael Holland. She is the co-author of Howdunit: Book of Poisons, with Serita Stevens, as well as author of the Freddie and Kathy mystery series, set in the 1920s, the Old Los Angeles series, set in 1870, and the Operation Quickline series, plus several stand alones. She and her husband live in Southern California with an assortment of critters.